CW01496846

# HAPPILY-EVER-AFTER AT THE DOG & DUCK

JILL STEEPLES

Boldwood

First published in 2018 as Happily-Ever-After at the Dog & Duck. This edition published in Great Britain in 2023 by Boldwood Books Ltd.

Cover Design by Head Design Ltd

Cover Illustration: Shutterstock

A CIP catalogue record for this book is available from the British Library.

Paperback ISBN 978-1-78513-850-8

Large Print ISBN 978-1-78513-849-2

Hardback ISBN 978-1-78513-848-5

Ebook ISBN 978-1-78513-851-5

Kindle ISBN 978-1-78513-852-2

Audio CD ISBN 978-1-78513-843-0

MP3 CD ISBN 978-1-78513-844-7

Digital audio download ISBN 978-1-78513-846-1

Boldwood Books Ltd
23 Bowerdean Street
London SW6 3TN
www.boldwoodbooks.com

*For my lovely family, as always, with love.*

# 1

The village green in Little Leyton was abuzz with activity on the afternoon of that sunny Sunday in August. It was the bank holiday weekend, the last hurrah of summer before the children returned to school, when the cooler autumnal days would move in around us. Soon the mad descent into the Christmas preparations would begin and, as much as I was enjoying this glorious weather, I felt a tingle of anticipation at the thought of the change in seasons. The run-up to Christmas was always my favourite time of year.

For now, I was content sitting beneath the shade of the old oak tree with little Noel on my knee, sporting a navy and lemon two piece with matching hat, and Digby, my labrador, at my feet, watching as the world went by. The villagers were out in force today to support the summer fayre, milling around the marquees, chatting to one another and visiting the cheerfully decorated stalls. At my feet was a wicker basket filled to the brim with the stash of goodies I'd collected on my way around the green: some jams and chutneys, a couple of paperbacks from the Mother and Toddler book stall and two pretty little floral tea plates from St Cuthbert's church bric-a-brac stall.

My gaze drifted across to The Dog and Duck pub where the front door was wide open and a steady flow of people wandered in and out, no doubt on the way to the barn at the back, which we'd decorated with bunting and balloons. When I'd popped in earlier the Pimms and summer cocktails were proving to be very popular and the walled beer garden, adorned with blooming hanging baskets from Polly's Flowers next door, was packed with happy customers taking a rest from the delights of the fayre and soaking up the sun and booze instead. Just how I, as landlady of the inn, liked it.

Since Noel's arrival eight months ago, I'd stepped back from the day-to-day running of the pub, leaving it in the capable hands of my barman, Dan, his girlfriend, Silke, and of course, Eric, who was the previous landlord and who was now living back at the pub, but I still couldn't stop myself from getting involved on special occasions like today.

In the main arena, where we'd already seen a gymnastics display from the local club, the school choir performing songs from their end-of-term show and the Mother and Toddler's fancy dress competition, which had brought forward a fetching array of sea creatures, a cacophony of barking broke out as the dog show got under way.

'Look, Noel. Can you see Daddy and Flora?'

I lifted him up for a better view and laughed as we watched Flora trying to go in every direction possible, blatantly ignoring any of Max's commands and getting her lead tangled around his legs, almost tripping him over, before becoming distracted by an extremely well-behaved and handsome German Shepherd to the side of her, who was clearly determined to remain immune to her charms.

\* \* \*

Max was dressed in cargo shorts and a white short-sleeved shirt, which only served to highlight his tanned and muscular arms and his face was set in an expression of determination. Well, he was nothing if not competitive, but, judging by some of the other dogs in the ring who were obviously much better trained than Flora, I really didn't reckon much to our chances.

Thankfully there were classes for waggiest tail, most appealing eyes, best OAP and best newcomer, although I don't think anyone was really too concerned about winning any prizes – certainly not the dogs, who were having too much fun together. Apart, that was, from Max.

'Prettiest dame,' he said, waving a rosette at me, when it was all over and he came to find us. 'Huh, she could have won any one of those classes. Best newcomer was the one we wanted, wasn't it, Flora? But it went to Captain, that German Shepherd.'

'It doesn't matter, Max. It's the taking part that counts. You both did really well. And we know that Flora really is the best dog in the village.' I covered up Digby's ears as I said the words.

Max looked marginally appeased. Honestly, talk about rose-tinted glasses. He was in love; truly, madly, deeply. With me, he assured me, but I suspected his head had been turned by the young English pointer, Flora, who we'd recently adopted from Spain. In fairness, I was pretty smitten too – with her big brown eyes and long gangly legs, she was funny and sweet, but she could be a little so-and-so when she wanted to be and hadn't quite grasped where she was in the pecking order in the house, seemingly believing she was top dog.

Our melded canine family of Max's two gun dogs, Holly and Bella, and my lovely labrador, Digby, who'd been my faithful companion since I'd returned to the village, tolerated the little whipper-snapper with remarkable sangfroid.

'Max! I thought it was you! Oh, you and your dog were brilliant in that ring. I think you should have won best in show. How are you?'

In a white gypsy skirt and matching broderie anglaise off-the-shoulder top, showing off a long slim neck and golden toned arms, the woman spoke in a breathy whisper and looked a vision of summer loveliness. It was only when she lifted her big-rimmed sunglasses off her face and rested them on her head that I realised exactly who it was.

'Hello, Darcy!'

She spun round to look down at me on the bench.

'Ellie, hi! I didn't notice you there.' That was hardly surprising, I mused, as I noted the disappointment in her voice. 'Didn't Max do well?'

I nodded, forcing a smile. Darcy was an old work friend of Polly's and a huge fan of Max. I'd first met her when she'd turned up for Polly's hen-do at the pub and she'd made a beeline for him, throwing everything from her extensive range of seduction techniques at him. Thankfully Max had been as resolutely immune to her charms as Captain had been to Flora's, not that it'd seemed to deter Darcy in any way. She'd told me exactly what she thought about my boyfriend and had even suggested she would be happy to take him off my hands if I ever tired of him. *As if that was really going to happen?* When she'd realised I wasn't about to go anywhere, she'd cast her attentions on one of the young waiters who'd been specially hired for the event instead. It had all got a bit riotous out in the barn with the champagne cocktails flowing all night long, the music stirring everyone's senses and some impromptu and sultry dance moves going on, involving various items of clothing being discarded across the room. Messy didn't really cover it. The next day, Darcy, who'd been unable to get home the previous night as she'd been in such a sorry state and so had stayed with us at the manor, had been contrite and apologetic for her behaviour and all had been forgiven.

Now, with her hand on Max's arm, I wondered if she'd come back especially to see if I had grown tired of Max after all.

'How are you?' she asked, plonking herself down on the bench next to me. My nostrils twitched as I caught a whiff of her heady exotic perfume.

'I'm fine, thank you. Enjoying this lovely weather.'

'You look tired,' she said, ignoring my comment and peering at me intently. 'Are you sure you're all right?'

Max glanced at me with concern in his eyes. It was funny, I'd been absolutely fine before Darcy'd turned up, but suddenly I felt tired and jaded against her shining luminosity. I knew from before that she said things as she saw them and I shouldn't let her off-the-cuff comments get to me but her arrival had definitely ruffled me.

'Yes, it's just what having babies does for you,' I said lightly, bouncing Noel on my knee.

'You won't have heard our news,' said Max, putting an arm around my shoulder in an obvious show of togetherness. 'Ellie and I are getting married.'

I gave him a sideways glance, thankful for the support.

'Oh, really?' Darcy's features dropped for the slightest moment before she quickly plastered on a smile. 'That's great news. Congratulations! When's the big day?'

'We haven't confirmed the exact day yet, but hopefully very soon,' said Max.

'If it was me, I'd do it tomorrow.' Darcy sighed heavily. 'Why wait? I'd love to be getting married soon.'

Our news seemed to deflate Darcy and she was lost to her own thoughts for a moment. Polly had told me that she'd spent most of her twenties in a fruitless relationship with her married boss and ever since she'd had a series of bad experiences with men. Darcy had admitted to me, that fateful morning after the night before, that she envied me and Polly, being settled and happy in our relationships.

'Anyway,' she said, shaking herself as if to put an end to her musing, 'I wanted to say hello to Polly. Have you seen her?'

'Yes, she was over by the shop with Sasha earlier.' My best friend, Polly, owned the florist's, Polly's Flowers, next door to the pub. I'd noticed the pair of them, heads together, deep in conversation. I'd waved to them and they'd waved back but I'd had the distinct impression they hadn't wanted me to be part of their tête-à-tête so I'd left them to it. I could always catch up with them later.

'I'll go and find her. Lovely to see you again,' said Darcy, wafting off in the direction of the pub.

When she'd gone, Max placed his hands on the tops of my arms, his dark brown eyes searching my face appraisingly. 'You know you shouldn't let her get to you.'

I pushed him away, feeling my skin prickle under the intensity of his gaze.

'I know.' I shook my head. 'It's not really Darcy. I suppose she just hit a nerve.'

'Hmm, well, I could have throttled her.'

'She wasn't to know.' I stood up with Noel in my arms and manoeuvred the buggy round so that I could strap him in, my hand unable to resist squeezing his little chubby legs, which were wriggling in delight, his gorgeous happy face smiling up at me.

'Ellie!' Max grabbed me by the arm and spun me round to face him again. 'Are you sure you're okay? You don't have to put on a front with me, you know that?'

'I'm fine. Honestly.' I shrugged. 'I suppose I'm just a bit sensitive at the moment. That's all.'

'And that's totally understandable. You know, I still think it would be better if you told your mum and dad. They would want to know. And you might find it helpful.'

'No!' I hadn't meant to sound harsh. I turned away, busying myself with Noel's baby bag, checking I'd packed away all his bits and doing up zips, anything to stop me from looking into Max's gaze. 'We've talked about this. You know what's she's like. She would only fuss and they've had enough to contend with this year.'

'But—'

'Please, Max, just drop it.' I straightened up and steeled myself to look at him, my expression clearly conveying the seriousness of my decision.

'Okay. Sorry.'

Max gave a small smile but I recognised the hurt in his eyes. He was dealing with it in his way and I was dealing with it in mine, it was just that our coping mechanisms were very different. The truth was, apart from my closest friends, Polly, Josie and Sasha, we hadn't told a soul. I suppose we'd been superstitious, waiting until that significant twelve week milestone before announcing to the world that we were expecting our second baby. Only we never made it to that point, my pregnancy coming to an abrupt end when I was barely eight weeks gone. In some respects, I think Max was finding it more difficult to cope with than me. It wasn't that I wasn't hurting and grieving, just that I didn't want to dwell on what had happened nor share it with the rest of the world.

'Right,' said Max, his voice sounding unnaturally bright. 'Do you want to make a move, then?' He leant down to ruffle Flora's head. I took the lead from him, while Digby walked obediently at my side and Max pushed Noel in his buggy.

The stallholders were packing up their wares and equipment, the visitors drifting away, making their way home or, perhaps some, calling in at The Dog and Duck for a drink.

'Do you want to stop for one?' Max asked when we reached the pub, as if reading my mind.

My gaze drifted up at the colourfully painted sign of The Dog and Duck hanging above the old eighteenth century building. Max had bought the place a couple of years ago when the future of the pub had looked uncertain. I hadn't known him well back then, but I wasn't the only one suspicious of his intentions, wondering if he might develop it into a luxury house or flats with the sole aim of making a quick profit. I hadn't realised that his love for the pub ran almost as deep as mine. His late grandfather, Noel Golding, had been a regular customer at the pub and the reason Max had come to the village in the first place was to nurse him through his last days. Max's gesture, saving The Dog and Duck and keeping it alive for the community, had marked a turning point, not only in our professional relationship, but also in our personal life too.

I'd accepted Max's offer to take over as manager and we became a couple at the same time. Seeing the renovated pub sign that first time had been a turning point for me and even now when I caught a glimpse of it, those feelings of love and gratitude came flooding back.

'Let's go home, shall we? What I could really do with is a nice cup of tea.'

Later, back at the manor, we had the place to ourselves. Katy, Max's teenage sister, was out with her boyfriend, Ryan, and Arthur, an old family friend and surrogate grandpa, who was living with us now, was still down at the pub with friends. Noel was fast asleep in his cot, worn out from all the shenanigans of the day.

'You know, talking to Darcy made me think,' said Max, handing me a glass of crisp white wine. 'Why haven't we set the date for the wedding yet? I know we spoke about doing it in the spring, but why wait? I feel as though I've waited long enough as it is. Let's get married this year?'

His words ignited a spark of excitement within me. He went across to the calendar, pulling up the pages to reach the month of December.

'A Christmas wedding?' I asked.

'Why not? It's a special time for us. It's the anniversary of when we first properly got together and Noel's birthday now, too.'

How could I ever possibly forget our son's unexpected and dramatic arrival on Christmas Day? 'But we've got our holiday next month and a busy time coming up at the pub.' My mind was contemplating all the things we would need to do. 'It doesn't leave a lot of time.'

'Enough time to organise a wedding.' Max ran his finger across the days of the month. 'The 20th of December? What do you say?'

I paused for only the briefest moment.

'Well, if we can get in at St Cuthbert's, then I can't see any reason why not.'

Max dashed over and lifted me off my feet, twirling me around and planting a kiss on my forehead.

'Perfect. Something for us all to look forward to.'

It was just what we needed. I gave a passing thought to Darcy, a smile spreading across my lips. She might not have realised it, but she'd given us a push in the right direction just when we'd most needed it.

# 2

Although I was itching to tell everyone our news, we kept the secret to ourselves for another few weeks until we were certain that we would be able to make everything happen for our chosen date in December. I got in touch with our friend, Reverend Trish Evans, from St Cuthbert's Church to ask if she would be able to marry us on that date, spoke to Dave at Yardleys, the butchers in the village, to see if they would be able to help with the catering, and checked the bookings for the barn at The Dog and Duck to see if it was free that weekend. With the stars conspiring in our favour it soon became clear that I needed to get a move on, as I had a wedding to organise, and in only three months' time too!

A few days later, with that in mind, I made the trip down to No. 2 Ivy Lane Cottages.

'Darling! Come in.' Mum's face lit up at seeing me, or probably more accurately, at seeing Noel. She bent down to unstrap him from his buggy and lifted his little body, clad in fetching blue shorts and matching T-shirt, up into her arms, showering him with an array of kisses. 'Look who's here, Malc!' she called through to my dad, who came wandering in from the garden.

'Ah, my two favourite people!'

Mum's brow furrowed as she chastised him with a dark look.

'Let me rephrase that. My three favourite people in the world, all in the same room. How lucky am I?'

I had to smile. In truth, I was the lucky one, having my parents back and living in the village. When I'd fallen pregnant with Noel they were out in Dubai, enjoying an ex-pat lifestyle in the sunshine, spending their time with their newfound friends, sipping cocktails and dining out at the yacht club. They'd been due to stay out there for another couple of years when suddenly they made the surprising decision to move back to Little Leyton shortly after Noel was born. There was no consultation or warning, they just did it, seemingly on the spur of moment, and I couldn't help wondering then what was behind, what seemed to me, a rash decision.

Had there been a falling out in Dubai, were they facing financial difficulties or did they feel they had to come home to support me with the baby? I'd had so many questions. As it turned out it was none of those things. It had been a few weeks later that I found out the real shocking reason for them coming home. Dad had been diagnosed with cancer. At first I couldn't believe it. That someone who had always been the strong one in our family, so vibrant and full of energy, could be susceptible to such a horrible disease. I'd believed my dad to be invincible and couldn't imagine a time when he wouldn't be around. Coming face to face with his mortality had been a huge shock to us all, bringing home the fragility of life and everything we had to be grateful for. The thought of losing Dad, and Noel growing up not knowing his grandfather, was heart-breaking.

Even now, when I thought about it, a cold shudder rippled through my body.

Luckily Dad was able to undergo treatment swiftly and – touch wood, fingers crossed and saying the occasional prayer to anyone who might listen – it seemed to have been a success. Now the hospital staff were just monitoring him at regular intervals.

'You all right, Dad?' It didn't stop me from worrying about him though, checking his face and looking into his eyes every time I saw him just to see if I could detect any changes. Today, with him in his shorts and T-shirt, his skin bronzed from the sun, you would never know there had been anything wrong.

'Me? I'm dandy. Shall we go and sit in the garden? I'll pop the kettle on,' he said jauntily.

Meanwhile, Mum was obviously doing her own familial checks and placed her hand on my shoulder, gazing into my face intently.

'Are you all right, love? I was saying to your father, you haven't seemed quite yourself in recent weeks. And you look a bit peaky. There's nothing wrong, is there?'

Honestly, I'd swear Mum had a sixth sense. She could always tell when something was bothering me or if I was under the weather. I loved her dearly but this was exactly the reason why I didn't want her to know about the miscarriage. She would be devastated and concerned for me, I knew, and dealing with her grief and sense of loss, on top of my own, was something I didn't feel strong enough for just now. We'd been through so much with Dad's illness that I didn't want to inflict any further worry or concern on them. Not when there wasn't anything they could do to change things.

'I'm fine, Mum, really.'

She raised her brow at me, clearly not convinced by my explanation.

'You're overdoing it, Ellie. You've not stopped since you've had this little one. And you've got Arthur and Katy to look after now too. Then there's all the work you do for the pub. Not to mention that mad dog you've taken on. No wonder you're worn out.'

When she put it like that it did sound a lot, but honestly, I'd felt perfectly fine when I'd arrived, only I was beginning to feel steadily worse by the moment. Mum was hardly to know though.

'Then there was all that time and effort you put into organising Polly's wedding,' she went on. 'It's hardly any wonder you're completely frazzled.'

'Oh, I know.' I nodded, glad Mum had steered the conversation in a different direction. 'But it was such good fun, I wouldn't have missed out on a moment of it for the world.'

'True. You did do an amazing job.'

Polly had married the famous writer, George Williamson, at St Cuthbert's church in the village and I'd organised a champagne reception for them in the old barn at the back of the pub, honoured to be chosen as Polly's maid of honour. The sun had shone all day and it had been the most perfect occasion.

'Well, actually... I'll be back in wedding planning mode very soon. Just as soon as we get back from our holiday.'

Mum's eyes widened and her face lit up.

'Don't tell me you've set the date at last?'

'Yes! That's what I wanted to talk to you about.'

'Oh, Malc! Forget that tea.' Thankfully Mum seemed to have forgotten her concerns about me, too. 'Open up a bottle of fizz. We've got some celebrating to do.'

Out in the garden, sitting around the circular wooden patio table, and with our glasses suitably filled with some fizz that Dad had found in the fridge, Mum and Dad were eager to hear all the details. Dad held Noel in his arms, jiggling him up and down on his knee.

'Well, we've decided on a Christmas wedding because it's such a special time of year for us. This Christmas will be the second anniversary of when Max first bought the pub.'

Admittedly, he'd immediately closed it for refurbishment and I'd been furious at the time, convinced he had some mad scheme up his sleeve to sell the pub on. I'd been devastated thinking the pub might never open again while all the time Max had been working night and day to get the place into a condition where we could reopen for Christmas Eve.

'It was such a magical moment when I finally realised Max wanted to keep the pub alive just as much as I did.'

'Yes, I remember that excited phone call you made to us, telling us the news. I think everyone in Little Leyton was so relieved to find out they wouldn't be losing their pub after all.'

'Yeah, and it made me fall in love with Max all the more. I could never have been with Max if he had sold The Dog and Duck. So, all this was obviously meant to be. And then with this little man coming along the following Christmas, it just seems that there's no better time for us to get married.'

'Well, I think a winter wedding will be perfect. Something a bit different. We got married in November, didn't we, Malc? It was a bitterly cold day and we all froze in the photos but none of that mattered. Just so long as we won't all get snowed in at the church!'

We shared a glance and grimaced. Mum was joking, but it wasn't beyond the realms of possibility, especially after last year when little Noel was born in the barn at The Dog and Duck on Christmas Day. We'd been hosting Christmas lunch for some friends when my bump had decided, totally unexpectedly, he wanted to put in an appearance for the festivities, a few weeks before schedule. With a fierce snowstorm raging outside there had been absolutely no chance of getting to the hospital and when it had become clear there was no turning back I'd had no other choice but to give birth in the barn. Thankfully, I'd had Max and Josie at my side and we'd managed to track down a retired midwife from the village, who had arrived at the last moment to see our baby into the world. A smile spread across my face at the memory. Noel really was our little Christmas miracle.

'Don't be daft,' Dad chastised Mum. 'It couldn't happen again!'

'Well, let's hope not!' Mum chuckled. 'I'm presuming you'll be having the ceremony at St Cuthbert's?'

'Of course. Where else?'

It was our village church, where I'd gone to Sunday School, participated in various harvest festivals and Christingles and attended several weddings and lots of christenings, too. I wasn't particularly religious but St Cuthbert's had played just as important a part in my growing up as the pub had done and I couldn't imagine getting married anywhere else.

'And what about the reception – where will you hold that?'

'Well, we were thinking about a drinks reception at the pub and then going back to the manor for the main event, but I'm coming round to the idea of doing it all at The Dog and Duck. We'll probably have fifty to sixty guests and they would easily fit into the barn. I want to keep it fairly low key and for the food to be simple, but delicious. Something like bangers and mash.'

Dad's eyes shot up and a big grin spread across his face.

'My favourite! Well, I think that's a jolly good idea.'

Mum dropped her head, clearly mulling over the suggestion until she broke into a smile, too.

'It is. You don't want everybody traipsing around your lovely home anyway and it will be far too cold for a marquee outside.'

'Exactly! And I've got some plans for how we might deck out the pub and the barn to make it really special.'

Mum rubbed her hands together and gave a little shudder of excitement.

'Something to look forward to, that's for sure,' she said. 'Of course, it'll be our big anniversary coming up this year. Thirty years married. So, it will be a double celebration.'

Dad shook his head, smiling indulgently. Mum had been talking about their pearl anniversary for months now. I'm sure there couldn't be a soul in the village who didn't yet know about their upcoming celebration. There was absolutely no chance of me or Dad forgetting about it either – if we did, Mum would never speak to us again.

'We need to get something organised for that, don't we, Dad?' I flashed him a glance.

'Well, don't go to any trouble.' Mum's laugh tinkled around the garden, but neither of us were in any doubt that we'd be in very serious trouble if we didn't! 'More important,' she said, brushing that aside, 'are the arrangements for your wedding. Let me know what you need us to do. Have you spoken to Caroline yet?'

Mum's good friend and next door neighbour was an amazing seamstress. She'd made my prom dress when I was at school and had made Polly's dress and my bridesmaid dress for her wedding this year.

'No, I'll do that this week. I need to speak to the bridesmaids first. Katy will be one, obviously, but I want to have Josie, Polly and Sasha, too. I've invited them round on Friday night to tell them the news. I can't have one without the others and they've all been such good friends to me.'

'Oh, it will be perfect!' Mum took Noel from Dad's arms and peered into his face, his little legs kicking in the air, his mouth opening and closing as though talking to her. 'What do you think to all this?' she cooed at him. 'Your mummy and daddy getting married. Isn't it exciting? Who knows? You might even have a little brother or sister on the way by then.'

'Mum!' I snapped, while Dad reprimanded her with a fierce glance over the top of his glasses.

'What?' she said, innocently. 'I didn't mean anything by it. All I was saying was that—'

'Yes, we know exactly what you're saying. But I'm not sure it's any of your business, Veronica.'

Mum huffed and stood up, grumbling to Noel about the unfairness of it all. Thank goodness for Dad. Her off-the-cuff comment had twisted at my heart like a knife. I took a deep breath. Best not to think too far in the future. Not this year at least. I had a wedding to organise and would be putting all my time and energies into that. After that, who knew what fate might have in store for us?

# 3

Later that day, back at the manor, I found Max, Arthur and Katy sitting around the kitchen table, the doors of the conservatory wide open onto the stone paved patio that offered views of the sweeping lawns, running into the distance as far as the eye could see. The days were still warm and bright, but the faintest of breezes provided a cool autumnal edge and the geraniums and blowsy petunias in the profusion of wood and stone planters were beginning to look a little straggly now.

After dinner I would go round and deadhead the plants, which was my one small contribution to the upkeep of the extensive grounds. I found it reassuringly therapeutic, giving me a chance to snatch some alone time and to reflect on the events of the day. Luckily, Max had a small team of gardeners who helped him out around Braithwaite Manor and it was their hard work that kept the gardens looking so plentiful. Of course, Max was head gardener and liked to get outside as much as his busy schedule would allow. He was never happier than when sitting upon his ride-on mower, his canvas hat perched on his head at a jaunty angle, whizzing across the lawns. Arthur was a keen gardener too, and was always ready with advice, even when it wasn't needed. He'd had an allotment for years, growing an assortment of fruit and vegetables, until a spate of ill health had meant he'd no longer been able to manage. When he'd fallen ill, Arthur had come to us to recuperate and the arrangement had worked so well that he'd never returned home. Braithwaite Manor was his home now and he was part of our family. He'd also taken on the role of Chief Adviser for Vegetable and Fruit Production.

Max's little sister, Katy, on the other hand, had no interest in gardening or the great outdoors, come to that. Spending the majority of her childhood growing up in Spain, she'd always told me how much she'd hated the heat, just one of the many reasons why she'd been desperate to come back to the UK to live. There'd been a big bust up with her mum, Rose, and her stepdad, Alan, and Katy had left under a cloud, coming to live with us for a while. Max had agreed to let Katy stay, and she was now happily settled in Little Leyton, attending college in town, working shifts at The Dog and Duck, back in touch with her biological father and in a steady relationship with her boyfriend, Ryan.

I pulled out a chair and sat down at the table to join them. Along with the four dogs, currently mooching beneath the table, this was our little melded family.

'So, how did it go?' Max placed a very welcome cup of tea in front of me. 'What did they think to the news?'

'What news?' asked Katy, sitting up to attention, her curiosity immediately piqued.

'Well... we were waiting to tell Veronica and Malc before making it common knowledge, but Ellie and I have set a date for the wedding. It'll be on 20th of December this year.'

'Really!' Katy jumped up from her seat, squealing. The dogs, alerted by her excitement, jumped up too, their tails wagging excitedly, and Flora darted between all our legs making us giggle with her antics.

'Ah, that's marvellous news,' said Arthur, standing up to shake Max's hand and giving me a hug. 'If you're half as happy as me and my Marge were, then you'll have some magic years ahead. It's what it's all about, isn't it? A happy family life.'

I squeezed Arthur even tighter and rested my head on his chest. I remembered Marge well. She was a kind hearted woman who welcomed all the village children into her home and in the summer months was happy for us to run wild around her playground of a garden. There would be home made cakes and biscuits, and fresh lemonade, and I would always come away with a bag of apples, or pears, a batch of scones or anything else that Marge might have whipped up that day. They never missed a birthday or Christmas, always sending a card and a small present. When Marge died, Arthur put on a brave front and carried on as best he could, but it was plain to see for anyone who knew him that he was struggling without the woman he loved at his side. That was the start of the deterioration in his health, I realised now. He hadn't looked after himself, not eating or drinking properly, and had slowly declined to a point where he couldn't manage on his own. Max and I were both so pleased and relieved when we were able to persuade him to come and live with us.

'It is very exciting, but if you could both keep it under your hats for another few days. I haven't mentioned it to the girls yet. I've invited Polly, Josie and Sasha round on Friday night for drinks and nibbles. I'll tell them the news then and ask if they'll be my bridesmaids. I can't wait to see their faces.'

'Your secret is safe with me,' said Arthur, tapping his nose. Katy glanced across at me, nodding her agreement before standing up and wandering over to Noel's rocker, lifting him out.

'Once we get back from our holidays it will be full steam ahead with the arrangements. When you think about it, it's not that far away.'

'When is it you're going?' asked Katy.

'In a couple of weeks. It's come round so quickly and I'm already feeling nervous about leaving Noel behind, but Max seems to think it's for the best.' I cast him a questioning glance, hoping he might have had a change of heart on that front.

'Look, Ellie, it's up to you. I really don't mind. And if you're not going to be happy leaving him behind, then of course we must take him with us, but you need a break and I think you'll get more of a rest if it's just the two of us. We'll be able to completely relax, go for some nice long walks, have some lovely meals, get some good nights' sleep, with proper lie-ins, and come back completely refreshed. Your mum and dad will be here to look after Noel and the dogs, so really there's nothing to worry about.'

'Good idea,' said Arthur. 'We'll manage, won't we, Katy?'

'Yes, well, you certainly don't need to worry about me! I don't need looking after. In fact, I might go and stay with Ryan,' she said airily, before handing Noel over to Max, and turning to waltz out of the kitchen, tension bristling off her shoulders.

'Katy! I don't think Max was suggesting you needed looking after for one moment.'

'And you won't be staying with Ryan, young lady. You'll be staying here. To give Veronica and Malc a hand if they need it.'

Max's tone was gruff and I could see Katy's hackles rise.

'We were hoping you might help with looking after the dogs and with Noel,' I offered. 'You're always so good with him when he's cross and tired, and doesn't want to settle. It will make me feel so much better knowing you're here with him.'

'Really?' She turned to me, her expression matching the sharpness of her tone. 'So, you want me to help out when it suits you, but otherwise you don't want to know me.'

'Katy! Don't speak to Ellie like that! What's got into you?' Max's brow furrowed, his puzzled expression mirroring my own confusion. Her face had lit up to hear our wedding news, but now it was as if she was having second thoughts about the whole idea. 'Do you not want us to go on holiday – is that it?'

'No, it's not that at all!' she said in frustration.

Max and I shared a glance and shrugged, none the wiser as to what had made Katy so angry.

'Oh, come on, Katy,' I tried to coax her. 'I know you and can tell when you're upset. How can we do anything to put it right if you won't tell us what it is?'

'It's you!' she said, glaring at me, as though it were blindingly obvious. 'You pretend that we're best friends and everything, but it doesn't mean a thing.'

I glanced across at Arthur, who was looking as perplexed as me.

'That's not true. Why would you even think that?'

'Huh!' She crossed her arms fiercely, her body held rigid.

'Katy? Tell me, what's all this about?' I went over to her, wrapping my arms around her, but she was unwilling or unable to accept my comfort. She pushed me away, still glaring at me.

Now I was totally confused, my mind trying to make sense of what Katy was saying. I'd been preoccupied these last couple of weeks, all my energies consumed by my miscarriage, trying to put on a brave front and carry on as normal. I thought I'd been doing pretty well, that no one noticed how much I was struggling inside, but Mum had clearly sensed something was wrong. And now Katy, too.

Had I been guilty of neglecting her? Things had settled down since she'd first arrived in Little Leyton but she was still vulnerable emotionally, her moods swinging from one extreme to another. She was in touch now with Andy, her biological father, but her relationship with her mum, Rose, and stepdad, Alan, had suffered. She confided in me, much more so than she did with Max, and I really loved how our relationship had grown in such a relatively short space of time. Not having any siblings of my own, I really did think of her as the little sister I never had, but now she was accusing me of letting her down.

'Don't be rude! Ellie's had a lot on her plate recently. She's—'

'Max!' I threw him a cautionary glance.

He was fuming, I could tell, a muscle twitching in his cheek and the set of his jaw giving away his true feelings. I didn't want him blurting something out we both might come to regret later and making matters much worse with Katy.

'Look, I know my head's been elsewhere, first with Polly's wedding, and then...' I waved my hand around vaguely '...well, there's always something going on around here.' I was hoping to gloss over what had really been distracting me these last few weeks. 'But I'm always here for you, you know that?'

She sat back down again, slumping in the oak carver, contemplating her fingernails.

'You still don't get it, do you?' She paused, looking up at me reproachfully. She took a big breath, clearly summoning up the nerve to say whatever it was that was bothering her. 'You promised me, Ellie. You told me I'd be your bridesmaid and now you seem to have forgotten all about that. You're having all your other friends instead.' Tears glistened in her eyes as she looked from me to Max.

'Oh, good grief!' This, with a roll of his eyes, was Max's helpful contribution to the conversation.

'What?' I had to press my lips together to stop myself from smiling because it clearly wasn't a laughing matter as far as Katy was concerned. 'Is that what you're upset about?' She dropped her gaze, unable to look me in the eye now. 'Oh, Katy! Of course you're going to be my bridesmaid, if that's what's worrying you?'

'Really?' Hope flickered in her big brown eyes. The corners of her mouth twitched, and for a moment I wasn't sure if she was going to laugh or burst into tears. 'Do you really mean that? You're not just saying it because I've made a fuss?'

'Don't worry, we're used to you making a fuss,' said Max flippantly.

'Take no notice of him. I'm having the girls, yes, but as well as you, not instead of. I mean, honestly, you've been telling me ever since we first met how you'd be my bridesmaid one day.'

'Yes, but that was only me dropping hints,' said Katy disingenuously.

'Ha! Not very subtle ones!'

Katy lifted her chin, deliberately ignoring Max's comment.

'Come here, you daft thing!'

Now, she was more than willing to accept my comfort and came across and dropped her head onto my chest as I wrapped my arms around her. Sometimes Katy was full of sass, confidence and attitude and other times, like today, her vulnerability was almost palpable beneath the surface. She'd been deeply hurt by the secret her mum had kept from her and now had trouble trusting anyone.

'You know, you should make sure you're here on Friday night. It's been ages since we've had a girly night and we'll definitely all be in the mood for celebrating.'

'Oh... well, I've already said I'd see Ryan. There's a gig on at Upper Leyton, but I could always cancel, I suppose,' she said, not entirely convincingly.

'No, don't do that! Go and have some fun with Ryan. There'll be plenty of other opportunities for wedding talk in the coming months!'

Max cast us a disapproving stare, before his eyes softened with an indulgent smile.

'You know, there's a lot to be said for the two of us just disappearing for a weekend and doing the deed. Maybe we should do it while we're away on holiday? Just think of the money we'd save. We wouldn't need any brides-maids or any fuss then. What do you reckon?' I suspected Max was only half joking but Katy and I were quick to shoot him down for even daring to suggest such a thing.

'Definitely not,' I told him. 'Obviously the most important thing is us exchanging our vows, but I want to be able to do that in front of all our family and friends, and to have a bit of a shindig afterwards. I want to wear the fairy-tale dress and to feel like a princess for the day. That's every girl's dream, isn't it? I only intend to get married once, so I want it to be as perfect and magical as possible.'

'Yes, Max, you wouldn't deprive Ellie of all that, would you?' said Katy, whose mood had lifted considerably since she'd discovered she would be a bridesmaid after all.

'Fair enough,' said Max, holding his hands up in a gesture of defeat, his eyes shining with affection. 'I'm happy to concede that one. So long as all I'm expected to do is turn up on the day, suited and booted, and with the ring in my pocket, then I'll be a happy man. Roll on our holiday, Ellie, so we can find some proper peace and relaxation before all the wedding madness threatens to send us all completely barmy!'

# 4

___

On Friday night with the imminent arrival of Polly, Josie and Sasha expected, Max didn't need any encouragement to take Arthur off to The Dog and Duck for a pint. Already he'd bathed Noel while I pottered around downstairs, the sounds of their giggles and the splashing of water reaching me, making me smile. Afterwards he'd given him his bottle of warmed milk, read a story with the addition of some very convincing bear voices and then put him down to sleep. I swear Max had a special touch because no sooner had he crept away and turned to look at Noel snuggled in his cot than he was fast asleep. We were in the middle of a good spell at the moment and with any luck he would sleep the whole night through.

Downstairs, with only the dogs for company, who'd spent most of the day out in the grounds running riot and who were now flaked out on their beds, I pulled out some plates and glasses and cutlery from the farmhouse dresser and placed them on the table in the conservatory overlooking the garden. Katy had already gone out with Ryan, but earlier she'd helped me prepare some antipasti of cold meats, cheeses, sun-dried tomatoes and filled peppers and I would put them out a little later with a basket of breads to soak up the wine I felt sure we'd get through tonight.

It was still light outside, but the nights were definitely becoming cooler now, the vestiges of summer hanging on by the wispiest of threads. I lit tea-lights in the filigree holders dotted along the windowsill and placed some on the table, uplifted by the prettiness of the scene. I'd been living at Braithwaite Manor for about a year now, but still there were times when I had to pinch myself to believe this really was my home, struck by the sheer scale and gorgeousness of the old Georgian building.

I poured myself a small glass of wine from the cold bottle I'd just taken from the fridge. I took a sip, the golden nectar hitting exactly the right spot. I loved these nights spent with my best girlfriends in the whole world, putting the world to rights, drinking far too much wine, being wholly inappropriate and laughing. Most of all it was the laughter that was the defining feature of these occasions.

Admittedly, we'd toned it down a notch from the days when we were all single and baby free. Then it would get very messy, as we lamented our sorry love lives and made plans for our around the world, gap year, retirement trip. If I could only go back and tell those girls – me, Polly and Josie – that within the space of a few years we'd all be in committed relationships.

Thankfully, Josie and Ethan were back together now, trying to make a go of their marriage after a trial separation and, from what Josie had told me, the time apart had done them both good. Polly still hadn't come down to earth after her fairy-tale wedding in the summer and Sasha, the newest member of our little clan, was in a budding relationship with my old school pal, Johnny Tay. Then there was me, planning my wedding to the father of my child, undeniably the most eligible man in the village, and, arguably, in the whole county, too.

We were all in a good place at the moment and although I'd had a difficult few weeks recently, I didn't want to dwell on that. I was determined to look to the future.

My phone rang and I searched around, spotting it on the opposite worktop.

'Polly!' I said delightedly, seeing her name flash up on my handset.

'Hi, Ellie, look, I know this is short notice and I'm really sorry but I'm not going to make it tonight. I'm feeling a bit rough so I'm going to take myself off to bed and hope I feel better in the morning.'

'No! Really? But you have to come. You don't think a couple of glasses of fizz might make you feel better? I was so looking forward to seeing you.'

Disappointment swam round my body. 'It seems like ages since we had a proper catch-up. And, well... I've got some exciting news to tell you all.'

'Have you? Oh, sorry, Ellie. You'll have to tell me some other time.'

Polly must be feeling ill if she wasn't even going to ask me what the surprise was. She sounded as though she couldn't get off the phone quick enough, but then I supposed she couldn't help it if she was ill.

'It doesn't matter, it can wait until some other time,' I said disappointedly. 'I really hope you feel better tomorrow. Why don't I call in and see how it's going?'

'What? No! I mean, I'd hate for you to pick up any lurgy I might have. Leave it for a few days.'

This wasn't like Polly at all. She did sound out of sorts. Ordinarily, she'd have been champing at the bit to hear my exciting news. And when had she ever worried about passing on her germs to me?

'Okay, then. Not to worry,' I said brightly. 'Sounds as though you could do with your bed.' Probably a bad case of post-honeymoon blues, I decided after we'd hung up. I looked at my phone oddly, shaking my head. Was I imagining it or was Polly being distant with me? I sighed and took another sip from my wine. No, of course not. She was poorly and I was being oversensitive, missing the closeness we shared when I most needed it. There was no need to read too much into it.

Thankfully I didn't have too much time to dwell on it as shortly afterwards there was a rap on the back door and the dogs roused, beating me in the rush to greet our visitors.

'Come in, come in,' I said, my mood lifting at the sight of Josie and Sasha. 'We're a man down, I'm afraid. Polly just rang to say she wouldn't be able to make it.'

'Oh, that's a shame. She mentioned something about that this morning.' Josie swooped in for a hug and kissed me on the cheek. 'Never mind, more wine for us!'

I laughed, but couldn't help wondering why Polly hadn't said anything sooner if that was really the case. I just hoped she wasn't tiptoeing around me after my recent loss. Surely not. That wasn't her way at all. And yet...

'How are you doing, now?' Sasha put an arm around my shoulder, and squeezed me tightly around the waist with her other arm, peering in my face intently. I smiled and shrugged her embrace away on the pretext of needing to sort out some drinks.

'Fine, absolutely fine,' I said airily.

With my niggles over Polly and now with Sasha and Josie's obvious well-intended concern in the room, I felt my resolve wobble for the briefest moment. It hit me like that. When I least expected it. I turned away and took a deep breath, setting my attention on the bottle of fizz waiting to be opened, and shook those feelings away.

'Right. Shall we make a start on this wine, then? I can't tell you how lovely it is to see you both.'

Within moments any doubts I'd been experiencing were swept away as I got caught up in the easy chatter between my friends. Obviously, it would have been even better if Polly could have been there, but that wouldn't stop us from enjoying ourselves, not when we had wine, nibbles and exciting news to share.

'How's it going with Ethan?' I asked Josie once we were gathered around the kitchen table, glasses in hand.

'Yeah, good. You know, I wasn't sure whether it was the right thing for us to get back together, but it just seems so natural to have him home again. He's got his faults and he can be bloody infuriating at times. Unlike me.' This part was said with a look heavenwards and a wry smile. 'But I hated us living apart. Stella needs to have her daddy at home and it makes life so much easier having an extra pair of hands around. I know he was pretty useless on that front before, but he really is trying now to do his fair share. My family is small enough as it is, there's only Dad and some far-flung cousins that I never get to see, so I desperately want to keep our little unit together if I can. Besides, I love him.'

'Aw, well, that's everything, then. Hey, and as far as family goes, you know you have us. We're family, aren't we? Well, as good as.'

It was true. It was one of the things I so appreciated about living in the village. Everyone looked out for one another; it was almost like having an extended family around you. Josie knew that better than anyone. With her parents running The Dog and Duck for many years, Josie got to know practically all the villagers. When Josie's mum died while Josie was still a teenager, the whole of the community came

forward to support Eric and his daughter through what was a very difficult couple of years.

'Oh, I know. And I wouldn't have it any other way.'

'Me neither,' said Sasha. 'I feel really lucky to have ended up here,' she
said, flashing me a wry glance. 'Just think, if it wasn't for Max I would never
have come to Little Leyton in the first place. Then I wouldn't have met Peter
and, although he was never going to be the right man for me, I could never
regret getting involved with him because he gave me my beautiful little
Ruby. I would never have found three new best friends either,' she said,
giving a wide smile in our direction. 'Honestly, you have to sometimes think
that these things happen for a reason.'

'Too true. You're definitely one of us now,' I said, laughing. 'You realise
you could never leave now even if you wanted to.'

'Don't worry, I wouldn't want to!'

'Although that probably has a bit to do with a certain Johnny Tay being
on the scene?' said Josie mischievously. 'How's it going these days?'

Sasha's cheeks reddened and she gave a telling smile. It was funny to
think that when I first met Sasha she was in a long-standing relationship
with Max, staying in this very house. By rights I should hate the girl but I'd
warmed to her from the start, taken in by her open nature and by her
natural good looks. I'd had an injured dog in my arms at the time and
Sasha had dropped everything to drive us both to the vet's. Definitely a case
of beautiful inside and out.

I couldn't have known then that Max and Sasha's relationship was in its
last throes and would soon be over and that my friendship with Max would
later develop and blossom into something more. Now Sasha was with
Johnny, my old friend from way back, someone I'd had a brief romantic
dalliance with myself in the past. To anyone who didn't know us, it might
seem strange that our lives and friendships were so inextricably linked, but
I didn't ever give it a second thought these days.

'It's going better than I could have hoped.' Sasha held her crossed
fingers in the air. 'He's so easy to get on with and he adores Ruby, too. He's
really good with her and makes her chuckle – she thinks he's hilarious. He
makes us both laugh actually,' she said, lost in thought for a moment,
before gathering herself. 'But it's still early days and I don't want to jinx

anything, so we'll just have to see how it goes,' she said, her voice taking on a sing-song quality.

'You two are just perfect together,' I said.

'Definitely,' agreed Josie, who'd known Johnny as long as I had. 'You're made for each other.'

'Oh, enough about me,' said Sasha, batting our attentions away. 'How are you and Max doing now?'

'We're fine.' I picked up my wine glass and clasped my fingers around the stem. 'Max has found it hard, not knowing how to react around me, but he's been really supportive. It's a good job I've had little Noel to focus on because I'm not sure how I would have got through these last few weeks without him. He's a great distraction and it's impossible to stay down for long when his little smiling face greets me each morning. Max has persuaded me to get away for a week so he's planning on whisking me off to the seaside for some rest and recuperation. I wasn't sure about it at first because it will mean leaving Noel behind with my parents but Max insists it's exactly what we need.'

'Too true! Max is such a sweetheart. Where's he taking you?'

'We're going up to the Northumberland coast to stay in a castle, apparently!'

'Of course you are!' said Josie, laughing. 'That's such a Max thing to do.'

'Isn't it?' agreed Sasha. 'Not a wet weekend in Wales in a tent for you two.'

'Ha, no, and I'm really looking forward to it now,' I said, buoyed by the girls' positive response. 'It will give us a chance to properly unwind before we gear ourselves up for... well, for the big event at Christmas.'

Two curious faces looked at me expectantly. I grinned, so excited now to tell them my big news.

'Yes,' I said, shuffling forward in my seat. 'That's why I wanted to get you round here tonight. To tell you we've set a date for the wedding. It's going to be on 20th of December.'

'About bloody time,' said Josie, with a huge smile on her face.

'Ah-h-h! That's just brilliant news,' swooned Sasha.

They both leapt up from their chairs, came over to my side of the table and hugged me in congratulations.

'I know. I can't tell you how excited I am to have some firm plans in place. December is such a special time for us, it holds so many memories, so we thought, why not?'

Josie grabbed the bottle of fizz and topped up our glasses.

'This definitely calls for a toast!'

'It's such a shame Polly couldn't be here,' I said, taking a moment.

'Oh, she's going to be absolutely made up when she hears the news,' said Josie. 'You know how much she's been on at you to tie the knot ever since she got married.'

'I know!' There'd been a concerted campaign from Polly to include me and Max in her wedding plans earlier in the year and make it a double celebration, but I wanted to be sure in my own mind that it was the right thing for us to do and not get carried away on Polly's wave of excitement. Now, I was in no doubt whatsoever that I wanted to spend the rest of my life with Max and couldn't wait to tie the knot. 'Don't worry, I'll catch up with her very soon. There's something else, you see. I wanted to ask you, my three best friends in the whole world, if you would do me the very big honour of being my bridesmaids on my special day.'

The resulting squeals and jumping up and down on the spot with some furious arm waving thrown in gave me the answer I needed to know.

'Really? I am so touched.' Sasha flapped her hand in front of her face. 'I've never been a bridesmaid before and... well, I never expected this. You've known Josie and Polly all your life, but, you and me, well, it's only been a couple of years.'

'But haven't we crammed a lot into those years?'

Sasha nodded, hugging me. Our connection had been cemented through our relationship with Max, but our friendship had grown independently of that. Admittedly I'd been suspicious when Sasha had returned to the village, heavily pregnant and looking for a place to make her home. I'd put two and two together and got five and for a while it had caused ructions between Max and me, but once I realised the truth of the matter, I decided the best thing to do was to be the bigger person and offer Sasha a friendly welcome to the village.

I'd visited her at her cottage in Bluebell Lane, with gift in hand, shortly after she'd moved in, but my timing couldn't have been worse! Whether or not it had anything to do with me turning up on her doorstep, I don't know, but she went into labour unexpectedly while I was there. With no family of her own in the area, she'd asked if I'd go to the hospital with her and be her birth partner. Well, it hadn't been so much a question, more a declaration of fact. I'd never been more ill-prepared for anything in my life, but I couldn't turn my back on her in her moment of need. Despite my panic and reluctance at the time, it had actually turned out to be a huge privilege being at Sasha's side for the birth of her baby and it had created a bond between us that could never be broken.

'Once I get back from my holidays we'll get together to discuss the arrangements. I'll be asking Caroline to make the dresses, seeing as she did such a fabulous job with the gowns for Polly's wedding, and besides, she and my mum would never forgive me if I even suggested going anywhere else.'

'I'm just imagining what they might be like,' said Sasha, going all dreamy. 'And a winter wedding will be magical, especially if it snows.'

'Well, after my last experience with snow I'm not sure I'll be wishing for a white wedding in that particular sense, but, whatever the weather, it's going to be a brilliant day. Fairly low-key, just a celebration with our friends and family, some gorgeous pub grub, plenty of booze and a good old knees-up.'

'Sounds perfect,' said Josie.

'I nearly blurted it out to Polly when I spoke to her on the phone but I could tell from her voice that she wasn't really in the right frame of mind. Besides, I want to see her reaction when I tell her.'

'Oh, don't worry about Polly,' said Sasha, taking another swig of her wine. We were on our second bottle now. 'She'll be fine and by the time the wedding comes around, she'll be over—' She stopped, wide-eyed, and then winced, grabbing at her shin, probably because she'd just felt the full force of Josie's foot against her leg.

'I mean... she'll be over this bug by then,' stuttered Sasha, sheer panic spread across her face.

'Well, I should jolly well hope so. It's three months away yet! Now either she's got some dreadful disease that I don't know about or there's something else going on?' I looked from Josie to Sasha expectantly, waiting for some kind of explanation, but there wasn't one forthcoming. 'Hmm, I thought something was up with Polly, but I couldn't put my finger on what it was. Do you want to tell me what's going on?'

I saw the surreptitious glance between the pair of them before Sasha dropped her head into her hands.

'Oh, God, I'm so sorry. Me and my big mouth.'

'Josie?' I asked, when I realised I wouldn't be getting any sensible answers from Sasha.

'Look.' She took a breath as if steeling herself. 'Polly wanted to tell you herself, in person, but I guess the cat's out of the bag now.' She glared at Sasha accusingly.

'Sorry!' Sasha shrank into her shoulders, slumped in her chair and found solace in her wine.

'The thing is, Polly's pregnant.'

'Wha-at?' I had to process those words for a minute. Make sure I knew exactly what they meant. 'Polly's pregnant? And you both knew about it? Why hasn't she told me?'

I fell silent, aware that the atmosphere in the room had changed, the laughter and happiness of a few minutes ago replaced with an embarrassed awkwardness. The thought that Polly hadn't told me, her best friend, when she'd told the others made no sense to me whatsoever. Feeling hurt and confused, tears pricked my eyes and I squeezed them away. I stared into the faces of Josie and Sasha, who were both looking as though they would rather be anywhere else in the world right now than sitting opposite me dealing with my incomprehension.

'She wanted to find the right moment. She's feeling really rough and wanted to wait until she was past this sickness stage.'

'But she had no such qualms about telling you and Sasha?' Now it was my turn to drop my head into my hands. 'Oh, I get it. She didn't want to tell me because she thought I'd be upset, after what happened, losing my baby, is that it?'

'Oh, Ellie.' Josie jumped up and came and put an arm around my shoulder. 'Polly didn't want to hurt you. She found out about her pregnancy just after you'd suffered your miscarriage and she didn't want to make you feel any worse than you already did by telling you her news.'

A rush of emotions swirled around my body. Hurt, confusion, sadness. Sasha picked up the wine bottle and refilled my glass, shaking her head and mouthing her apologies.

'Well, it was hardly as if she was going to keep it secret for very long, was it?' I grumbled. 'I'm just upset that she didn't feel she could tell me. We're supposed to be best friends.'

'And you are,' said Josie, squeezing me tighter. 'Maybe she didn't handle it in the best way but that came from a place of concern and love for you. Nothing else. And I know how excited she's going to be when she hears that the wedding date has been set.'

I sat pensive for a moment, battling with my emotions, not really sure how I should be feeling until I recognised the pang of loss I felt inside, not only for our lost baby but for Polly too, not being here at my side. She must have felt awful at what should have been one of the happiest moments in her life and instead she was preoccupied, worrying over my feelings. My heart twisted for her. I'm not sure I would have handled it any differently in her shoes.

'I know.' I sighed. 'And to think she's got a little baby growing. It's the best news ever. I'm really happy for her. Honestly, I am. I just hope she doesn't think I might not be.'

'Listen, once you get to see and speak to her, all of this will be forgotten. When you think about it, there's so much good news around here right now and we need to celebrate that. Come on,' said Josie, raising her glass in the umpteenth toast of the evening. 'To weddings, friendship, babies and... new beginnings.'

# 5

We were lingering over the coffee I'd made, and the girls were just making the first mutterings about going home, when we heard the roar of a distinctive motorbike and the scrunch of gravel on the driveway.

'That sounds like Ryan,' I said, jumping out of my chair to peer through the window. 'What's he doing here?'

Seconds later, Katy came running into the kitchen, pulling off her motorcycle helmet, her jet-black hair sticking up at all angles now.

'Katy! What's going on? If Max finds out you've been on that bike again, he'll go spare.'

'Ellie!' Her breath came in short sharp bursts. 'I need Max. Where is he? There's a fire in the high street. We could just see it from the top of the lane. Smoke billowing up in the sky. I don't know where it's coming from but it looks as though it might be the pub.'

'What?' I shook my head, not really believing it. 'How come?'

'I don't know. But Max needs to get down there right now. Ryan says it's definitely the pub that's burning.'

'But Max is already there. At the pub with Arthur. Oh, God!' Panic swept through my veins as I tried to make sense of what Katy was saying. She must be mistaken. The pub would be full of customers tonight. There couldn't be a fire.

'Dad's down there too,' said Josie, concern etched over her features. 'I've got to go, to see what's going on there.'

'I'll come. Can you stay here, Katy, and look after Noel?'

Her face fell, but she nodded her agreement. I knew she'd want to turn right round, get back on Ryan's motorbike and see for herself what was going on, but if there really was a fire blazing at the pub then it was better if she stayed well out of the way.

'Oh, do be careful,' said Sasha, pulling on her jacket. 'I'll get home and tell Johnny. He'll want to help. Let us know if there's anything we can do.'

Josie and I quickly grabbed our coats and rushed outside, the cold air and the thought of what we might encounter when we reached the pub immediately sobering us up. I turned down Ryan's offer to jump on the back of his bike as, for a start, I was terrified of that big black hulking machine, but also because Josie and I wanted to be together for this. We watched the lights of the motorbike disappear up the drive in the direction from which it had come and we linked arms, following the beam of the torch, walking as quickly as we could, occasionally breaking into a trot in our haste to get there.

'It'll be all right, won't it, Josie?' I asked.

'Look,' she said, pointing into the distance. 'You can see the fire.'

As soon as we reached the high street, any hope that it might have been a false alarm was dashed when we saw a swarm of people milling around outside The Dog and Duck, against the backdrop of flames and plumes of smoke reaching up into the night sky.

'Oh, God!' We ran the rest of the way, my heart thumping hard in my chest and my stomach churning over and over. Bile rose in my throat and I gulped the sensation down, not wanting to throw up over the pavement. Dave, one of the regulars at the pub, was the first person we saw as the sound of sirens drew ever closer.

'What's happened?'

'Aw, Ellie.' He wrapped his arm around me. 'To be fair, I still don't know. Dan started shouting for us all to get out, saying the barn was on fire. We couldn't get out of there fast enough.'

'Did they get everyone out?'

'Yeah, I think so.' I cast him a questioning glance. He didn't sound entirely convincing but he just shrugged away my unasked question.

My gaze roamed the melee trying to pick out the familiar faces. Someone had found a chair for Arthur and he was sitting on the verge on the opposite side of the road, looking bewildered at the scene unfolding.

'Where's Max and Eric?'

Dave grimaced, confirming my worst suspicions.

'They went round the back to see if they could put out the fire. We told them to leave it, to wait for the fire service, but you know what Max is like. There was no stopping him.'

'And Dad went with him? The idiot! He's almost seventy. What was he thinking?'

Fear gripped my body as there was no mistaking the acrid stench of smoke filling the air. I grabbed hold of Josie's hand and squeezed it tight, craning my head to see through the crowds in search of Max and Eric. It was nothing less than I expected from those two. Max wouldn't have stopped to think, acting entirely on instinct, believing he was invincible. And Eric would have been the same, determined to do whatever he could to save his beloved pub. The stupid bloody idiots.

I pulled Josie by the hand and we edged forward, seeing if we could get a better view and find out more information about what exactly had happened, but we were stopped in our tracks.

'You can't go any further, love. This whole area is being cordoned off. You need to move right back. In fact, you'd be better off going home and leaving us to do our job.'

'But this is my pub. And my husband and her dad are still in that build-ing. You have to get them out!'

Okay, so it wasn't strictly true that Max was my husband but he was as good as, and if anything were to happen to him, then... well, it just didn't bear thinking about.

'Don't worry, we'll do everything we can.'

The men and women from the fire service piled through the side entrance to the pub, with their ladders and hoses. Our attention was distracted as two ambulances came speeding along the high street, drawing to a halt outside the pub, my heart filling with dread at the sight. The paramedics jumped out and purposefully made their way across to the chief fire officer, who seemed to be coordinating the proceedings.

'Has someone been injured, then?' I asked, hearing the panic in my own voice.

'We're doing an initial survey. Could you give me the names of the missing persons you mentioned, please?'

I gasped and glanced at Josie. They weren't missing people. It was just Max and Eric who'd nipped outside to the back. Any moment now they would reappear along the cobbled path, laughing and joking at their lucky escape. The fire officer quickly scribbled down their names in his notebook before striding off, leaving us horrified and adrift.

'Ellie. There you are!' I turned round to see Darcy, who'd sidled up next to me. My heart sank. She was the last person I wanted to see right now and it briefly crossed my mind that she'd been spending an awful lot of time in the village recently. 'What a thing to happen, eh? Mind you, it's not all bad – I do love a man in uniform,' she swooned, her gaze following the rear of one of the male firefighters. 'Although I promise you I didn't have anything to do with this.' Her high pitched laughter went straight through me and elicited some deathly stares from some of the other villagers standing around us.

'Darcy! How could you even think about something like that at a time like this? The whole pub could be destroyed and we still don't know if anyone's been injured.'

'Oh, Ellie, don't be so melodramatic.' She waved a manicured hand around in the air. 'Those hunky firemen will have it all under control. Don't you worry about that. You know, Max was such a hero. I was talking to him when that barmaid started shouting about a fire. He didn't think twice about jumping up and running round the back.' She made a flapping motion with her hand against her chest. 'He's a proper all round action man, isn't he?'

'Darcy, get out of my bloody sight, would you, before I say or do something I might regret.'

'Ooh.' She pursed her lips and widened her eyes. 'I was just trying to make you feel better, that's all. There's really no need to be quite so rude.'

'Just...' I held up the palms of my hands to her, floundering as to what to say. 'Please just go.'

Josie grabbed my hand and pulled me to one side, away from the annoying Darcy.

'Look, Ellie, over there. It's Max and Dad, and Dan. They're okay. They're actually okay.'

'Oh, thank goodness.' Relief flooded through my body, my legs feeling as though they might give way beneath me. We barged our way through to try and reach them and stopped to speak to one of the firefighters on the way. 'Do you think everyone's out now?'

'Yes, and we're hopeful that we've got the blaze under control.'

'Really?' It didn't seem possible. Everything seemed so desperately out of control. People milled around on the pavement outside the pub in shock, the grey smoke billowing into the night sky, the sickening smell filling our lungs. 'Thank you. Thank you so much,' I said, squeezing the man's arm. 'Max! Eric! Over here.' Josie and I both waved madly to catch their attention.

'Ellie!' Max's face was smudged with black smoke marks, matching the darkness of his expression. 'What are you doing here?'

'Katy came home and told us there was a fire. I couldn't not come. I had to make sure everyone was okay.'

He wrapped his arms around me, my head falling on his jumper, his whole body reeking of smoke and burning, the smell catching at my throat. I pulled away to look up at him.

'Oh, God! Are you all right?' My gaze darted from Max to Eric, who was looking equally bedraggled and utterly defeated.

'We were lucky.' Max raked a hand through his mussed-up hair. 'It could have been so much worse. The fire took hold really quickly. There was nothing we could do to stop it. Those small extinguishers didn't even touch the flames.'

Eric coughed and spluttered, shaking his head.

'I've never seen anything like it.'

Just then one of the paramedics who'd spotted Eric struggling with his breathing came over to talk to him.

'I know you don't want to, but I think it might be best if we get you to the hospital to have a proper check-over, just as a precaution.'

'No, I'm not going,' said Eric firmly. 'I'll be absolutely fine. I've got my daughter here. She'll look after me.'

'Well, if anything changes, if you feel at all unwell or if your breathing gets any worse, then you must get to the hospital straight away. Okay?' she said. 'You, too,' she said, including Max in her advice.

'Come on, Dad, let's get you home.' Josie put her arm through her dad's. Eric glanced up at The Dog and Duck, the colourful painted sign still swinging defiantly against the smoky sky. This was Eric's home for many years. How must he be feeling knowing it had come very close to being destroyed in a matter of minutes? If it weren't for the pungent smell and the swarm of emergency vehicles and activity outside, you wouldn't be able to tell what had gone on. One thing was for sure, Eric wouldn't be sleeping here tonight. Or tomorrow. And when the pub might be able to open again, well, that was anyone's best guess.

# 6

Back at the manor, despite the late hour, no one was ready for their beds, our thoughts and minds preoccupied with the lucky escape we'd had tonight. I suspected we were all still in a state of shock. I made coffee, pouring in a nip of brandy for those who needed one. Poor Arthur looked worn out as he sat huddled in one of the oak carvers, a blanket round his shoulders. He'd got so much more tonight than the enjoyable pint of beer he'd bargained for. Ryan had returned and was offering some moral support to Katy, the pair of them curled up together on the cushioned window seat in the kitchen, holding hands.

'What will Dan and Silke do?' Katy asked.

'Well, fortunately their boat is back on the water, just this week, after being at the repair yard for a couple of months so they've gone back to the canal tonight. Eric went home with Josie. I expect he'll be all out of sorts.'

'How bad was the damage?' asked Ryan.

'We'll have a better idea tomorrow when we get to see it in daylight,' Max said. 'But I don't think there's much left of the barn and the fire spread to the kitchen of the main building, too. Thank God the fire service turned up when they did or else it could have been a whole lot worse.'

'I know. It could so easily have spread to Polly's shop and the antiques shop too.' The full impact of what could have happened was only just resonating with me.

Josie had rung Polly to tell her what was going on, but had assured her that the florist's wasn't affected by the fire – the last thing we wanted was for her to come rushing out late at night in a panic. The fun and frolics of earlier tonight with the girls seemed like a lifetime away.

'So what exactly happened?' Ryan asked. 'Does anyone know?'

'It was Silke who raised the alarm. She was up in the bedroom and looked out the window and saw that the barn was alight. She called out to Dan and that's when we all went dashing round the back. I don't know what caused the fire, but once it took hold it went up like an inferno. It all happened so fast. There was nothing we could do to stop it.'

'I still can't believe it.' I shook my head. 'It was a good job the barn wasn't full with customers or else we might be in a very different situation now. We have to be grateful that there weren't any injuries or fatalities even.'

'Definitely. Although if we had been using the barn then we might have been able to detect the fire earlier and put a stop to it before it really took hold.' Max gave a resigned shrug. 'Who knows? It's all just speculation at the moment.'

'What does this mean for the pub? How long do you think it will be out of action?' Katy voiced the very concerns that had been troubling me, too.

'Well, it will have to stay closed until the authorities have declared the place safe and that won't be until the surveys on the building are done. They'll need to assess the damage and find out what might have caused the fire in the first place.'

'Oh, God.' I let out a heartfelt sigh. 'We had so much planned at the pub for these coming weeks. There's the quiz on Tuesday, the book club on Friday, and I'd taken so many bookings for the barn lately.' That side of the business had really grown in recent months as people came to know about the barn and what a great space it was for functions. We'd hosted a wide range of events including christening receptions, hen nights, birthday parties and weddings too. 'I'll have to ring round tomorrow and let people know what's happened. It'll mean cancelling lots of events.'

'So long as it doesn't mean cancelling your wedding,' said Katy.

Our wedding was three months away – surely that was enough time to get everything back to normal. I flashed a glance at Max hoping for his reassurance, but instead he just shrugged non-committally.

'It's too early to say.'

'What?' I said, horrified.

He nodded. 'Look, we're all just surmising, but you saw the state of the pub tonight. Until we know the full extent of what we're dealing with we can't make any plans, but I think it's safe to assume that the pub will be out of action for a few weeks or even months. We'll just have to wait and see.'

*Out of action for months*? It was difficult to comprehend such a thing. That could feasibly take us beyond Christmas. It had been bad enough when the pub was closed for a few weeks in the run-up to Christmas a few years ago when renovations were being done. To have the pub closed again over the festive season would be gut-wrenching.

'You know what that means, don't you?' I said sadly, my voice wavering with emotion. 'We're going to have to postpone the wedding!'

Katy's face dropped, to match the sinking of my heart, but it seemed churlish to be thinking of something so frivolous at a time like this. However inconvenient it was, I was just so grateful that the pub and our customers had got off relatively scot-free.

'Come on,' said Max, standing up. 'We should all get to bed. We're going to have a busy few days ahead.'

A moment later, upstairs, I hovered at the threshold to Noel's bedroom. I tiptoed in, careful not to rouse him, and I melted at the sight of him, my heart overflowing with love. His body was encased in a pale blue Peter Rabbit Babygro, his arms flung above his head, his top lip quivering faintly as he breathed in and out. Totally oblivious to the drama that had been unfolding tonight. Tears pricked at my eyes and I couldn't help myself from reaching out a finger to run down his cheek. Even from a distance I could detect his sweet vanilla scent. From behind me I sensed a movement and turned round to find Max. He came over and slipped an arm around my waist and bent over to look at Noel. We exchanged a look of relief and love, grateful that the most precious thing in the world to us was safe and that no one had been hurt in the blaze. Wasn't that all that mattered?

So we might have to put our wedding plans on hold until next year, but that was a small price to pay when it all might have been so much worse.

# 7

The next morning, after a fitful night's sleep and an almost welcome five o'clock alarm call from Noel, when I brought him into bed with us for a much needed cuddle, Max got up and disappeared out into his office in the gardens, spending a few hours on the phone speaking to the insurers and various other people who needed to be consulted about the fire. I made us coffee and bacon sandwiches, before I sat down at the kitchen table and went through the bookings calendar for the barn, ringing round everyone on the list, cancelling their functions. It broke my heart to have to do it, but there was no other option, not when we didn't have a room for hire now.

'You could try the community centre,' I told each of our customers, half-heartedly, sharing in their disappointment. I'd only recently started on the arrangements for our wedding, and now I would probably need to cancel those too, so soon after I'd booked them. I picked up the pen and scribbled at the bottom of my notebook.

*Cancel catering*
*Speak to Rev. Trish Evans*
*Rearrange date?*
*Discuss with Max!*

I sighed, that would all need to wait until some other time. Now, we had other more pressing matters to see to.

Later, leaving Noel at home with Katy, Max and I took a walk into the village to visit the pub in daylight to see for ourselves the full extent of the damage. As soon as we reached the high street the stench of burning assaulted our senses and my hand flew to my mouth and nose, the pungent smell of burnt timbers hitting the back of my throat and making me gag.

As we stood in front of the historic eighteenth century building my heart twisted at the palpable sadness wafting in the air.

Across the front of the pub and the main front door polythene tape was draped with the words 'Fire Service' emblazoned across it. For what seemed like minutes, but could only really have been seconds, I was frozen to the spot, shocked at the reminder that something like this could have actually happened.

'I just can't bear it.' I groaned. Max came across and put an arm around my shoulder, squeezing it tight.

The pub had been at the centre of village life for years and had hosted so many memorable events in that time. It had been a happy family home for Eric, his late wife, Miriam, and Josie, who'd been a dear friend since I was about four years old. This place had practically been my second home when I was growing up, I'd spent that many hours here with Josie. It was why I'd been so determined to keep the pub open when it had looked as though it might be sold to private developers. It was devastating to think that it might be out of action now indefinitely.

Max wandered across to the wooden side gates, standing on tiptoe to peer over the top into the beer garden.

'Come on,' he said, beckoning me over. I took hold of his hand and we wandered over the cobbled side path, a lump lodged in my chest as I prepared myself for what was waiting for us.

'Oh, no!' I cried. 'It's all gone!'

I knew that, of course. Max had told me the barn had burnt down, we'd been talking about it all night long, and yet it was still such a shock to be confronted with the actual physical aftermath of the fire.

The old barn, or what was left of it, was unrecognisable. There was just a black charred mess of broken and scorched timbers left in its place. The acrid bitter smell of smoke hung in the air. There was no sign of the long trestle tables and benches; no doubt they were in amongst the pile of ashes smothering the ground. Max strode around, clearly with his property expert hat on, looking up at what remained of the shell of the building and then peering in at the blackened kitchen of the main building.

'Blimey, it's worse than I thought. We're lucky that the whole pub didn't go up in the blaze.'

'I suppose,' I murmured. Although it didn't feel very lucky to me. The barn had been such a special space, an integral part of the pub's success, but it wasn't only because it was the venue for so many happy occasions, but also, more poignantly, it was where our baby was born.

It was just soul destroying to think that it had been completely wiped away in the matter of an hour or so. Now the authorities had closed down the pub until all the investigations were complete and who knew how long that would be? Contractors had been in already to put scaffolding up around the rear of the pub by the kitchen as a precaution so that any visiting surveyors would be safe as they undertook their work.

We didn't hang around, it was far too depressing, and we wandered back out to the front of the building. The florists to one side of the pub and the antiques shop to the other had stayed closed today as the whole area had been cordoned off by the authorities. A steady succession of villagers came along, hugging us, passing on their sympathies, offering words of comfort.

'Don't worry, it seems terrible now, but at least no one was hurt. It could have been so much worse.'

The sentiment was repeated over and over by well-meaning friends and, while it was true and I was grateful for their concern, at the moment I was struggling to see a way beyond all the mess and devastation. Ordinarily we would have been gearing up for a busy day at the pub but now it was as if our whole lives had been put on hold as a result of the fire.

'Ellie. There you are! I've been trying to call you.'

I turned round, hearing Polly's familiar voice.

'I'm so sorry.' She threw her arms around me and squeezed so tight that

I had to extricate myself from her over zealous embrace. If there'd been a moment last night when I'd been worried that things might have changed between us, seeing the concern in her eyes now reassured me that everything was as it had always been.

'What happened? Do you know?' she asked.

'They're not sure, but it's been suggested it might have been an electrical fault.'

'Crikey, you would never believe that it could have such a devastating effect.' She linked arms with me as we surveyed the scene.

'I know. And I'm just relieved that it didn't spread to your shop. That doesn't bear thinking about. I'm sorry you've not been able to open up today.'

Polly waved a dismissive hand.

'Don't worry about that. It's only for a day. They've said we should be able to open up again on Monday.'

'And are you feeling better now?'

'Oh, Ellie, I'm so sorry about that. I know you've got so much going on now with all of this but I really need to talk to you some time. There's something I need to tell you, and I feel really bad that I didn't mention it sooner. It's just that...' She looked around at the locals swarming the high street, at all the activity going on in front of us. 'Look, now's not the time. Could we grab a coffee together some time soon?'

'It's all right, Polly. You don't need to worry.' I took hold of her arms, my gaze scanning her face. 'I know. About the baby.'

Polly's face clouded with confusion.

'You do? Oh, God. I'm so, so sorry. Who told you?'

'Stop it!' I scolded her, lightly. 'You don't need to apologise. It was Sasha – she let it slip last night, after far too many glasses of wine. She didn't mean to. She felt terrible when she realised.'

'Oh, I didn't want you finding out like that, but it's not Sasha's fault, it's mine. I wasn't deliberately keeping it from you. I wanted to tell you, but it didn't seem right to be feeling so happy when you'd been through such a shitty time. And now this has happened on top of everything else.'

'It's okay, Polly. I'm thrilled for you, really I am.' I pulled her into my embrace, hugging her tight. 'Look, if you're free now, why don't we go back to the manor and have a proper catch-up? I could do with a coffee. You can tell me how it's all been going.'

'Yeah, good idea,' said Max, who'd swooped in on our conversation. 'I've still got a couple of things to sort out here but I shouldn't be too long. I'll see you back there later.'

Back at the manor, Katy was keen to get down to the village to meet her friends who had all converged in the high street, so she quickly left, and I made coffee for Polly and me, and a cup of tea for Arthur who was taking his time this morning after all the drama of last night.

'So, do you know how long the pub will be closed for?' Polly asked as she sat down at the kitchen table, holding Noel in her arms.

'No idea yet. I'm just pleased Max is dealing with the authorities and the insurers. I think I'd find it far too stressful. Phoning around everyone this morning telling them the pub and the barn would be closed indefinitely was bad enough. So to have some good news to share...' I nodded my head in the direction of Polly's non-existent bump '...is just lovely.'

She smiled, ruffling Noel's fine hair.

'Honestly, Ellie, you were the first person I wanted to tell, but I didn't know how, knowing you had lost your baby when we might have shared our pregnancies together, and thinking how it would make you feel seeing me go through mine. I know I shouldn't have presumed to know how you were feeling, but I was just trying to make sense of my own emotions really before I spoke to you.'

'It's fine, really it is. I understand,' I said, detecting the faintest quiver in my voice and hoping Polly wouldn't notice it. It had been an emotional twenty-four hours, after all. 'It just wasn't meant to be for us this time around. But this, you expecting your baby, is a small silver lining that we could never have anticipated. Just think, I'm going to be an honorary auntie. I'm pretty chuffed about that.'

'Good. I'm so relieved. I was worried that this would come between us or things might be awkward now.'

'Never! Anyway,' I said, keen to move the conversation on, 'how are you feeling?'

My gaze ran down her body. There was no sign of any bump yet, but her skin had a sheer translucence to it that accentuated her freckles. There was a definite glow about her – an inner pregnancy glow combined with... an all too familiar greyness. She exhaled a big sigh and grimaced.

'Terrible. Why didn't you tell me it was so awful? I feel sick the whole time. Not just in the morning, but all day. And so exhausted too. I wasn't lying about how terrible I was feeling when I spoke to you yesterday. I couldn't have come last night even if I'd wanted to. Just the whiff of food is enough to make my stomach churn.'

'It'll all be worth it. In a few weeks' time you'll be feeling more like your normal self and you'll be in that lovely blooming stage.'

'I do hope so! I don't want to feel like this for the next six months.' She paused, then cringed. 'Listen to me moaning on. Sorry. I shouldn't—'

'Stop it,' I said, probably more harshly than was necessary. 'You can't tiptoe round me, watching what you say for the rest of your pregnancy. I want to hear all about it. The good bits and the bad bits. Isn't that what friends are for? I'll be really sad if you feel you can't talk to me honestly any more.'

'Oh, I will, Ellie,' she said, reaching across for my hand. 'Once I get my head around all of this. Anyway, enough about me. What was the news you wanted to tell me?'

'Ah, yes, that! I think my good news might be on hold now, after last night's fire. We'd set a date for the wedding.' Polly's face lit up. 'It was going to be on 20th of December and I wanted to ask you to be a bridesmaid, along with Josie, Sasha and Katy. Only I'm not sure it'll be happening now.'

'Oh, Ellie, really? What bloody bad timing. But don't let this stop you. You can still get married. Hell, you have to go ahead with the wedding. Especially now you've asked me to be your bridesmaid. Or else I'll be really disappointed.' She flashed me a smile. 'Honestly, Ellie, it will be fine. And thank you. I can't wait to be your bridesmaid! I'd have been mightily offended if you hadn't asked,' she said, giving me a cheeky wink. 'You might just have to change the venue, that's all – I'm guessing you were going to have it in the barn?'

'Yes. But I'm thinking it might be easier to put it off now until next year when things have settled down a bit.'

'What, are you kidding me? As bridesmaid, it is my responsibility to make sure the wedding takes place as planned. So, we're going to make it happen, one way or another. Do you understand me?'

I laughed and shook my head. Sometimes there was no arguing with Polly.

# 8

It turned out to be one of those days. The phone didn't stop ringing and we had a constant string of people popping by wanting to find out the latest news about the pub. No sooner had Polly left to go home, muttering about all things bridal, than Max returned, bringing with him Dan and Eric, too. Mum and Dad had called in as well and Katy had brought Ryan along to join in with the post-match analysis.

'What I can't get over,' said Eric, clearly reliving every awful moment, 'is how quickly that fire took hold. In all my years at The Dog and Duck, I've never seen anything like it. We heard Silke yelling from upstairs about a fire. She came rushing down and we all shot out the back to see what was going on but by then the whole barn was ablaze. The force of it was staggering. There was nothing we could have done to stop it.'

'Oh, goodness, Eric, we know that. And you mustn't blame yourselves. If the three of you hadn't been there and acted so quickly in calling the emergency services then the whole pub could have burnt down.'

'I know, but I can't help feeling responsible. That we could have done more.'

'We did everything we could.' Max reassured him.

Eric shook his head and I felt so desperately sad for him. I'd been lost in my own feelings and what it would mean for me but Eric would have suffered an equal sense of loss. After he'd returned from his travels after his retirement he'd moved in to live with Josie and Ethan, but when their marriage had hit the rocks he'd made his excuses and moved out, into the spare room at The Dog and Duck. He'd said he'd wanted to give them the time and space to sort out their difficulties and I was sure that was true but I suspected there was also an element of him wanting to get back to the pub. To the place where he felt most at home.

'How's Silke doing?' I asked Dan.

'She's fine. A bit shook up. We're both the same really. We can't help thinking what might have happened if the fire had started a couple of hours later when we were all in bed.'

'It doesn't bear thinking about,' said Eric gravely.

'Well, we'll do what we can to get the pub up and running as quickly as possible,' said Max. 'Just as soon as we get the go ahead then we can make a start on the refurbishment. It will need a complete new kitchen before you guys can move back in.'

Max owned the freehold of the property while I ran the pub. Ordinarily, he didn't get involved with the day-to-day goings-on at the pub, that was my responsibility, but who knew when I might be able to get back to doing the job I loved. I was only thankful that Max was on hand to deal with all the practicalities of dealing with the aftermath of the fire.

'Of course, we'll pay your salaries while you're off work,' I told Dan and Eric.

'Don't worry about that, love,' said Eric.

'Well, we'll sort something out. It's hardly your fault you can't work. I've cancelled all the bookings we had for the barn, although I think word had spread pretty rapidly anyway,' I said.

'Probably like wildfire.' Eric raised his eyebrows, a rueful smile playing on his lips.

'It's such a shame.' I sighed.

'Were there many bookings?' asked Dan.

'At least one each week, but there were more events that I wanted to organise, like a Halloween party and a Bonfire Night bash. It would have got so much busier in the run-up to Christmas. Oh, and there was the small matter of a very personal wedding in December, too. We won't be able to go ahead now.'

'There's always next year,' Max said, which prompted an involuntary roll of the eyes from me.

'It's disappointing,' he said, 'but it can't be helped.' It wasn't that he was unsympathetic, only that he wasn't one to wallow. All he was focussed on was putting things right. 'Think about it, Ellie. We've been here before. We closed the pub down a couple of years ago for refurbishment and that came right in the end.'

'Yeah,' I agreed, half-heartedly.

I was feeling sorry for myself. What with losing our baby and now the pub being closed for the foreseeable future it was as though we'd hit a run of bad luck. I'd been doing my utmost to be positive, not dwelling on what had gone wrong, but trying to focus instead on everything we had to look forward to. This just seemed like an extra kick in the teeth, as though events were conspiring against us. It felt selfish with Dan and Eric sitting around my table, when they'd gone through such an awful ordeal, that all I was thinking about was how it would affect my big plans for my wedding day.

'You know, there's always the village hall.'

'There's no way I'm holding my wedding in the village hall!'

'I wasn't suggesting for one moment that you did.' Max shook his head ruefully. 'I meant for those people whose events you had to cancel.'

'Oh, right, I see,' I said, my cheeks flushing at my outburst. Everyone sitting around the table gave me a sympathetic look, making me feel worse than I already did. 'Yes,' I said, trying to recover the moment. 'Well, I did point them in the direction of the community centre, too.'

'Although it's hardly the same, is it?' said Katy, who was definitely batting on my side, just as disappointed as I was.

It didn't really matter. Not in the grand scheme of things. You just had to get these things in perspective. We had only just decided on getting married this year, so it wasn't any real hardship to have to move it to next year. A summer wedding, as Polly had, would be lovely. Although if I was really set on a Christmas wedding, then there was always, as Max had suggested, next year. Even if it did seem an impossibly long way away.

Later, when it was just me, Max and Noel left alone together – Katy and

Arthur had disappeared off to their respective bedrooms – we were just debating on what we might have for supper, deciding fish and chips from the mobile van would be the best option for tonight, when another thought popped into my head.

'Something else we haven't done,' I told Max. 'If you give me the number of the hotel I'll ring them and cancel the booking.'

'What?' Max grabbed my arm and spun me round to face him. 'But why? Why would we want to do that?'

'We can't go away, Max, not when we don't know what's happening with the pub. We need to get everything sorted with all the different agencies involved. We'll have to put the holiday off until next year too.'

'There'll be nothing that pressing to do while the investigations are still going on. And if there is, well then, we're always contactable on the end of the phone or by email.' Max stroked a finger down my cheek. 'I think, after everything that's happened, we both need a holiday now more than ever.'

He kissed me and pulled me into his chest and I melted into his warm and supportive embrace.

'This is a blip, Ellie. One we could have done without but we'll get through this. Honestly, we will.'

Just as his lips met mine again and I felt my body relax into his, there was yet another knock at the door and Max reluctantly extricated himself and went across to answer it, while I went off in search of my handbag, looking for my purse for the fish and chips.

'Good grief!' Max's voice was incredulous and I spun round wondering what this latest unexpected turn of events might be.

'Who is it?' I called.

'Mum?'

'Hello, Max. Ellie!' Rose lugged two suitcases, a rucksack, some carrier bags and her handbag over the threshold, dumping them on the floor and then turned to the driver of the taxi. 'Could you please bring my other bags through?'

'What are you doing here, Mum?' Max's voice reflected the shock I was feeling. 'You never said you were coming. And where's Alan?'

'Oh...' she waved a hand around dismissively '...I've left him.' She took in our stricken faces, looking from me to Max, then to Katy and to Arthur, who had both joined us in the kitchen, hearing our surprise visitor's arrival. 'I hope this isn't a bad time. What's happened at the pub? I noticed that it was closed when we drove past. Anyway,' she went on, not waiting for our explanation, 'sorry for just turning up like this but I'm hoping I might be able to stay. Just for a few days. Alan and I are finished. He can't understand that I want to be close to my family. I mean, what's wrong with that? It's only natural, isn't it?'

She seemed to be directing her question at me, so I nodded in agreement. Katy, who hadn't always enjoyed the easiest of relationships with her mum, seemed to have been rendered speechless.

They'd all been through a difficult time since the truth about Katy's biological father had been revealed. Alan, Katy's stepfather, had blurted out the facts in the middle of an argument. The man she always believed to be her father, Max's dad, wasn't her father after all, and Katy's world, everything she'd known to be true, had unravelled around her. That was why she'd left her home in Spain with her mum and Alan to come to live with Max at the manor. She was well and truly settled now in Little Leyton and her relationship with her mum was almost back to what it had been before the fallout, but Katy had never forgiven Alan, directing all her hurt and anger in his direction. Now, it seemed as if Rose and Alan's relationship hadn't survived the fallout either.

'Don't worry,' she said, giving a light laugh as the taxi driver struggled with the last of the bags, looking relieved that he could finally make his escape. 'I won't stay long, just until I can find myself somewhere more permanent, like a room in a house somewhere.'

I detected the imperceptible lift of Max's eyebrows as he surveyed the huge collection of luggage on the hall floor. I didn't know about a room, she needed an aircraft hangar to store that little lot. With Arthur, Katy and Rose living in the house and my parents coming to stay to look after Noel very soon, it looked as though life at Braithwaite Manor might become even more interesting over the next couple of weeks. I sighed and pulled out another chair at the table, this time for Rose.

A week away by the seaside seemed very appealing indeed.

# 9

'Do you really think this is the best idea? Maybe we should go home. We could always postpone our trip and rearrange it for some other time when things have settled down a little at home?'

'Ellie! Stop it! We're barely out of the village yet. Besides, when is life ever going to settle down in Little Leyton? No, this might be the last chance we have to get away together for a long time. Besides, they'll all be fine,' he said, chuckling.

I sat on my hands, trying to settle my inner panic, and gazed out of the window of the car, wondering how I would ever get through a whole week without seeing my little boy. My empty arms ached, I was missing him that much already. If it had been down to me I would have probably turned back right there and then and gone home.

It had been a bit frenetic getting away. Mum and Dad had arrived earlier in the morning, despite Rose's insistence that there was no need for them to come as she was more than capable of looking after her grandson herself. It had taken some careful handling to circumnavigate that little one, but in truth Noel knew my mum and dad so much better, having seen them on a regular basis since he was born, and Mum knew his routine as well as I did.

Mum and Rose had got to know each other better and had grown closer during Rose's last visit just after Noel was born, but I wasn't sure how they would fare being under the same roof for a week, vying for top grandmother slot.

Katy was already finding it hard living with her mum again and seemed to have reverted to being a sulky teenager in her presence. Max had taken Katy to one side and told her that she wasn't to kick off or to get into any arguments with her mum while we were away. Rose was going through a rough patch and she needed time to clear her head and decide what she was going to do next. Max was hoping that by the time we returned from holiday she would have realised just how much she was missing Alan and would be on the next flight back to Spain.

Arthur had wished us well cheerfully but I suspected he was putting on a brave front. He'd come to rely on me for, not only practical support, but emotional support too, and I knew he'd miss me being around every day, so I'd given him a big hug and told him I'd be back before he knew it. Still, Katy would keep a close eye on him. Those two had formed the most unlikely friendship and she popped into his room each morning, before going off to college, for a natter and a catch-up.

Digby had got wind of the fact that I was going away and had followed me around morosely. His big brown eyes had looked up at me accusingly and I'd felt terrible that he wasn't coming with us. I had suggested to Max that we take him, knowing he would love the long sandy beaches on the coast, but Max had quickly put paid to that idea. This time was for just Max and me without any other distractions. Besides, the other dogs hadn't had any such concerns about our imminent disappearance and had been lolloping around the kitchen, excited by all the activity in the house.

On the way through the village we slowed down as we passed The Dog and Duck and I felt a pang of sadness on seeing the old place looking empty and forlorn.

'Don't worry, Ellie, it will be up and running again before you know it.'

'Oh, I know,' I said, looking over my shoulder to see the distinctive old building disappearing into the distance. The sooner the better as far as I was concerned.

\* \* \*

'Come on,' said Max, grabbing hold of my hand and leading me away from
the car. It had been a long journey, almost seven hours, and it was a relief to
be able to stretch out my legs and to feel the cool nip of the air on my skin
as we clambered over the grassy bank. Autumn had arrived with a
vengeance. The sky was cloudless still but the wind whipped off the sea
invigorating my senses. I dug my hands into the front pocket of my hoodie,
glad of the warmth it offered. We followed a rough narrow path that grew
increasingly sandy and as we reached the top of a dune a beautiful stretch
of coastline, as far as the eye could see, revealed itself.

'Look at that!' I said, my mouth dropping open at the sight. The wide
sandy beach swept away from us in both directions, reaching the expanse
of sky.

'Isn't it beautiful? I've always loved it up here.'

'It's breathtaking,' I agreed. In the far distance there was a lone dog
walker with two springer spaniels who were dashing in and out of the
water, chasing waves, but aside from them there wasn't a soul in sight.

'Even in high season this beach is pretty much deserted, which is why I
love it so much. It's so remote and peaceful. You can walk for miles without
bumping into anyone.'

'Wouldn't the dogs love it here?'

'Yes. Well, we must come back some time. We can rent a cottage and
bring Noel and all the dogs, or maybe just Digby,' he said, clearly thinking
about that scenario for a moment. 'Now, though, it's great that it's just you
and me.' He squeezed my hand. 'We don't often have a chance to spend
time alone, just the two of us.'

I looked across at his profile, the strong cut of his jaw, his roman nose,
the set of his wide mouth and my heart lifted. Sometimes it was hard to
believe that we'd only known each other a couple of years, we'd been
through so much together in that time, and for a long while I'd been
tormented by doubts over whether he really was the right man for me. My
attraction to him had been instantaneous and all-encompassing but I
hadn't trusted the strength of my feelings, unsure whether they were based
purely on longing and lust for Max who was, well, unlike anyone I'd ever
met before. He'd had an aura about him that was dangerously enticing but
his lifestyle was so far removed from mine that I couldn't think what we

could possibly have in common. He was a property developer, successful, his huge restored manor house in the country testament to just how successful he was, but he was also enigmatic, sometimes distant and detached, his emotions guarded beneath a cool and confident exterior.

Thankfully he'd hung around long enough to convince me that my feelings were real and, more importantly, his feelings for me were the genuine article too. Once I'd got to know him properly, I'd realised how unjust I'd been in my assumptions. Max was many things but underneath he was honourable, kind and loyal, he would do anything for anybody and, yes, he was sexy as hell to boot. That was never more apparent than now as he strode out over the beach, the sea breeze lifting his hair off his collar.

'Oh, I know. And this is lovely,' I said, meaning it, glad we were here now. I snuggled into Max's side as he wrapped his arm around me, realising it must have been a whole five minutes since I'd thought of Noel, the pub and everyone back at home. Max was right. It would all work out fine. We needed to make the most of the time we had alone together in this beautiful part of the world. It would be over before we knew it and we'd be back having to face all those problems of our daily lives.

Before I'd met Max, he had been living alone in the sophisticated minimalist splendour of his Georgian country mansion and now it was filled with people and dogs and babies and clutter. No wonder he'd suggested getting away from it all.

'You don't really mind, do you?'

Max looked at me perplexed.

'How do you mean?'

'Well, that our life at home is pretty hectic these days. There's always something going on, some drama or another, people turning up randomly.'

'Are you kidding? I love all the craziness of the manor, the constant visitors and the high jinks of the dogs, but most of all I love that you are at the centre of it all, holding it all together. If it all gets too much for me then I can disappear out into my office, but if it wasn't for you, then I'm not sure where we'd all be. Katy and I would have fallen out ages ago, that's for sure, and Arthur would still be living in that cottage of his, alone and unhappy. You've turned all our lives around, Ellie. Noel's growing up in a happy and supportive household and that's so important to me. Okay, it's a bit manic at times, but that's family life for you. We've been through a really rough time recently, with one thing and another,' he said, stroking my face with his thumb, 'but we still have so much to be grateful for.'

'I know. It's good to be reminded of it, too.'

We walked down to the sea, the sand soft and giving beneath our feet, stopping occasionally to marvel at the shells wedged into the ground. The gentle swell of the tide greeted us and we laughed as the sea washed around us, making our feet wet.

'Come on,' said Max, some time later. 'I spotted a cafe on the road where we parked the car. Let's go and have a cup of tea.'

Fifteen minutes later, with our shoes damp and full of sand, we were back on the coastal road and we walked the short distance across to The Driftwood Cafe. A single storey building with full length glass windows all the way around, it offered views of the surrounding sand dunes and to the sea in the far distance. I was sure if I worked there I would spend the whole day gazing outside at the spectacular landscape. The small lobby to the cafe housed a selection of information leaflets and postcards, while inside the main seating area there was a welcoming wood burning stove, which was alight, and a selection of tables and chairs, comfy armchairs and a sofa adorned with bright cushions. The pale blue walls displayed a variety of seaside artifacts including fishing nets, starfish and shells. On the main serving counter were several glass domes with an enticing selection of cakes and biscuits. The place was empty, save for us, and I was beginning to wonder if they were just closing up when a young woman wandered out from behind the scenes to greet us.

'Hello! Can I help you?'

'Can we get a pot of tea and some cream scones?' Max asked.

'Yes. Sure. Take a seat and I'll bring them over.'

With a choice of seats, we plumped for the comfy sofa next to the stove, which was beside a low table covered with the day's newspapers and some magazines. It was such a lovely quiet oasis away from the rest of the world that it was easy to sink into the cushions and forget about everything else outside this warm and cosy snug. Apparently, the castle we were staying in was only down the road so there was no rush for us to get away.

'They look gorgeous,' I said to the woman when she brought over a plate of sultana scones with a tub of clotted cream and a pot of jam. 'It's very quiet in here today.'

'Yes, thank goodness!' She gave a tentative smile. 'I mean, you're very welcome and everything but I'm new around here so I'm really pleased I'm not rushed off my feet. I'm looking after the place for my aunt and uncle. They've gone to Australia for a month to see their new grandchild. My cousin has just had a baby girl. They were going to close the cafe down for the winter season, but I... well, I was at a loose end so I said I'd come and look after the place. It'll give me something to do and take my mind off things.' She paused, looking as though she might have said too much. 'Mainly it's to help out my aunt and uncle.'

'How lovely,' I said. My mind flirted for a brief moment with the idea of running a seaside cafe. I could just imagine myself behind the counter serving up light lunches and delicious cakes. I knew all about running a pub, ordering supplies and customer service. It couldn't be too much different from that – *could it*? – and you had the beach on your doorstep. Then I realised it would only work if I could bring all my friends and family from Little Leyton with me and that was probably too much of a tall order. 'We have a pub in the village where we live so I know what it's like to run something like this.'

The girl nodded. I guessed she was about twenty-four or five. She was petite, only about five feet tall, I suspected, with blonde highlighted hair piled up on the back of her head in a messy bun. She had a pink gingham pinny wrapped around her skinny body which was clad in jeans and T-shirt.

'Are you on your honeymoon?' she asked, looking from me to Max.

'No, we're not married. Well, not yet. We're actually getting married in December.'

Were we? I cast Max a questioning glance. It was news to me.

'Or rather we were getting married in December,' I explained. 'We're not sure if we'll be able to now. It's been a bit mad at home and everything's up in the air at the moment.'

'Oh, right...' The girl looked embarrassed, as though she might have said something out of turn, causing awkwardness between us, but it wasn't anything like that. It was just talking to the girl made me realise that Max and I hadn't had a proper conversation about our wedding plans in the light of the fire and what we might do about it now. I'd just assumed we would put off the date to a more suitable time.

'Of course we're still getting married this year,' said Max.

I laughed.

'As you can see we've got no idea what we're doing,' I said, trying to smooth over the uneasiness. 'It's one of the reasons we've come away. To have a bit of a breather and to discuss our plans. Not that we'd be having one of those huge fancy dos if we do decide to go ahead. It'll be just a village affair at the pub with all our friends and family.'

'Sounds lovely,' said the girl wistfully. 'I thought it must be something like that. You look like a newly married couple, very much in love.'

'Aw, thanks.'

Max looked across at me and placed a hand on my thigh, giving it a squeeze.

'We are,' he said, with that distinctive, familiar smile.

# 10

---

After that first time we seemed to gravitate towards The Driftwood Cafe every day, usually after a long walk along one of the deserted beaches. The castle where we were staying had been transformed into a luxury hotel and stood on a headland overlooking the sea and was all wood panelling, high ceilings and dark wood furniture. With the addition of luxurious drapes in velvet, and ornate trailing rose and ivy patterns on the walls, it gave the accommodation a sophisticated and luxurious feel. There was no expense spared and the service was second to none, but if I was being truthful I think I preferred the cosy, welcoming atmosphere of The Driftwood Cafe. It was a highlight of our day, kicking off our shoes and curling up on the old squishy sofa to have a read of the papers. We'd got to know Fliss, the young woman running the cafe, and I looked forward to seeing her and catching up on the news. Like the first time we visited, we found the cafe pretty much empty on most days; sometimes there would be the occasional dog walker who'd dropped in for some sustenance before going on their way again, but generally we had the place to ourselves. Fliss would always come and join us for a natter.

'How are the wedding plans going?' she asked, with a wry smile one particular afternoon, bringing us over a pot of tea and some fruit cake. It was my mission to sample as many of the cakes and biscuits as I possibly could so I plumped for something different each day. So far, they'd all been equally delicious.

Max chuckled.

'Well, at least we're agreed now that it will be this Christmas.' After talking to Fliss on the first day of our holiday we'd carried on our conversation back at the hotel and Max had persuaded me that there was no reason for us to change our plans. The wedding would go ahead as we'd arranged even if we might need to find another venue for the reception. Although Max was hopeful that we might have the barn rebuilt by then, which was exciting even if I didn't share his optimism. 'It's a special time for us,' he explained to Fliss now. 'Our son was born on Christmas Day last year.'

'Really? The best Christmas present ever, I bet.'

'Yes.' He nodded. 'Anyway, I'm leaving all the wedding arrangements to Ellie. That's her speciality. Apparently, all I have to do is turn up on the day, suited and booted, with a ring in my pocket.'

'Make sure you do!' said Fliss jokingly. 'My fiancé couldn't even manage that.'

'Oh, I'm sorry to hear that,' I said, exchanging a glance with Max. Fliss's tone was light-hearted enough but I wasn't sure of the meaning behind her comment or if it was just a throwaway remark. I didn't want to embarrass her by delving any further.

It made me realise that Fliss knew an awful lot about us and our life back in Little Leyton. I'd told her about what had happened at the pub, shown her photos of Noel and the dogs and discussed what we might have to eat at our wedding, but it was only now that I realised I didn't really know the first thing about her or her background.

'So, did you grow up here?' I asked her now, deciding that it was much safer territory than asking about her fiancé. She certainly didn't have a local accent.

'No.' She shook her head. 'I used to come and visit most summers though. My cousin, Clover, the one who's just had the baby, is the same age as me and she was an only child too, so it was nice for us to get together and spend the holidays with each other. Her mum and dad would be here at the cafe and we would go down to the beach each day or walk along the coastal road into town. Happy days!'

'So where did you grow up then?'

'In Birmingham. It couldn't be more different than this,' she said, gazing out of the window wistfully. 'I loved it though. My home was there, my school, all my friends, my mum and dad, and Brad, of course.'

'Brad?' I asked, and Max flashed me a warning glance. I knew exactly what that look meant. It meant I was overstepping the mark, poking my nose into business that had nothing to do with me. It was a habit that came with running the pub. I really didn't mean to be nosey but I did find people would confide in me and they'd know whatever was said would be kept in confidence. Now, I wasn't at work though, and I was afraid I might have been intruding.

'My boyfriend. Or should I say my ex-boyfriend.'

'Ah, I see.' I let it go, zipping my mouth tight so that I wouldn't ask any more awkward questions while Max delved deeper into his newspaper.

'We were childhood sweethearts,' she volunteered. 'We got together when we were fourteen. He was my first and only boyfriend, we were together for over ten years.'

A bad feeling swept over me and I sensed she was about to tell me something terrible, that he'd died perhaps from some awful disease. I cursed myself for asking about him and wished I'd stuck with platitudes about the weather and the beautiful views. I looked to Max for help, but he was absolutely refusing to lift his head in our direction.

'We were meant to be getting married too, this year.'

'Oh, goodness, were you? What happened?' I asked, unable to stop myself.

'Well, he decided, at least not at the altar, but at the eleventh hour, that he didn't want to marry me after all.' She smiled ruefully. 'Three weeks before the big day, would you believe? Everything was booked. I had the dress, the bridesmaids all in place and the reception arranged.'

I grimaced.

'The bastard! What reason did he give?'

She shrugged, as though she barely had an idea herself.

'He said that he couldn't go through with it. That he hadn't really experienced enough of life to make that final commitment to me.' Her mouth twisted involuntarily. 'I think that was code for he hadn't been out with any other girls other than me.'

'That must have been devastating,' I said, trying to imagine myself in Fliss's shoes.

'It was. I thought that was what was so special about our relationship. That we'd known each other since we were kids and would grow old together. But it wasn't meant to be.'

'Crikey. When did all this happen?'

'A couple of months ago.'

'Oh, Fliss! I'm so sorry. That's such an awful thing to happen. And there was me banging on about our wedding and all the things we have planned. You must have wanted to throttle me.'

'No, not at all. In some ways it's helped. I look at you and Max and it's obvious how much in love you are. I recognised it the very first day I met you, the way you look at each other, laugh at each other's jokes and finish each other's sentences. It's so lovely. It made me realise that Brad and I weren't like that at all. We'd been together so long that we took each other for granted. It's sad, but I think it's probably for the best that we broke up.'

'So that's why you've come here.'

'Yes, I had to get away. I couldn't stay in Birmingham, dealing with everyone's sympathy and the pitying looks.' I knew exactly how that felt. Fliss seemed eager now to continue her story. 'To make matters worse, I worked for the same company as Brad – it was his dad's electrical installation company – so I got to see him every day. I couldn't stay there any more, not after what happened, so I left, after five years of working there. So, I lost my fiancé, my job and my home – Brad and I were living together in a small flat – all in the space of a couple of weeks. When Joe and Annie heard, they immediately invited me to come and stay. So here I am!' She looked as though she still couldn't quite believe it herself. 'I'm not sure what I'll do next or where I'll go, but for the time being this is as good a place as any to be. You can't stay down for too long when you look outside to see that view.'

Max and I both turned to see the rolling sea in the distance and the wide golden sands and let out a collective sigh of appreciation.

'That's true. And if it's any consolation, it's his loss,' said Max firmly.

'Definitely. It reminds me of a friend of ours, Johnny. I went to school with him and we went out very briefly when we were teenagers. Anyway, he started seeing my best friend, Polly, a couple of years ago and they had a whirlwind romance. They were both madly in love and it looked as though they would end up together. Then, just as things were becoming more serious Johnny decided he couldn't take it any more, upped and left and went backpacking around the world.'

I shook my head at the reminder, still hardly able to believe that it had happened. It was so out of character for Johnny.

'Men, huh?'

'Not all men!' Max piped up.

'Polly was heartbroken. I felt so sorry for her because she truly believed Johnny was the one and I hated him so much for hurting her like that. He went off for six months and came back having got his head in order. He seemed to think he could pick up where he left off with Polly but in his absence she'd moved on. She'd met someone else. The bestselling crime novelist actually, George Williamson, have you heard of him? Anyway, they fell madly in love and the pair of them got married this year and now she's expecting a baby.'

'Really? How lovely! So, there's hope for me yet, then?' said Fliss, with a resigned smile.

'Of course there is. There are only bigger and better things ahead for you,' I said, with a smile.

'I hope so. Thanks for listening, Ellie, and you, Max. I'm not sure what Joe and Annie would think if they knew I'd been boring their customers with the sorry tale of my life history.'

'You've not been boring us at all.'

'It's really helped though, talking everything through. It's set a few things straight in my mind. Mainly that there's no way I'd ever want to get back with Brad. I'm looking for the real thing now, something like you two have together. Something I never shared with Brad. Of course, all my friends and family at home have been great and have rallied round, but they all know Brad and had their own views and assumptions on what happened, why he did what he did, what I should do about it. They were full of well-meaning advice and good suggestions. Do you understand what

I'm saying? It's nice that I can talk to you and you have no pre-judgements on the situation. Or on me.'

I nodded, knowing exactly what she meant. Sometimes facing the people you loved most in the world, revealing your innermost hurt, was much more difficult than opening up to a stranger.

# 11

Later that night, after a dinner of pan fried sea bass and rosemary infused sautéed potatoes in the Michelin starred restaurant of the hotel, Max and I took a short walk in the floodlit gardens of the castle. Holding hands in such a romantic setting, sharing one-on-one time together, was just what we'd both needed. Despite my reservations about coming away I realised now it was the best possible thing we could have done. The miscarriage and then the fire had seen our hopes go up in smoke, but coming here, rediscovering each other, had given me some much needed perspective. We'd suffered a couple of setbacks, but we'd get over them and move forward, as Max kept on reminding me. Instead of dwelling on what had gone wrong, I needed to focus on the good things.

I breathed in the cool evening air and turned to look at Max. He was definitely one of the good things. My heart galloped as his gaze latched on to mine, and he took hold of my hand, interlocking my fingers with his. Whilst I'd loved being here in this beautiful part of the country, I would also look forward to getting home to see the dogs, my parents, Rose, Katy and Arthur, and most of all my little boy, Noel. I couldn't wait to hold him in my arms and to squeeze him tight. I missed the scent of him, his happy chuckles in the morning and his smiling little face looking up at me. Seeing him over Zoom every day only increased my longing. Mind you, Mum was doing a great job in looking after Noel as it seemed he wasn't missing us in the slightest and was having a whale of a time with all the attention he'd been receiving.

'So, you're glad I managed to persuade you to come along, after all?' Max asked as we meandered along the pathway overlooking the coast, the swell of the sea fierce tonight.

'Yes, I wouldn't have wanted to miss a moment of this.' A shiver ran along the length of my arms and I snuggled into the warmth of my cardigan. 'It's reminded me that there's a whole other world outside the sometimes claustrophobic confines of Little Leyton.'

'Hey, you're not getting fed up with your home village? We could always jack it all in and come somewhere like here to run a hotel or cafe – what do you say?'

I laughed, suspecting Max was only half joking.

'While that's a lovely idea, I'd miss everyone too much. And I want Noel, all our children, to grow up in a friendly village just like I did, having their family close by and making life-long friends.'

'Me, too. It was something I never had.'

Max and his family had moved around a lot when he was growing up so he'd never really experienced that sense of community, not until he'd moved to Little Leyton. I suspected he'd be as reluctant to move on from the village now as I would be.

'There will be more babies, won't there, Max?'

'What?' He stopped and pulled me round to face him, looking intently into my eyes. 'Of course there will be.'

'I just worry that the same thing will happen again. I couldn't bear to go through it for a second time.'

'You can't think like that. There's no reason why it should. That's what the doctors said. And we need to keep on believing that. It'll be fine. I've got a good feeling in here about it.' He tapped his hand against his chest.

'Oh, yeah, I'm sure you're right. I'm just having a moment.'

'Come on,' he said, slipping an arm around my waist and squeezing me tight. We walked on. 'We should make this a regular thing, you know. The two of us getting away together, at least once a year. What do you think?'

'I'd love that.'

'Me, too. Let's make it happen, then,' he said, turning to me with a smile. 'And as far as more babies go, you must be the one to decide when you think we're ready to try again.'

I nodded.

'Next year, I think.' I'd already given it plenty of thought. 'Once we're married and the pub is up and running again. Once all the problems are out of the way.'

'Ah, we'll just have a different set of problems then,' he said with a wry smile. 'But I think it's a good idea. Starting the new year afresh. Although there's nothing to stop us from practising in the meantime.'

I laughed and stood on tiptoe to kiss him on the lips. His gaze roamed my face before he kissed me back, more fervently this time, his tongue on my lips tasting deliciously salty. The wind whistled around us and goose-bumps ran along my spine, which I suspect were heightened by being held close to Max's strong, hard body.

'I can't wait to get married,' I said, swept away by the romance of our surroundings, my hair blowing off my face in the breeze of the cool night air. 'It really isn't that far away now. And something to look forward to after everything that's happened this year.'

'Too true,' he said, running his hands over my fingers. 'Blimey, you're freezing. Let's get back to our room.'

On the way we stopped for a hot chocolate in the hotel bar and a chat with the owners and some other late night guests who were taking a night-cap. With the sound of chatter and laughter ringing around me I could almost imagine we were sitting in the snug bar of The Dog and Duck, that the fire that had closed its doors hadn't really happened. The only differ-ence being here was the view outside of the rolling dark sea, which looked really quite forbidding tonight. It was truly mesmerising to watch, any time of the day. With the wide sandy beaches it would be the perfect place to bring Noel for his first trip to the seaside and I was already making plans as to when we might be able to do that. Maybe next year in the spring.

Absent-mindedly I pulled my phone out of my bag and started scrolling through my messages. Mainly from Mum telling me what Noel had been up to that day, lots of photos of him too, some from Polly asking me the best remedy for morning sickness and a couple of terse messages from Katy asking what exactly we intended to do about Rose.

'Anything pressing?'

'Not really,' I said, deciding not to mention Katy, knowing it would only rile Max. 'Noel's doing fine apparently.'

'Well, in that case put that phone away. We'll be home soon enough and all this will just be a hazy memory.'

That was true. Although we'd have plenty of great memories to take home with us, I realised as I snuggled up closer to Max in bed later that night. The queen size bed with its duck down pillows and duvets was the most comfortable bed I'd ever slept in; my whole body sank into its deep recesses and the crisp Egyptian linen and the plethora of velvet and silk cushions only added to the feeling of luxury. I stretched out, my naked body wrapping around Max's, our limbs entangling naturally, adopting the familiar positions from past intimacies. It was a treat to be able to lose myself in the moment, to focus all my attention on Max and the proximity of his body next to mine. At home, I'd have one ear open for Noel or be listening for Katy to come home or bracing myself for little Flora to have escaped from downstairs and to come charging into the bedroom with the other dogs following. Here, I didn't have to worry about all that, I could just focus on the gorgeous man in my arms. Now, all I had to concentrate on was the effect Max's hands were having on me as they gently caressed my body and that delicious feeling of anticipation in my tummy.

He stroked the hair away from my face and looked intently into my eyes, before dropping kisses along the length of my neck and along my collarbone, making me squirm.

'I love you, Ellie Browne.'

'I love you too, Max Golding.' I sighed, my body melting into the bed as I succumbed to a further barrage of delightful kisses.

\* \* \*

The next day was the last of our holiday and after a full English breakfast at the hotel we checked out and drove down to the quay in the fishing village. It was such a picturesque spot we'd made a habit of coming down here every morning for a meander along the front, stopping to look at all the boats as they came and went on their fishing trips. We'd been talking about taking a trip of our own out to what was affectionately called 'Puffin Island', although Max told me that we'd be lucky to see any at this time of the year.

'We should go anyway. Hopefully we'll get to see some seals on the rocks around the islands and some resident birds. Another good reason to come back again. To see the puffins when they're nesting.'

We jumped on an open top boat and sat port side and I was grateful that I had several layers of clothing on as it was bitterly cold out on the sea. The wind buffeted our progress and a drizzly but insistent rain assaulted us. I hung onto Max for dear life, trying to find some warmth from his broad body, but the cold still reached the very core of my bones. Even so the squally weather couldn't dampen the beauty of our surroundings and my gaze was transfixed by the unfolding views of the rocky islands in front of us and the shoreline behind, with the imposing castle towering above us from high up on the headland.

'Look, Ellie,' said Max, diverting my attention, when we must have been motoring for about thirty minutes. 'Can you see the seals?'

I turned my head and gasped, my heart lifting at the sight. There was a whole colony of them on the rocks and even some bobbing up and down in the sea around us, their little faces observing us curiously before they disappeared beneath the water again. Max laughed at my attempts to take a photo of them as no sooner had I got my camera out of its bag and lined up the shot, than the little blighters had done their disappearing act again and all I'd managed to get were several photos of the grey and forbidding sea. Luckily there were plenty more photo opportunities once we'd landed on the jetty and we climbed off the boat and hurried along the pathway that wound its way around the entire island. Arms wide to my side, I took a moment and spun round three hundred and sixty degrees, soaking up the atmosphere, even revelling in the bitter cold stinging at my cheeks. I pulled out my camera again and snapped away happily at the rugged scenery and the wildlife, including some shags, perched on the rocky outcrops.

'I love it here. It's so remote. You can feel the sheer power of the sea and the elements. It makes you feel so small and insignificant against the force of the world.'

'It's wonderful, isn't it?' Max put an arm around my shoulder and we gazed out to sea together. 'If you come earlier in the year, say May or June, the whole island is covered with birds. It's a magnificent sight to see all the puffins – they're such comical birds to look at, and kittiwakes, fulmars, guillemots, razorbills.'

'Really? I haven't heard of half of those birds. I definitely want to come back and see the puffins.'

'We'll do that, but be warned. You'll have to wear headgear because the terns get very aggressive when they're guarding their nests. They will dive bomb humans to protect their chicks.'

'I know exactly how those birds feel,' I said, chuckling. 'I'd do exactly the same to protect my little chick.' I glanced at my watch. By the time we got home tonight, Noel would be fast asleep in his cot, although there was a part of me that hoped he might wake up, stirred by our arrival, so that I could hold him in my arms and kiss his squidgy neck, breathing in the delicious scent of him. It would be agony to see all his cuteness in his cot and not be able to lift him out.

After the return boat trip back to the mainland I dragged Max into the little gift shop at the top of the quay. It was full of trinkets, jewellery, postcards, soft toys and colourful kitchenware. I picked up a cute plush puffin for Noel and found some pretty glass necklaces for Mum, Rose and Katy and some jars of chutney and boxes of biscuits. I could have spent all day in there, mooching around, picking up gifts for the entire village, but Max quickly became impatient and shooed me along.

'Come on,' he said. 'Do you want to pop into The Driftwood Cafe for one last time?'

'You bet I do.'

Arriving at the cafe, I found it hard to believe that it was only a week since we'd first come here. It was as though we'd been visiting this place for years. Pushing open the front door, hearing the old fashioned bell tinkle and feeling the blast of warm air from the wood burning stove provided such a welcoming atmosphere that I couldn't help but be reminded of The Dog and Duck.

Today, four of the tables were occupied and Fliss was talking to a young man at the counter. He was wearing a waterproof bib and braces, blue wellies and a jaunty hat, from under which damp black curls escaped. He took the bacon butty wrapped in a brown paper bag and the polystyrene cup from Fliss and thanked her with a wide smile and a small wink that elicited a shy smile from her. She spotted us and waved.

'You're busy in here today.'

'I know! Never too busy for you two though. Go and grab yourself a seat and I'll bring some menus over.'

The fisherman guy called out to Fliss as he pulled open the door.

'See you soon, Felicity!'

I raised my eyebrows and gave a questioning smile. Fliss shook her head indulgently.

'Oh, that's Davey. Take no notice of him. His sole purpose in life seems to be to wind me up. He went to school with Clover so I've got to know him over the years. He knows how much I hate my real name so of course he insists on calling me it.'

'Ah, right.'

'We used to go rock pooling together as kids. He was annoying then and he hasn't changed much since.' Her tone was dismissive but there was a smile on her face as she spoke. 'Still, he's made a point of calling in every day for a chat and his butty, so I shouldn't complain about him too much.'

It was good to see Fliss looking so animated and upbeat and reassuring to know she had some friends in the local community. Soon, people at the other tables departed, leaving us as the only customers in the cafe. Fliss brought over our ham and cheese toasties and mugs of hot chocolate with marshmallows and whipped cream. Very decadent, but I reckoned it was the last day of our holiday so it was definitely allowed. And there was even room for one of the delicious flapjacks afterwards.

'So, you guys are heading home shortly, are you?'

'Yes! I can't wait to get back to see everybody but I shall be sad to leave this beautiful place. And we'll certainly miss our daily visits to The Driftwood Cafe, and seeing you especially, Fliss. I really hope things work out for you.'

'Thanks. I'm sure they will. It's been a godsend coming here. Birmingham and Brad seem another lifetime away now.' She stretched her arms out wide, encompassing the cafe. 'You know, I enjoy running this place much more than I ever did working in a grotty office, chasing invoices and doing vat returns. I must have been mad to do it for so long.'

I gave a rueful smile, knowing exactly what she meant. I felt the same after working in a soulless office in corporate London for so long.

'This place, the sea and the landscape get beneath your skin after a while. I won't ever want to go back, that's for sure. Well, certainly not yet. There are too many reminders at home. I suppose once Joe and Annie come back I'll have to decide what I'm going to do but I might stay around here. Find a job if I can.'

'I can't think of any better place to make a new start,' I told her. 'Anyway, Max and I have already decided that we're coming back next year and bringing Noel and the dogs with us, so we'll definitely be calling in here, to see your aunt and your uncle, if you're not around. And remember, if you're ever down our way then do come and see us at The Dog and Duck. You'd be very welcome. We can't offer you sea views but the village is very pretty in its own way.'

'I might just take you up on that,' said Fliss, laughing.

'Come on,' said Max. 'We ought to be making a move. We've got a very long journey ahead of us.'

We all stood and Fliss threw her arms around me, squeezing tight.

'Safe journey home. And thanks for listening to me,' she called as we made our way to the door. 'Oh, and good luck with the pub. I hope you're up and running again very soon.'

I hated goodbyes at the best of times. I turned and waved before hearing the shop bell tinkle for one last time and followed Max over to the car. I took a moment, my gaze drifting one hundred and eighty degrees around me, committing the breathtaking landscape to my memory.

Already I was looking forward to our next visit here.

# 12

The journey home was every bit as long as Max had suggested. As soon as we'd left the north-east coastline I was impatient to be home. My bottom grew uncomfortable in the passenger seat and my feet restless so at the first opportunity I took over the driving from Max, while he had a doze. Even though I'd enjoyed every single moment of my holiday, I couldn't wait to get back home and into a routine with Noel and the dogs, and to start making plans for when the pub could re-open, hopefully in time for our busy season in the run-up to Christmas.

Outside, the sky was darkening and my concentration was waning so I pulled into the next service station, the car gliding to a halt in the car park bringing Max out of his slumber.

'Ah, a coffee?' he said, looking across at me affectionately as he stretched out his long body, his arms and legs overfilling his side of the car, making me smile. 'My turn back behind the wheel, I reckon. You know, you should try to get some sleep on this final leg of the journey home. Noel will probably keep us awake every night this coming week to get his own back for not taking him away with us.'

'Ha, you're probably right there.'

Long lazy mornings and drawn out breakfast feasts would be things of the past now. It would be back to a snatched piece of toast in between exercising the dogs, seeing to Noel, popping in on Arthur and getting Katy off to college on time.

After a revitalising coffee and a walk around the dreary service station we were back on the road, with Max still insisting on driving and urging me to catch up on my sleep, but there was no chance of that, not when my mind was already switching back into Little Leyton mode and filling with all the things I would need to do when we got home.

'Are you all right, Ellie?' Max said a little later. 'You seem miles away.'

'Just thinking about being back home and all the things I shall need to do once we get there. I wonder how it's going with the pub, if there'll be any more news about what caused the fire.'

'I'll get onto the insurers first thing in the morning for an update.'

I rested my eyes; I wondered too, how Rose had been getting on. I was worried that she had been upset about her separation from Alan, with no one to talk to about it. She wouldn't discuss it with Katy, knowing her strong feelings about Alan, and she wasn't close enough to my mum to confide in her either. I just hoped Rose and Alan would have been in touch with each other while we were away and were working through their problems. It would be one of the first things I did when I got back: have a proper heart-to-heart with Rose to see if there was anything we could do to help. I would pop in to see Polly, too – hopefully she would be feeling better now – and I would need to start making lists for Christmas, Noel's birthday and the wedding, too. I felt a little flutter of panic in my chest, as all the thoughts threatened to overwhelm me, but I knew as soon as I made a start and got everything written down in my notebook it would all seem much more manageable.

I must have eventually nodded off because it was an hour later when Max nudged me in the side.

'We're nearly home, Ells.'

I shifted up in the passenger seat, peering out of the window, pleased to recognise the increasingly familiar landmarks whizzing past until we came upon the welcoming village sign for Little Leyton. I wriggled my shoulders to rid myself of the tension in my joints, my eyes alighting on all the shops and houses I knew so well. There was something about coming home after a break away that made everything look different somehow. As though it had been shifted slightly or as though you were seeing it through another set of eyes.

Max slowed right down as we drove along the high street and we both craned our heads to see the pub, which was looking cold and neglected in the darkness.

'I know it's crazy, but I half hoped that we'd get here and find the place open, the lights on and the pub filled with people enjoying themselves.'

'Don't worry.' Max reached across and squeezed my knee with his hand. 'It honestly won't be long until that's happening again.'

Back at the manor, before we'd even managed to get out of the car, we received the biggest welcome as all four of the dogs came galloping out, swarming round the car to greet us.

'Hello, hello,' I said, laughing, as I clambered out. Flora went mad, jumping up at my legs, while Digby waited patiently for some attention. Holly and Bella weaved in between our legs, intent on tripping us over, and herded us towards the back door as though we might not know where to go.

Inside, Mum, Dad, Katy and Arthur were all waiting for us, and the dogs were still going crazy at our arrival, especially Flora, who was scooting around maniacally, depositing a little welcoming present for us on the floor in her excitement, while Digby looked up at me with brown soulful eyes, chastising me for my absence.

'I'll grab the mop.' I laughed.

'I'll pop the kettle on and make you both a cuppa,' said Mum. 'I expect you could do with one after that long journey. There's a pile of post for you over there. And there were some phone messages too. I've written down the details on that notepad.' She gestured in the general direction of the kitchen table. 'In fact, we haven't stopped here all week. You've had lots of visitors too, mainly just the villagers wanting to offer their help with the pub – oh, and that Darcy turned up. She brought you that gorgeous bunch of flowers. She seems like a lovely lady.'

The abundant arrangement in the vase, a palette of dusty pink, rich red and purple flowers accentuated by dove grey foliage was stunning, and totally unexpected. Maybe Darcy had a guilty conscience, who knew? Whatever the reason for the kind gesture, I would have to track her down and offer her my thanks.

'Anyway, I shall have to get off to bed,' Mum said now. 'I'm completely exhausted. We can have a proper catch-up in the morning.'

'How's Noel been?' I asked her, before she disappeared upstairs.

'He's been absolutely delightful. And such a good lad for his nanny and granddad. Every night Malc's been reading him a bedtime story and he goes straight off to sleep, not waking once in the night, even if he is up and raring to go at six o'clock in the morning.' She laughed. 'I have to go. I need my beauty sleep.'

Poor Mum! She looked shattered and very pleased to have us home again. There were some weeks when I'd been completely frazzled come the weekend so I knew exactly how she felt, but then again I was used to it and had to remember that Mum was that much older than me. She'd be in need of a holiday herself by the sounds of things.

'It's lovely to have you home again,' said Arthur, easing himself out of his chair. 'I shall have to get to bed myself though because I've got a blood test early in the morning. I forgot to arrange a taxi but I can do that in the morning.'

'What time's your appointment, Arthur?'

'Eight-thirty.'

'Well, don't worry about a taxi because I'll be able to take you now,' I told him as he trundled along behind his walker in the direction of his bedroom, putting paid to any hope I might have had of a lie-in in my own bed.

I exhaled a sigh of satisfaction mixed with contentment at being home again, sitting around my own kitchen table, my hands clasped around a warm mug of tea.

'How's your mum?' I asked Katy, when it was just the three of us left together. The dogs had finally settled and were slumped around my feet, blocking my escape, in case I had any ideas about leaving them again.

'Oh, she's absolutely fine,' she said, pointedly. 'She's completely rearranged that guest bedroom of hers. She's put all her clothes in the wardrobes and put all her little trinkets and photos out on the dressing table and windowsills. Talk about making yourself at home. I told her she doesn't need to unpack everything if she's only going to be here for a while, but she doesn't seem to have any plans to move on.'

'It doesn't matter,' said Max. 'It's not as though we're short of space here.'

'Yes, but...' Katy went on to regale us with a further list of crimes that Rose had committed in the short space of time she'd been staying at the manor, and we listened sympathetically, nodding in all the right places, until a very familiar wail of protest came from upstairs.

'Really?' I said, looking at Max, laughing. 'He sleeps perfectly well all the time we were away and as soon as we're back, he decides he needs to wake up in the middle of the night.'

'He just wants to say hello.' We both stood up, eager to see our little boy again, and giving us the perfect excuse for escaping from Katy's complaints.

The charms of Northumberland, the huge expanses of beach, the beautiful seaside cafe and the peace and solitude seemed a million miles away now, but it didn't matter. It was really rather lovely to be home.

## 13

'Stop going on at me!' Katy's voice rang out from the landing, a door slammed and she came stomping down the stairs, a thunderous expression on her face and a rucksack hanging over her shoulder.

'What on earth is going on?' I asked, greeting Katy as she lugged her bad temper with her into the kitchen.

'It's Mum! Errggh...' She literally grabbed at the hair at her temples. 'She's been driving me mad. She thinks since you two have been away she can tell me exactly what to do. When she can't.' She folded her arms crossly, her chest heaving.

'Well, without wishing to state the obvious, Katy, she is your mum and therefore I think she might have a point. She's probably within her rights to tell you what she thinks you should do. Besides, I'm sure she only wants what's best for you.'

'No, she doesn't! And this isn't her house. She can't make the rules. She's only a visitor. This is my home now. She can't just waltz in here and act like she owns the place.'

'Oh, Katy!'

Really, I could have done without this today. It was a couple of weeks since we'd returned from holiday and Max was preoccupied with sorting out the insurance, speaking to assessors and surveyors, loss adjustors and loss assessors. He had several other projects on the go too, an office block redevelopment in London and the refurbishment of a row of cottages he owned in the village. He was working fourteen hour days, out first thing in the morning and back late at night. The only time we had for each other was late at night when we would share a cup of cocoa or a glass of wine and have a quick catch-up of the day's events. The intimate time we'd shared on holiday was just a fading memory now. I gave a fleeting thought to Fliss and what she might be doing, conjuring up the view she would be looking out on through her tall windows. What wouldn't I give to wander into the cafe right now for a coffee and a bun?

'Your mum's going through a difficult time, Katy. I thought you might appreciate that.'

'Well, that's her own fault. I don't know why she stayed with Alan for as long as she did. I never liked him. He always gave me such a hard time and Mum always took his side and never backed me up.'

I wasn't sure that was strictly true. Katy had told me that she'd got on well with Alan when she was little but when she'd reached the teenage years, the pair of them had clashed terribly, with the arguments becoming ever more frequent and fierce. Once Alan had revealed the truth about Katy's real dad, she'd never wanted anything more to do with him, directing all her hurt and anger in his direction as though he was solely responsible for what had happened.

'Why should I be on her side now?' Katy demanded of me.

'Because she's your mum? She needs your support. She doesn't want you giving her even more grief to deal with while she's here.'

'That's the thing. How long is she staying for exactly? Max needs to say something to her. She keeps telling me that she won't be going back to Spain to be with Alan again, but where does that leave us? What are we going to do? I can't live under the same roof as her indefinitely. I'll end up murdering her.'

I pulled Noel out of his high chair and gave it a wipe down, trying to stop myself from laughing. I suspected Katy was only half joking.

'Do you want any breakfast before you go?'

Katy shook her head. It seemed with the distance of a few hundred miles between them, Katy and her mum had overcome their differences, but living under the same roof for a couple of weeks had brought all those issues to the fore once again. Where was Max when you needed him?

After seeing Katy off to go and catch the bus from the village, I fed the dogs, took a mug of tea in to Arthur, placed Noel in his playpen and sat down at the conservatory table for a much needed mug of coffee. A moment's peace to take in the view of the extensive gardens, not quite on the same scale as Fliss's view of the rolling sea, but pretty nonetheless. The sound of footsteps behind me made me spin round.

'Is it safe to come in now?' Rose was smiling wryly. 'Sorry about the commotion this morning. I can't seem to say anything to Katy these days without her flying off the handle. You would think she'd enjoy having her mum around, but oh, no!'

'I'd say it's typical teenage angst and tantrums. I can remember being the same with my mum. I'm sure it will pass.'

'Hmm...' Rose looked unconvinced. She made herself a mug of tea from the recently boiled kettle, before coming through to join me in the conservatory, stopping to coo over Noel for a moment. 'You told me that last time I was here, Ellie! Just when I think Katy and I are getting somewhere, something else happens and all the old grievances are brought up again and we're back where we started. I thought she might have forgiven me by now. I'd hoped that she might think about coming to live with me again, if I find the right place, but that doesn't look very likely, does it?'

'Are you sure that's what you really want, Rose? Have you spoken to Alan? Is there no way you two can get back together?'

Rose shook her head firmly.

'No, I wouldn't want to now. All of this has caused such a rift between us. There's no going back. I should never have kept it a secret from Katy, the identity of her real dad, but you can't turn back time, can you? What's done is done. And I have to live with the consequences. I'm afraid my relationship with Alan is one of them. I'm determined that Katy won't be another.'

'What will you do, then?' I asked.

'Don't worry, love. I'll be out from under your feet just as soon as I can.'

'No, that isn't what I meant. You're welcome to stay here for as long as you like. I just wondered if you had any plans.'

'Well, I shall have to find myself a job, I suppose.' Her laugh tinkled around the kitchen nervously, at the preposterousness of her own suggestion, no doubt. It was several years since Rose had held down a proper job. 'And find a place to stay. I can't stop here forever.'

'Well, we'll help you in any way we can, you know that.'

'Yes, and who knows? Perhaps Katy will want to come and live with me at some stage? You two have been marvellous in providing a home for her, but you've got your hands full enough as it is.'

It was funny really because many people had commented on how hard it must be, bringing up a baby while having a hormonal teenage girl, a frail pensioner and four boisterous dogs living with us, too. Only I didn't view it that way. And neither did Max. We relished having a full and busy household and I liked the fact that I didn't have to worry about the dogs when I went out, as well as having a live-in babysitter in the shape of Katy.

'Katy's place is with me really, isn't it?' said Rose.

I could see why she would think that but Katy loved living at the manor and I could imagine what her reaction might be to the suggestion that she moved back in with her mum. That was a conversation for them to have later. With me well out of the way. Instead, I said neutrally, 'I'm sure things will be so much better for the pair of you, living in the same area.'

'I hope so,' said Rose with a pensive smile.

Just then there was a rat-a-tat on the back door, followed by the door opening and someone calling, 'Hello there, it's only me!'

I knew exactly who it was, recognising the familiar tones of the voice, and I looked, startled, across at Rose. She shrugged her shoulders, answering my unasked question. Of course she had no clue who it was – why would she after so many years? I jumped up and dashed out into the kitchen to greet our visitor, thinking I might be able to shoo them out the way they'd come, but sadly, it was too late for that. Instead I stood rooted to the spot for a moment, wishing the ground would swallow me up or hoping that Rose might have taken it upon herself to slip out of the conservatory doors into the garden, but why would she? That was just wishful thinking on my part.

'Hope I'm not disturbing you.' He wandered straight on in. 'Oh...' It took him the briefest moment. '...Rose? I wasn't expecting to see you here.'

Rose's eyes widened and her mouth gaped open. Her hands reached out to grab the edge of the table for support. She went to say something, but only a funny squeaking noise came from deep down inside her chest. After a heavy pause she managed to say, 'Andy?'

'Should I go?' He looked to me for guidance. 'I'll go. I'll come back some other time.' Andy backed out through the kitchen, a look of frozen panic on his face, but I jumped up and beckoned him back towards us.

'No, don't go. Not now you're here. Come through. I mean, you know Rose, don't you?'

*What a stupid thing to say!* They both looked at me, disbelievingly, but I'd had to say something to fill the heavy, intense silence hovering in the air. Rose stood up and wandered across to greet Andy. I wasn't sure if she was going to punch him on the nose, kiss him on the cheek or shake his hand. I mean, what exactly is the protocol for meeting up with the father of your daughter after eighteen long years?

Apparently, in Andy and Rose's case, it was an awkward sidestep shuffle with embarrassed laughter.

'Sorry, I didn't realise you'd be here.' He turned to me. 'I've been working away for a few weeks and only just heard about the fire so I wanted to pop in and pass on my sympathies and to see if there was anything I could do to help.'

'That's really kind of you but there's nothing anyone can do at the moment. Max is just waiting for the go ahead from the insurers to start on the repairs.'

Rose fidgeted uneasily from foot to foot, clearly itching to say something. Suddenly she burst out a garbled flurry of words.

'Look, Andy, I'm really sorry. For everything. I know sorry doesn't really cover it, but I hope you'll understand that I didn't deliberately set out to hurt you or Katy. I did what I thought was the right thing at the time but eventually everything unravelled around me. I was wrong to keep the truth from you both. I realise that now. You can't base your life on a lie. People only end up getting hurt. If I could relive my time and do things differently then I would, but you can't turn back time. I've spent so many sleepless nights wondering—'

'Stop.' Andy held up his hand. 'Look, Rose, it doesn't matter. You're right, we can't turn back the clock. What's done is done. Admittedly, when I first received your letter telling me I had a grown-up daughter, it was a complete shock. In fact, I couldn't believe it at first. I thought it must have been some sort of hoax or a way of getting some money out of me. Although you wouldn't have had much joy there,' he joked. 'It really didn't seem possible that I could have my own child out there somewhere, but, once I got my head around the idea, I realised it was the most amazing thing that could ever happen to me. Like winning the lottery. I still didn't believe it was true though. That's why I had to come and see Katy for myself. I was intent on getting DNA tests done, seeing the truth down on paper, but as soon as I set eyes on her all my doubts and reservations evaporated into thin air. I knew instantly that I was looking at my daughter.'

Rose's chin wobbled. I could tell she was trying valiantly to hang onto her emotions, not wanting to cry in front of Andy, but she was in every danger of breaking down at any moment.

'Let me pop the kettle on,' I said, as a distraction. Rose turned away from Andy and gave me a grateful smile of thanks.

'I think it's probably better if I go.'

'You don't need to go on my account,' Rose was quick to reassure Andy.

'Well, if you're sure.'

Over a mug of tea, Rose continued to pour her heart out.

'I'm just so sorry that I deprived you of all those years when Katy was growing up. She'd always believed that Max's father was her dad and in fairness he doted on her, accepted her as his own. After he died there never seemed the right moment to tell Katy the truth. When I met Alan, he stepped into the role of stepfather, and in the early years it worked out fine, but as soon as Katy hit the teenage years, well, that's when things started to go wrong. You know what teenagers are like, she started answering back, smoking and drinking, and it all became a bit too much for Alan. I suppose the truth was bound to come out at some point. I just didn't expect it to be like that, out of the blue, in the middle of an argument.'

Andy nodded.

'I'm not here to judge you, Rose. You're her mother. You did what you thought was right at the time. That was your call. I'm just glad I've had the opportunity to get to know Katy now. Obviously it was difficult at first and I wasn't sure she'd even want me in her life, but, you know, we're getting along fine now. I couldn't be a part of her childhood but I'm determined to be there for her in the future. That's if she wants me, of course.'

Andy was certainly true to his word. Ever since he and Katy had got to know each other he'd been a regular visitor at the manor and Katy had been to visit him at his home too, and met his family. With Rose living in Spain and only coming for occasional visits it had never occurred to me that Andy and Rose would ever bump into each other here. Although thinking about it now, I supposed it had only been a matter of time before the pair of them came face to face.

'Oh, she does, that much I can tell. Not that she really talks to me about it, but it's good that everything's out in the open. Our relationship is still a bit shaky, but I suppose it's going to take a little while for Katy to trust me again.'

Part of me wondered if I should make myself scarce so that the two of them could have a proper heart-to-heart, but I didn't honestly know how Rose, or Andy, might feel about that. Instead, I hovered around, seeing to Noel, paying attention to the dogs, with one ear out to the conversation, just in case I needed to step in to soothe any frayed emotions. In fact, I was surprised at how honestly and genuinely they opened up to each other, talking to each other as parents to Katy, and not as ex-lovers. It must have been strange for them though, after all this time.

'I'm sorry all this has had such an impact on your relationship with Katy. And I guess with your partner, too. Alan, is it?'

Rose gave a rueful shrug.

'Yes, my husband actually, but we've separated now. No, don't worry.' Rose held up a hand, responding to Andy's stricken expression. 'It wasn't only this business with Katy. Things have been tricky for a while and this simply tipped us over the edge. I'm only staying here until I can find something more permanent, although hopefully I'll be able to find somewhere locally.'

'Ah, right, I see,' said Andy. And I couldn't tell from his intonation whether he thought that was a good thing or a bad thing. With Rose, Andy and Katy all living within close proximity of each other, it either meant that Katy would find that happy family scenario that she'd been searching for all her life or that there'd be even more fireworks lighting up the sky over Little Leyton.

## 14

<hr>

After seeing Andy off, and with Rose announcing she was going into town to sort out her banking arrangements, I decided to get out of the house as well. I needed to clear my head after the emotionally charged encounter in my kitchen this morning. It had been the last thing I'd expected. At least it hadn't come to blows and I was hoping it would be a relief for Katy that her parents were back in touch and being civil towards one another.

Outside I breathed in the woody autumn scent. The days were much cooler now and the change in seasons was evident in the lanes and countryside surrounding the manor with the leaves on the trees and bushes having turned a golden and russet hue. I loved this time of year, a time for reflection on the events to date and that delightful sense of anticipation in preparation for the looming end of year festivities. I exhaled deeply, feeling the cold nip at my cheeks. Until I knew for certain when the pub would open again it was difficult to make any firm plans.

It was part of my daily routine to put Noel in his buggy and take the short walk into the village, usually with Digby at my side, to call in at The Dog and Duck and to chat through any issues with Dan or Silke. Not today though, what with it being still closed. The pub looked so sad and unloved with the windows boarded up. I had to stop myself from badgering Max all the time about when the work might start, but the longer it went on, the more concerned I became about the money we were losing.

The next best thing to visiting the pub was popping into Polly's Flowers next door. It was only a very small shop but chocolate box pretty with black mullioned windows and the name of the shop inscribed in fancy ornate lettering above the door. As I entered the bell tinkled and Polly came out from behind the scenes.

'Ellie! How lovely to see you. I can't tell you how much I've been missing our daily chats.' She wrapped me in a hug. 'Come and tell me all your news.'

'Oh, me too. It seems like ages since I last saw you.' We'd spoken several times on the phone in the intervening weeks but it wasn't the same as meeting in person. If there'd been any ill feeling from the misunderstanding over Polly's pregnancy, then that was all well forgotten now. 'This isn't a bad time, is it?'

'No, not at all. The morning rush is over.' She glanced at her watch. 'In fact, it would be around about now that I would be popping into the pub for my daily cappuccino or glass of fresh orange juice. It seems strange around here with the pub still closed. I know it's not the same but I could offer you a mug of instant. How does that sound?'

'Go on, then,' I said, smiling. I parked Noel, who had obligingly fallen asleep in his buggy, behind the counter and perched my bottom on one of the high stools. In the galvanised steel buckets on the rustic wooden display shelves were a selection of different blooms in pinks and reds and creams and yellows, their sweet scent wafting in the air. 'I needed to get out of the house today. Sometimes all the trials and tribulations of the manor get on top of me. You'll never guess who turned up this morning.'

'Who?'

'Andy. Just wandered straight in while I was sitting there talking to Rose. In fairness, that's what he always does when he visits, but it just hadn't occurred to me that he might do it when Rose was there.'

'Really? That must have been awkward? When did they last see each other?'

'Oh, years ago! When they had their fling so at least eighteen years.'

'Blimey, that must be so weird. Can you imagine? How did Andy react? Did he have a go at Rose?'

'No! It was all very civilised. I mean, I didn't really get involved. I just hovered around and let them get on with it, ready to jump in if it became heated, but it didn't. Rose was very apologetic and emotional and Andy was very gracious actually.'

'That's good. I bet Katy was pleased.'

'Well, she doesn't actually know about it yet. I hope it will bring her some peace of mind, knowing that her parents are back in touch and being reasonable with each other, but you can never really tell with Katy!'

Polly handed me a mug of coffee, her body brushing up against mine as she placed it on the counter.

'Hey, look at you!' I said, reaching out for her arm. 'You're definitely showing now.'

'I know.' She looked down, pulling her pinny tight over her tummy to show off a little bump, the sight making me smile. 'Aw, Ellie, I hope this doesn't make you feel sad,' she said, her gaze searching my face.

'No,' I replied honestly. 'It's bittersweet obviously, but I'm really thrilled for you and George, and seeing your pregnancy grow, well, it's a good reminder that life goes on, right? I can't wait to meet this little person,' I said, reaching out a hand to feel her stomach. 'For me and Max, though, it just wasn't the right time. When it happens again for us, then it will be all the more special for what we've been through.'

'Definitely,' said Polly, with a wide smile. 'Oh, by the way, did you like the flowers?'

'What flowers?' I asked, confused.

'The ones from Darcy? She asked me to do a lovely bouquet for you because she thought she might have upset you. What was that all about?'

'Ah, of course. Well, you know what Darcy's like!' I rolled my eyes. 'It was the night of the fire and she caught me at the wrong moment. I was worried sick about Max because he hadn't come out of the pub and she was wittering on about what a hero he was and how it wasn't all bad if she got to ogle at hunky firemen. Honestly! I'm afraid I snapped at her.'

Polly winced. 'Don't worry. I'd have done the same. She can be good fun sometimes but she isn't always the most sensitive of people.'

'I know. I don't like the way she's got a thing for Max either. I sense her hovering on the sidelines, just waiting for Max and I to fall out, so that she can swoop in and take my place. Mind you, I shouldn't be too critical of her. It was after we bumped into her at the summer fayre and told her about our marriage plans that we decided we wanted to do it sooner rather than later and set the date for December.'

'Is there any progress on that front?'

'Not really. Everything's on hold until we know when the pub will be ready, but I'm getting a bit anxious now as it won't leave us a lot of time to get everything organised.'

'Are you still thinking of postponing it?'

'No, I really don't want to now.' I sighed. 'After everything that's happened, I just want to get on with it and marry the man I love. Is that too much to ask?'

'Not at all. You could always run away one weekend and get the deed done.'

My face must have given away exactly what I thought of that idea.

'Hey, I was only joking.' Polly laughed.

'Hmm, that was Max's idea, too. I suppose the thing is I've set my heart on marrying at St Cuthbert's and having the reception in the barn, only there isn't a barn now. We might have to make do with a marquee at the manor instead.'

'Oh, la-di-da!' said Polly, mocking me. 'What a terrible shame that would be. A wedding in the grounds of a stately home!'

I felt suitably chastised and blushed, feeling foolish. Polly was right. Did it really matter where we held the reception? Exchanging our vows was the most important thing.

'I told you, you should have got married with us in the summer, made it a double wedding.'

Polly had been serious at the time, but back then I'd still been dithering over whether it was the right thing for Max and I to do. I'd wanted to be 100 per cent sure that we were marrying for the right reasons, and not because it was the expected thing for us to do. When I thought of the number of times I'd turned down Max's proposals, I was lucky he hadn't grown impatient with me and hot-footed it in the opposite direction.

Fortunately, it looked as though he had no intention of going anywhere.

Over coffee, I was able to briefly forget about the pub and the manor as Polly had me in stitches as she regaled me with the intimate details of how her pregnancy was progressing and the odd symptoms and cravings she was experiencing. She'd developed a passion for pickled gherkins, straight from the jar, waking in the middle of the night, unable to get back to sleep until she'd satisfied her craving. George, her husband, was elbow deep in edits of his latest book in his cosy crime series and wasn't providing Polly with nearly as much sympathy and attention as she felt she deserved.

'I'm not even sure he likes my changing body. He doesn't want to kiss me at the moment.'

'Well, I'm not surprised if you've got stinking pickled gherkin breath all the time!'

'Hmm, yes, do you think that might have something to do with it?'

'Never mind, if he gets this latest book out of the way before the baby arrives, then he'll be able to give you and the baby all his attention when you most need it.'

'Yes, well, he'd better or else I might be writing my own murder mystery novel with George as the victim!'

Polly liked to grumble about George, but beneath the minor niggles and gripes I knew they were absolutely solid and still as much in love as when they took their wedding vows. Later, as I wandered home, my mood high from spending time with my best friend, I was feeling suitably determined to get on with firming up the wedding arrangements. I'd get on the phone as soon as I got home to organise the marquee. But as I walked down the driveway to Braithwaite Manor, I had the distinct impression that my good mood wasn't going to last much longer.

Rose came running towards me, her face ashen, her gaze searching out the landscape around her.

'What on earth's the matter?' I asked, a feeling of dread rising in my chest.

'It's Flora. I can't find her anywhere. I put all the dogs out in the gardens and the other three came back when I called them but she wasn't with them. I've searched all the grounds, blown the whistle, even looked around the house thinking she may have snuck back in, but there's no sign of her anywhere. You didn't see her on your way in?'

I shook my head, panic filling my bones.

'Oh, God! Flora,' I yelled, hoping she might respond to my voice. I spun round, looking far into the distance, hoping I could spot her distinctive white tail held straight behind her, but she was nowhere to be seen. All sorts of scenarios passed through my mind. Flora was a gun dog, bred to hunt and run across fields. Probably she'd gone off in chase of a bird or a squirrel but she had absolutely no road sense at all. If she'd reached the main road, well, it didn't bear thinking about at all. 'How long ago did you last see her?'

Rose sighed and tears filled her eyes.

'I'm really sorry, Ellie, but it was about half an hour ago now.'

# 15

'This is all your fault, Mum! Why didn't you check the side gate when you put the dogs out?'

'I didn't realise I had to,' Rose said, with a stricken expression.

'Is that how she got out?' I asked Katy, who ran over to join us.

'Probably! How else could she have managed it? I've only just got home myself. Mum was supposed to be looking after the dogs. This has never happened before.' Katy glared at her mum, her dark expression full of recriminations.

'Well, I didn't do it on purpose, Katy,' Rose pleaded, clearly distraught. 'If that's what you think.'

'Look, this isn't helping. It isn't anyone's fault. We just need to find Flora. Rose, can you take Noel and the dogs inside? I'll go into the woods to see if I can find her. Katy, have a walk down the lanes, see if she's wandered down there.'

My heart was thumping in my chest; I was wondering what I would tell Max if we couldn't find her. I knew I complained about that dog, chastised her when she got under my feet, or when she tripped me up and ran off with my bra or knickers, but she made me laugh constantly and gave me such unconditional love. Despite my impatience with her, the thought of something bad happening to her tore at my heart. More than that, she'd been a gift to me from Max. I'd always wanted an English pointer and Max had found little Flora, rescued from the streets of Spain, in a rehoming centre. He'd presented her to me as a surprise and I'd been overwhelmed by the unexpected gesture. That hadn't been the only surprise though. I'd quickly discovered she was wearing a cute little red collar with a name tag on it that spelled out the words, *'will you marry me?'* It still made my heart skip a beat to think about that day.

Now my heart skipped for a completely different reason. Where could Flora be? I ran back the way I'd come, calling out her name. If only the pub were still open I could ring and tell them to spread the word, even get some of our regulars out looking for her. Panic was shooting around my body, making me indecisive as to what to do for the best. I ran through the woods, part of the route of our usual walk, over terrain that Flora loved. Her nose would always track the ground, picking up the scent of the wildlife – squirrels, rabbits and muntjac deer – that frequented Bluebell Woods. She often ran off, chasing after a bird, disappearing into the undergrowth in pursuit of her prey, oblivious to my calls, but she would come back eventually, tail wagging furiously, eager to rejoin me and the other dogs.

'Flora!'

Today, my calls, increasingly urgent, went unanswered. I was just making my way back through the woods, stopping to peer beneath some bushes to no avail, when my mobile buzzed and, seeing Katy's name on the display, I stabbed at the answer button.

'Katy?'

'Any news?' she asked me and the small spark of hope that had risen in my chest quickly deflated.

'No. You neither, I'm guessing?'

'Uh-uh. Oh, Ellie. What are we going to do?'

'Let's meet back at the manor and we can ring round a few people in the village, get them to keep an eye out for her. She'll be getting tired now, so hopefully she'll make her own way home.'

That was wishful thinking on my part but I wanted to keep positive for Katy's sake. Would Flora even know how to find her way back to the manor, especially if she'd ventured far away? What if she'd been involved in an accident, or got stuck in some barbed wire fencing in one of the remote fields – that had happened to Amber once, one of the dogs I'd cared for when I was running my doggy day care business – too far away for anyone to find her. Or perhaps she was lying hurt on the side of a road somewhere or someone could have stolen her. There'd been a spate of dog thefts in the area recently. Every scenario that popped into my head was a bad one. Now, I just wanted to get home and speak to Max; he'd know exactly what to do.

Back at the manor, Rose's pale face told me that Flora hadn't returned.

'I'm so sorry. This is all my fault. If I hadn't let the dogs out when I did or if I'd called them in sooner, then this might never have happened.'

'You can't blame yourself, Rose. It could have happened at any time, to anyone. All that matters now is that we find her.'

Katy stood in the corner of the kitchen, arms folded, scowling at her mum. There was clearly no doubt in her mind as to who she believed was to blame for Flora going missing.

'Now, try not to worry,' said Arthur, who'd been alerted to the commotion. He'd sat himself down at the kitchen table, holding onto its edge, as though he would jump up at any moment and go out looking for her himself. He would if he could, I knew. 'Someone will find her and bring her home. You'll see.'

'I really hope so. She's got a collar on and has been microchipped so we'll just have to keep our fingers crossed.'

Rose made a pot of tea while I rang around people I knew in the village who might be out and about with their own dogs. Katy did the same with her friends. I also put a call in to the vets, who told me they would put her details on the register of lost dogs and let me know if they heard anything. Unable to settle, I paced up and down the kitchen, peering outside at the ominous dark sky, my heart sinking at the rumble of thunder in the distance. Rain started to fall, not a gentle spotting shower, but heavy sheets of rain that ricocheted off the path outside and clung to the windows.

'Oh, no, the poor love, she'll be soaked through.'

'Let's hope someone's taken her home and they're just working out how to get her back to us.'

Arthur was trying to put a positive spin on the situation but with each passing moment with no news about Flora, I was feeling worse and worse. Digby, who had always been so sensitive to my moods, stuck firmly to my side looking up at me with sorrowful brown eyes. I reached a hand down to ruffle his smooth soft coat and he rewarded me with a wet kiss, his way of telling me that everything would be all right.

'This has gone on far too long. I'm going to have to phone Max. It's getting dark out there. If she doesn't come back soon we'll have lost her forever.'

Thankfully, Max picked up straight away. Hearing his voice made me wobble, my words coming out between the sobs that I could do nothing now to control.

'Hey, slow down, tell me again, what's happened?'

'It's Flora, she escaped from the garden and we can't find her. She's been gone a couple of hours now. We've searched all around the woods and the lanes. I don't know where else to look. I'm so scared for her, Max!'

'I'll come straight home. Try not to worry. Flora will probably be back before I am.' Max's voice was authoritative and reassuring, but even his positivity couldn't bring Flora home. Half an hour later his Jeep screeched to a halt on the gravel driveway and he came flying into the kitchen, his expression expectant and hopeful. I shook my head.

'She's not been found, Max. We've rung round everyone we can think of. No one's seen her. If anything's happened to her, I don't know what I'll do.'

Max came to my side and wrapped me in a hug.

'It's Mum's fault. She was the one who let the dogs out. You stupid woman! You should have kept your eye on her. She's still just a puppy.'

'Katy!' Max and I chastised her together.

'I'm so sorry, Max. I didn't think to check if all the gates were locked.' Poor Rose. She hadn't stopped wringing her hands since Flora had disappeared and however much Katy blamed her for what had happened, I knew Rose blamed herself even more.

'Mum, it's not your fault. You know what I think's happened? That little scallywag has jumped over the side gate. I caught her attempting to do it the other day, but she couldn't quite manage it and I pulled her back by her tail. She's obviously had another go at it. Look, Ellie, do you want to come with me in the Jeep? We can have a drive around the village and go across to Upper Leyton too, see if there's any sign of her.'

'Yes, could we? It's driving me mad just sitting here and waiting, not able to do anything. Will you be all right looking after Noel, Rose? His tea's in a Tupperware box in the fridge.'

'I can do it,' piped up Katy immediately.

'Of course we'll be all right,' said Rose. 'You get off. Don't worry about anything here. We'll hold the fort, won't we?' said Rose, addressing both Katy and Arthur.

In the Jeep, Max turned the headlights on and put the windscreen wipers on full power, but their frantic swishing could barely keep the driving rain at bay. Visibility was poor, even with Max taking it slowly around the country roads. I peered out of the window into the hedgerows, hoping I might catch a glimpse of Flora, but it was almost impossible to pick out anything in the darkness. We drove around for what seemed like hours but there was no sign of her anywhere.

'We've lost her, haven't we?'

'It's too early to say that. We don't know what's happened. You have to remember she's a gun dog. She was brought up outdoors and lived on the streets for months. If any of our dogs can cope with being outside, it's her.'

'Yes, but that was in Spain in a warm climate. She's not used to this rain. She'll be soaking wet. She'll probably get hypothermia.'

'Look, Ellie, this isn't helping. We have to keep positive until we know exactly what has happened to her.'

I couldn't share Max's optimism. Flora might have come from the streets of Spain, but ever since she'd been living with us she'd been a totally pampered pooch, sleeping exactly where she wanted to sleep, which usually meant on one of the cream sofas in the living room. The other day when it was raining I'd opened the back door to let her out. She'd peered out from between my legs, taken one look at the miserable conditions outside and then done an about turn, returning to the comforts of her bed. I could just imagine her out in this rain, shivering and cowering beneath a bush somewhere, wondering what she'd done wrong.

When we reached Upper Leyton we climbed out of the Jeep and knocked on the doors of some of the old cottages overlooking the green. Max handed over his business card to everyone we spoke to, just in case of any sightings, but I think we both felt it probably wouldn't lead to anything.

I gave Katy a call to see if there'd been any news in our absence but there was nothing from their end either.

'Come on,' said Max. 'Let's go home. There's nothing we can do at this time of night. We can get up early tomorrow and resume our search.'

'But, Max, the thought of her staying out overnight breaks my heart. She'll be so frightened, if she runs out in front of a car in the dead of night she won't stand a chance.'

'Well, we'll just have to hope and pray that doesn't happen. If anything had happened to her, we would have heard. She's got our contact details on her collar. I bet she's found herself a nice cosy barn to settle down in for the night.'

On the way home we picked up fish and chips for everyone back at the manor, as I was in no mood for whipping up a meal. We all sat around the kitchen table morosely, picking at our chips half-heartedly. Everyone seemed to have lost their appetite, all distracted by our own thoughts as to what had happened to Flora.

'Oh, Katy,' I said, trying to distract us all. 'I forgot to mention your dad called in this morning. He'd heard about the fire and wanted to see if there was anything he could do to help.'

'Really?' Her face lit up. 'Yeah, I was filling him in on the Little Leyton news in a text the other day. He's been away for a while. It was a shame I missed him. I'll have to give him a call, see if we can fix another time.'

'Well, I must admit it was very strange coming face to face with Andy again after all these years.' Rose laughed lightly. She'd barely touched her fish and chip supper.

'What?' The hackles rose immediately on Katy's collar as she glared at her mum accusingly. 'You saw Dad too? Why didn't you mention it?'

'Well, in fairness, we've all been a bit preoccupied tonight, Katy,' I butted in.

'Huh, well, I hope you weren't horrible to him. I don't want him thinking he won't be able to come here now, now that you're here. Really, you should have nothing to do with him. I don't understand why you would even want to speak to him? You didn't want to for eighteen years, went out of your way to avoid him, in fact, so you have no right to expect to have anything to do with him now. You shouldn't be interfering and making things worse between the pair of us.'

Rose sighed exasperatedly.

'How many more times do I have to apologise to you? I had no idea Andy would turn up here today. If I had, I would probably have made myself scarce and kept out of the way until he was gone. But, in fact, it worked out absolutely fine. I felt a bit awkward when I first realised who it was but Andy was perfectly charming. Wasn't he, Ellie?'

I nodded, but Katy was clearly not convinced.

'There was absolutely no bad feeling between us.' Rose added.

'Well, just stay away from him. He's settled now. He's got his own family. He's not going to be interested in you any more.'

'Oh, for goodness' sake!'

'Look, emotions are running high tonight after everything that's happened today.' Max pushed his chair back and stood up and I was grateful to him for stepping in. All I could think about was Flora. I didn't want to be dealing with Rose and Katy's grievances, not tonight. 'Save this for some other time. We've got an early start in the morning if we want to find Flora. We'll need all the sleep we can get.'

# 16

Sleep was a great idea, but it was never going to happen, not as far as I was concerned. It had long been a source of amazement to me that Max could fall asleep within a matter of minutes, regardless of any worries that might be troubling him. I snuggled into his back, wrapping my arms around his firm body, drinking in the delicious scent of him, feeling the gentle yet steady rise and fall of his chest. Ordinarily I would have found it a comfort, soon falling asleep myself, but not tonight. Every time I closed my eyes I pictured Flora, out in the cold and rain, terrified and alone. All sorts of horrific images taunted my mind as I tossed and turned and fought with the pillows and duvet. Then I imagined I could hear her, whimpering outside, but when I strained to make out any further noises, there wasn't anything there at all. Still, just the faintest idea that she might be outside made me unable to stay in bed.

Carefully, so as not to wake Max, I eased myself out of bed, pulled on my dressing gown and my slippers and tiptoed out of the room, along the landing and paused to peep into Noel's room, my heart squeezing at the sight of him sleeping peacefully in his cot. I crept past, not wanting him to detect my presence, and made my way downstairs. Digby and the other dogs greeted me from their beds with a wag of their tails, looking at me as though they thought I was mad to be up at this unearthly hour. I wondered if they'd noticed Flora's absence; normally she would be snuggled up close to one of the other dogs.

In the boot room, I found my wellies and pulled on Max's old wax jacket, finding a torch in the old chest of drawers. Outside it was pitch dark, but the sensor lights along the edge of the house came on as soon as I stepped out.

'Flora!' I called her name into the stillness of the night, hoping she would come scampering around the corner. The cold whipped through my coat and dressing gown and my teeth chattered as I wandered around the garden, hoping against hope that she might be sheltering under a hedge. I flashed the torch across the lawns and under the bushes but it was hopeless. If she was here somewhere she'd have come running up to greet me by now.

Back indoors, knowing there would be no chance of me getting to sleep if I went back upstairs, I flicked on the kettle and made myself a mug of tea. At the kitchen table I wrapped my hands around it and stared out of the window, willing our lovely little Flora to come home. Where could she be? If and when we did get her home I would never let her out of my sight again.

I sighed, despair and exhaustion making my whole body weaken. I placed my mug to one side and dropped my head into my hands; the emotion that I'd been holding inside today, and probably over the last few weeks too, escaped from my chest, first in gentle sobs and then in heartfelt tumbling ones that I thought, once the torrent had started, might never stop. My mind turned to the baby we'd lost, her life over before it had even started – we hadn't known if our baby was a girl or a boy but my instinct had been that it was a little girl – and I wept for the child we would never know or see grow up or become part of our family, even though there would be a place in our hearts for her forever. I hadn't been able to do anything to save our baby but I was determined to do everything to bring little Flora home.

'Oh, Ellie.' I looked up, tears running down my face, to see Max standing in the shadows, wearing only his boxers and a black T-shirt.

'Sorry, I didn't mean to wake you,' I said, wiping my face with the arm of my dressing gown.

'You didn't. I turned over in bed and there was a cold and empty space next to me. I was worried about you,' he said, with a half-smile. 'Are you okay?'

I sighed heavily, sniffing back the tears.

'Look at me, crying over that silly dog. I couldn't sleep so I decided I might as well come down. I thought Flora might be waiting outside the back door but of course she wasn't.'

Max came over and wrapped his arms around me. He kissed me on the nape of my neck and I reached up my hand over my shoulder to find his, squeezing it tight.

'We can do a proper search for her tomorrow. It'll be okay. She'll turn up somewhere.'

'Do you think? I've just got a very bad feeling about this. It'll break my heart if anything's happened to her.'

His hand massaged my hair.

'Everything seems so much worse in the dead of night. When daylight comes it will look more hopeful.'

'I really hope so. I'm not sure how much more I can take. First we lost our baby, then the pub goes up in flames and now we've lost Flora. What have we done to deserve all this bad luck, Max? It's as if someone somewhere is trying to tell us something.'

Max walked round to the front of the chair and pulled me up on my feet, clasping my face in his hands.

'You can't think like that. It's a bad patch we're going through. I know how you feel. I feel exactly the same. Losing our baby was the single worst thing that's happened to me, to us, but there's nothing we can do to change that. We have to move on with our lives and look to the future. Of course, we'll never forget about the baby we lost, but we have so much to be grateful for: our little boy, our families and a wedding to look forward to.'

I rested my head on Max's chest, his heartbeat resounding in my ear.

'I can't think about planning a wedding, not all the time Flora is missing. It wouldn't be right. She's so sweet and played such a big part in the proposal. We couldn't just forget about that. How would we feel getting married without her being around?'

'That's not going to happen, Ellie. She'll be back, don't worry. And we're not changing our plans. You did speak to Trish Evans about saving the date at St Cuthbert's?'

'Yes.'

'Well, that's it, then. All booked. I've waited long enough to persuade you to walk down the aisle with me. I don't want to wait a moment longer.' He looked at me imploringly. 'The longer we leave it, the more chance there is of you changing your mind again.' This was delivered with that familiar crooked half-smile of his that made me forget all our troubles for the briefest moment.

'Whatever happens, our wedding is going to take place and, I promise you, we'll make it a day to remember with Flora at our side and at a venue to be confirmed.'

His words soothed and calmed me. Max was right. After everything that had happened it only mattered that our wedding actually went ahead. In fact, I made a pact with God, there and then, I would hold my wedding reception in the old telephone box on the high street if he wanted me to, if he would only return Flora safely home again.

\* \* \*

Afterwards I managed to get a couple of hours sleep – Max chivvied me to go back to bed and held me in his arms until I dropped off – although we were up early the next morning and more determined than ever to find Flora. The rain of yesterday had given way to a cloudless sky and the promise of a clear and bright day ahead.

While I fed Noel and then changed him, Max took the dogs out into the gardens, walking around the entire estate, checking to see if Flora might have returned. Digby, Holly and Bella galumphed across the lawns in their usual comedic way but my heart twinged knowing that Flora should be with them, scampering around their legs, getting in the way and making a general nuisance of herself. I loved that dog but I realised I'd spent most of my time chastising her and shooing her away. What wouldn't I give to have her back again being a perfect little pest?

After coffee and toast, Max and I headed off out in the Jeep, leaving Rose to look after Noel and to man the phone in case of any news. We'd put

messages on the local Facebook pages and contacted most of the dog chari-
ties in the area, but none of those had brought us any news.

'A dog can't just disappear off the face of the earth,' I said to Max as we
ventured further afield and explored the countryside to the north of Upper
Leyton. 'Someone must have seen her somewhere.' But even as I said the
words, I realised that it wasn't necessarily so. Not if she was lying injured, or
something unimaginably worse, in a ditch somewhere.

Neither of us wanted to stop our search but we were running out of
places to look and I could sense that even Max's unerring optimism was
beginning to waver.

'Let's go back to the manor,' said Max when we found ourselves travelling along the same road for about the third time. 'We can have a bite to eat
and then maybe get the maps out and see if there's anywhere obvious that
we've missed.'

'Yes.' I fell silent, my gaze staring fixedly at the passing landscape, realising time was running out on us. What were we supposed to do? Just stop
looking for her? I couldn't imagine ever being able to do that or how we
might be expected to carry on with our lives normally as though nothing
had happened. It was as though time had come to a complete and utter
standstill. We wouldn't be able to move on until we discovered what had
happened to Flora. 'We could make some posters when we get home. Take
them around to the shops in the villages and put them up on the telegraph
posts on the circular route walk.'

'That's a great idea.' Max jumped on my suggestion with enthusiasm
and for that moment we held a brief ray of hope again. It was that feeling
that we were doing something to bring her home to us.

Back at the manor, Rose had prepared us some ham and cheese toasties
and mugs of tea, although we both struggled to finish our sandwiches,
preoccupied as we were with the thought of Flora and where she could
possibly be and what more we could do to find her. Noel was completely
oblivious to the tensions around the table and greedily gobbled up his
butternut squash and sweet potato purée, fed to him by Rose. Arthur joined
us and encouraged us to keep positive.

'I've known dogs who've been missing for days before returning home.'

'Really?' I asked, ready to grasp at any grain of hope.

'Oh, yes. Sometimes when dogs pick up a scent that's it. They're off. And she is a gun dog.'

'I know,' I said, 'but she's only very young still and she hasn't got a lot of sense. I'm sure she'd never find her way home.'

'Don't underestimate her. She'll come back when she's good and ready.'

Arthur was just trying to make me feel better but there was no way Flora was still out there somewhere of her own free will. She was too attached to us and the other dogs and enjoyed her creature comforts far too much to not want to come home. No, she had to be lost or injured somewhere. It was the only thing that made any sense.

After lunch we put some posters together, showing a heart-rending photo of Flora looking directly into the camera, and put them into polythene folders so they would withstand the rain. We were just getting ready to leave when Max's phone went off and my heart skipped when he immediately picked up the call – he'd not been answering any of his business calls this morning so I naturally got my hopes up thinking it must be someone calling about Flora, even more so when I heard the nature of the conversation.

'Yep, that's right. Uh-huh. You have? Well, that's great news, a big relief.' His face broke out in a huge smile as he faced me. 'Thanks very much.'

'Has she been found?'

'What? Oh, no, but some other good news. That was the insurance company. They'll be making a full pay out on our claim. They've just got to get the paperwork signed off. It was an electrical fault in the lighting system that caused the fire apparently, so now we've got the go ahead to start on the refurbishment.'

Max looked at me expectantly, clearly wanting me to be as enthused about this latest turn of events as he was, but all I felt was a sense of crushing disappointment. The pub and what had happened to it had been at the centre of my world only a couple of days ago, but now it wasn't even remotely important. All that mattered was Flora. All the time we were hanging around here, we were never going to find her.

'Shall we go?' I asked, biting on my lip to stop my tears of disappointment from falling.

I knew none of this was Max's fault but I couldn't help my resentment towards him building as we set off in the Jeep again. Why couldn't he understand just how wretched I was feeling? How could he even think about the pub at a time like this? Flora wasn't just a dog, she was the embodiment of our commitment to each other and this, well, it seemed like a very bad omen to me.

I sat in silence, not trusting myself to say anything as we bumped along the drive and down to the lane out of the village. We revisited all those places we'd been to this morning, handing out posters to anyone we came across and dashing in and out of the shops, begging them to display them in their windows. At one point we got out of the Jeep and walked across the fields over stiles and through kissing gates, putting the posters up on tele-graph poles and prominent trees. I felt sure there could be no one in the county unaware now that Flora was missing.

Still, though, our attempts to find her proved futile and, after a couple more hours, Max was the one to suggest that we might as well go home. I couldn't bear it. To think that Flora would be spending another night out in the cold, all alone. When we got back to the manor, Rose, Katy and Arthur were all waiting for us, looking at us expectantly in the hope that we might have some good news for them. I simply shook my head, and went across to Noel, lifting him out of his rocker and cuddling him tight.

'Look, I think I might go and have a bath, if you don't mind?'

'No, not at all,' said Rose. 'You go and sort yourself out. Noel's perfectly happy down here with us.'

I felt guilty disappearing so soon again, especially when Rose had done more than her fair share of holding the fort, but I just needed a bit of time for myself. Even the spacious surroundings of the manor could feel claus-trophobic when we were all huddled together in the kitchen going over and over the same conversation.

*'She'll turn up soon.'*

*'She's probably found a doggy friend to hang out with and is having a wow of a time somewhere.'*

*'What an adventure she'll be having!'*

All comments delivered to make me feel better, but they didn't help in the slightest because the longer we went without any news of Flora, the more reason we had to feel less and less optimistic about the likely outcome.

I was just padding up the stairs when I heard a telephone ring and I stopped in my tracks, my whole body frozen to the spot. Then I made out Rose's voice.

'Yes, that's right. A-ha. Oh-h-h!' There was an exclamation, a huge exhalation of breath, but at that point I couldn't tell if it was a good or bad one until she let out a further cry. 'You've found her? Well, that's just brilliant news.'

I went bounding down the stairs and stood on the threshold of the kitchen, checking Rose's expression for clarification.

'It's the most wonderful news, Ellie. Flora has been found!'

## 17

Within minutes and after a lot of hugging and laughing, Max and I were back in the Jeep and on our way to collect Flora.

'West Wytton? Where even is that?'

'Well, according to the satnav, about twenty-five miles away from here.'

'Oh, my goodness, how on earth did she ever end up there? And did they say she was all right?'

Max shrugged.

'I don't know, Ellie. I didn't speak to them, remember? I know as much as you do, but if there'd been anything seriously wrong, then I'm sure they would have warned us. We'll find out soon enough though, I guess.'

*And relax...* Well, maybe just a little bit. I wouldn't be able to fully unwind until I saw Flora for myself.

'I honestly thought we'd lost her forever,' I said aloud as we drove out of the village.

'Did you? You should have more faith, Ellie,' he said, turning to raise his eyebrows at me and laughing.

It wouldn't be the first time he'd said those words to me and I was beginning to realise that maybe I should be more like Max and not always think the worst.

But what a difference a day made. For the last twenty-four hours I'd been in the pits of despair and now I was overcome with excitement at the prospect of seeing Flora again. Now, hopefully, life could return to something approaching normal.

\* \* \*

'Oh, Flora, look at you!'

At the vet's practice she came sliding out from one of the back rooms, her feet skidding across the floor in her haste to get to us, her tail wagging tentatively between her legs.

'What happened to you?'

She looked diminished somehow, as she looked up at me almost apologetically. Her coat, normally sleek and shiny, was now caked in mud, and there were dark streaks of tear stains beneath her eyes. More noticeable was the way she was cowering and trembling, looking all around her, uncertain of what she was supposed to do next. The veterinary nurse handed me the lead and showed us through to a consulting room to see the vet.

'Thank you so much,' I said before she had a chance to say anything. 'Where was she found?'

'A local farmer found her on his land last night. I think she gave him a bit of a runaround in one of his fields but finally he was able to coax her over with some treats. He said she was frightened and soaking wet so he took her back to the farm. She hasn't got a name tag on so there wasn't anybody he could call. He brought her along to us as soon as he could today.'

'Oh, Flora!' I couldn't resist picking her up, even though she was filthy and far too big to be picked up in my arms, but we were both in desperate need of a cuddle. She wriggled to get closer to my face and proceeded to lick me all over, which, with the overriding whiff of fox poo wafting up my nostrils, was pretty disgusting. Still, none of that actually mattered. All that mattered was that we had her back. 'What happened to your tag?'

'We've given her a thorough checking over and it looks as though she lost some fur around her collar and there's some grazes and cuts on her tummy and paws. I imagine she's picked those up by either getting caught on some fencing or maybe in some brambles. That's probably how her tag came off too. We've cleaned her up, well, her wounds at least, and I had to stitch together a slightly bigger cut on her shoulder, but other than that she seems to have come out from her adventure relatively unscathed. We'll give her some antibiotics just as a precaution.'

'We can't thank you enough,' said Max, who was looking as relieved as I was feeling, 'and of course we'd like to pass on our thanks to the gentleman who found her.'

While Max settled the bill I took Flora outside where the sun had come out in recognition of this important occasion.

'You haven't stopped smiling since we collected her,' said Max on the way home.

'I know. I still can't really believe we are lucky enough to have her back. I was preparing myself for the worst possible news, so this is just the best thing ever.'

'To be honest with you, there was a moment last night when my mind was entertaining some pretty dark scenarios too.'

'Really? And yet you kept on telling me you were confident she'd be found?'

'Well, what else could I say? I'm just mightily relieved she's back with us.'

Flora received a welcome befitting royalty back at the manor. She was smothered in hugs and kisses from Katy, Arthur shook his head indulgently and sneakily fed her digestive biscuits when he thought no one was looking and Rose apologised profusely and promised she would never let anything like that happen again.

Max shook his head.

'I've checked the gardens, Mum. There was some distinctive white fur on the top of the gate. That's how she got out. She leapt over it, the little so-and-so. It wasn't your fault at all so don't go blaming yourself. I've got my guys going round the grounds now, just to check the fencing, and to put up some additional trellis where necessary so she won't be able to repeat that little trick. Although I suspect she may have learnt her lesson now.'

After gulping down her dinner, as though she hadn't been fed in weeks, she curled up next to Holly and Bella in their bed in the utility room and looked as though she wouldn't be going anywhere soon, although I was relieved to see that her heartbreaking and incessant shaking had finally stopped.

'Right,' said Max with an exaggerated sigh. 'Where were we two days ago before this wild dog chase took over our every waking moment?'

Arthur had returned to his bedroom and Rose had made herself scarce too, probably relishing the opportunity for some alone time now she didn't have to look after Noel, just leaving Katy slouched at the kitchen table, scrolling through her phone.

'Max, I've been meaning to ask you, how long is Mum staying for, do you know?'

'I have no idea,' he said wearily, as though it was the last line of conversation he wanted to be having right now. 'As long as she wants to, I guess.'

'Really?' Katy's limbs seemed to have a will of their own and they stretched out over the chair and table in a languorous fashion. 'Well, she can't stay here forever, can she? I was thinking perhaps you should say something to her. She needs to find her own place some time.'

Max raised his eyebrows at Katy, his expression stern.

'Were you, now? Well, I hate to disappoint but Mum is welcome to stay here as long as she likes. That's what family is all about, isn't it? Helping out when our nearest and dearest most need our support.'

'Huh. I'm not sure Mum has the greatest grasp on the concept of family.'

'Honestly, Katy. I really don't know what your problem is with Mum. She's going out of her way to be lovely to you and you're just not having it, are you? I thought you two had got over your differences.'

I could hear the barely concealed exasperation in Max's voice. I focussed my attentions on Noel, not wanting to be dragged into this particular family spat.

'Well, we had. All the time she was living in Spain. But now, well, it just feels weird living under the same roof as her. She treats me like I'm fourteen years old or something, when I'm not. I'm a fully grown adult!'

'Well, then, start acting like one!' He softened his tone. 'All I'm saying is that you should try cutting Mum some slack. You might discover that you'll get on better.'

'It's isn't fair,' whined Katy, sounding, in fairness to Rose, very much like a young sulky teenager. 'We were all getting along fine until Mum turned up. And now she's gone and ruined everything. This is my home. Not hers.'

'It's my and Ellie's home actually, Katy. And your home too, all the time you want it to be. And Mum's. You're both welcome to stay for as long as you like, but I do expect you to make an effort to get along together all the time you're living here.'

Katy crossed her arms, clearly unimpressed with Max's stance.

'Well, if Mum's going to stay then maybe I should move out?' she said airily, challenging him with a defiant stare. I turned away, stifling a smile. Honestly, had she learned nothing about handling Max in all the months she'd been living with us?

'If that's what you want to do then obviously we'd be disappointed to see you go but we would understand, wouldn't we, Ellie?'

'Um, yes, whatever's best for you, Katy,' I said noncommittally.

'Although, of course, I'm not sure how you'd manage to pay rent, it's not as though you're earning any money from the pub at the moment,' Max said. 'I mean, you've still got at least another year at college before you can find a full time job.' Max tilted his head to the ceiling, as if deep in thought. 'I suppose you could always ask Mum if she'd help you out. You might be able to find a small room in a shared house or something.'

Katy's face literally dropped, until she quickly gathered herself, her eyes wide and unblinking.

We both knew how much Katy loved living at the manor; she had her own large and airy bedroom with a walk-in wardrobe, en-suite bathroom and marvellous views across the valley. How many teenage girls were as fortunate? This place was such a beautiful and special home that I could never imagine a time when I would take any of it for granted and I suspected Katy felt the same way too. She'd told me on several occasions how much she loved being part of a busy household and how she relished the chaotic family environment that she'd never really experienced at home.

'It feels as though I really belong here,' she'd told me not so long ago, 'and I love that. I've never had that sense of belonging before.'

Now you could see the cogs in her brain whirring as she realised she'd backed herself into a corner.

'Huh! Well, I shall just have to... well, I will just have to think about that!' she said, standing up and sauntering out of the kitchen with a disdainful look on her face.

'Oh, dear,' I said, chuckling when Katy was out of earshot. 'I don't think that was the answer she was looking for.'

Max shook his head.

'She's out of order and she knows it. She can't dictate who we have living here and as for the way she talks to Mum, there's no need for it.'

'I know. I do feel sorry for Rose at times. I don't like to interfere because it's something only they can sort out for themselves, but it can't be very pleasant for either of them.'

'Or the rest of us! It's not fair on you, Ellie. You've got enough on your plate without having to referee domestics between my family. I'll sit down and have a chat with Mum and see what she wants to do. The refurbishment on the cottages in the village is well under way and they're due to be ready in about six weeks' time. I wanted to offer Mum first refusal on one of those but I'll be pulling the guys off those soon to start work on the pub now we've got the go ahead. It'll mean that completion might be delayed a while.'

'Well, I'm sure we can muddle through here for a few more weeks. We'll just have to make sure we don't leave them alone together for too long or else they might come to blows.'

To be honest, I enjoyed having them both around. It meant there was always someone around to have a chat with, to share a cup of tea with, to help me out with the dogs or with Noel if I needed it, and boy, had I needed it this last couple of days. They were both only too keen to help out on that front, often vying with each other to be the one to give Noel his bath or feed him his tea.

After everything she'd been through I felt privileged that Katy trusted me enough to confide in me, talking to me late into the night, telling me her secrets and worries but also her hopes for the future in a way she never did with Max and certainly not with her mum these days. She'd really opened up to me about what had gone on with her mum and the way she'd felt about meeting her biological father after so many years of not even knowing of his existence. She'd brought a lot of drama to the manor but also a lot of laughter and her love for Noel was wonderful to witness.

The nature of my relationship with Rose was different because I'd only got to know her from her infrequent visits to the manor, which had always been with her husband, Alan, and at a time when she was still dealing with the fallout of the breakdown of her relationship with Katy. It had been a difficult time for everyone concerned and I'd always found Rose reticent and guarded in the company of Alan. This time around, on her own, she'd been more open and relaxed and I'd got to know and like her much more. I could sense that her focus now was on her relationships with her children, Max and Katy, and Noel too, but Katy certainly wasn't making matters easy for her mum.

'Anyway, have you sent those invitations out yet?'

'What?' I said, looking at him open-mouthed.

'Haven't we got a wedding to organise?'

'Give me a chance. I don't know if you've noticed but I've been preoccupied with a certain four legged creature these last few days.'

'Exactly. With our wedding mascot back in place there's no reason why we can't forge ahead with the arrangements. Work will start on the pub tomorrow. The priority is to get the kitchen gutted and refitted so that Eric, and Dan and Silke if they want to, can move back in and get the place reopened as quickly as possible. And then we can talk about what we want to do out the back.'

'How do you mean?'

'Well, we've effectively got a blank canvas out there. We're not restricted to what we can do, other than by planning requirements. But one idea would be to build a more permanent structure, like an orangery or a conservatory. Although obviously we wouldn't be able to complete something like that in time for the wedding.'

'No, exactly! Besides, the barn was a pretty permanent structure until it burnt down. It'd been there for hundreds of years.'

'I know, but if we utilised the space better, it would give you more flexibility for your events or for whatever else you might want to do out there. You could have a permanent dining facility if you wanted to go down that route? Get someone in to run the restaurant.'

'No!' I said, probably too vehemently. I didn't like to sound ungrateful when Max was putting all his other work commitments to one side to concentrate on The Dog and Duck, but I wanted the barn to be built to exactly the same specification as before, only obviously with better wiring.

'I don't want us to be like all the other pub food establishments out there. They're ten a penny. What makes The Dog and Duck so special is that it is primarily an old fashioned pub where people from the local community can come and meet their friends for a drink or join in with whatever's going on that day. If it becomes a restaurant then the whole essence of the place will change. Besides, you should know how important that old ramshackle barn is to us. It's always been such a cosy and inviting space. Think about it. It was where our baby was born!' I couldn't help becoming animated when I was talking about the pub. 'Where Josie held Stella's christening party, where Polly had her wedding reception and where I want to have our wedding party too. If we turn it into a restaurant or if it becomes a designated function room then it will lose all its charm, what it is that makes the place so special.'

'Okay, okay,' said Max, holding up his hands in a gesture of defeat. 'I get it. You want us to put the barn back to exactly how it was before.'

'Yes.'

'Fair enough,' he said, shaking his head indulgently. 'Your wish is my command, madam!'

I breathed a sigh of relief.

'How long do you think the work will take?'

'Hmm, well, that depends on a number of things. On whether we can get the subbies in, if we can get hold of all the materials, if the weather holds.' He shrugged, in that telltale way of seasoned contractors wanting to manage their customer's expectations. But I wasn't any old customer, for heaven's sake. I was his bride-to-be!

'Max!' I cried, punching him playfully in the arm.

'Hey, that hurt!' He laughed. 'Well, we have a firm deadline in place, don't we? The main pub work should be completed in three or four weeks. And the rebuild of the barn? You have my word, it will all be done for the 20th of December.'

## 18

Later that week, leaving the dogs safely secured at the manor, I headed outside into the now much noticeably cooler air. My old and much loved cream puffa jacket had emerged from the wardrobe and it was lovely to feel its comfortable warmth around my shoulders again, like reuniting with a faithful old friend. Noel was wrapped up in his new fur trimmed snuggle suit, a present from his Nana Rose, and was enjoying the ride in his buggy as we made our way to Josie's house on the new estate on the other side of the village. I hadn't seen her since the evening at the manor when I'd asked her to be my bridesmaid so we had lots to talk about and lots of plans to put in place if we had any chance of getting everything organised in time for my big day.

'Come in.' She beamed when we arrived at her house. 'We've been so excited, haven't we, Stella?'

My gorgeous little god-daughter, with her curls of auburn hair, suddenly went all shy and hid behind her mum's legs, peeping out at us warily.

'She's funny. Ever since I told her you were coming, she's been saying, "Door, Mummy, door." She's been peering out of the window saying, "Noll, Noll," too so I'm very pleased you've arrived at last,' she said, tickling Noel under his chin.

Josie took Noel from my arms and Stella followed her mum, eager to say hello to Noel beneath all his layers of padding.

I was just hanging up my coat in the hallway when Eric came down from upstairs and reached for his jacket on the coat hook.

'I do hope you're not leaving on our account.'

'Hello, sweetheart,' he said, giving me a massive hug. 'No, I thought I'd leave you girls to have a natter. I'm going for a walk before it gets too dark out there. I like to have a wander past the pub to get my daily update on how the work's progressing.'

'Isn't it exciting that things are actually starting to happen now? Max says it shouldn't be too long before we can open up again. That's going to be a special night.'

'I can't bloody wait!' said Eric, his face lighting up.

'Honestly, Ellie,' said Josie after Eric had left. 'He doesn't know what to do with himself these days. He's taken it very hard, the pub not being open. I thought he might enjoy the enforced rest, but I'm not sure he knows how to exist outside the four walls of that place.'

It was hardly surprising. After he'd retired as landlord, Eric had taken off, travelling around Europe to satisfy his wanderlust, but he seemed to have got that particular bug out of his system, and all he wanted to do was to potter around the pub chatting to his customers, old and new, without the responsibility of actually managing the place. The enforced closure of The Dog and Duck had impacted on so many people's lives.

'He can't wait to get back to the pub. Mind you, we'll miss him when he goes. Stella loves having him here. Those two have a mutual admiration society going on!'

I laughed, looking across at Stella now, who was delighted to have a captive audience in Noel. She was bringing him all her toys, one by one, and sitting them in a circle round him on the play mat. He flapped his little legs and arms around, laughing as he tried to reach them, knocking them over when he could.

'Anyway, how are things with you, Ellie? You must be completely frazzled. You've had such a lot to contend with these last few weeks,' she said with a sympathetic smile. She handed me a mug of tea and sat down beside me on the sofa.

'It's been mad, I must admit. Honestly, I was okay, thought I was on top of everything and then when we lost Flora that day, it was like the final straw. I just went to pieces. It didn't seem fair after everything we'd been through that we could lose her forever, too. It was heartbreaking and I'm not sure how I would have coped if we hadn't got her home again.'

'That little minx, putting you through all that worry!'

'I know. I'm not sure she'll do it again though. She stays close to me and the other dogs when we're out now. I think we all learned a valuable lesson that day. Now, touch wood, everything's back on track and the only thing I have to worry about is organising a wedding.'

'You must have tons to do. If there's anything I can help with, then just shout.'

'Well, I've already sent most of the invitations out so that's a start. Max assures me that the barn will be ready in time.' I crossed my fingers up in the air just to be extra safe. 'But I do have a marquee lined up for the manor in case of any last minute hitches. The food is going to be simple, home cooked fare and Yardleys, the butchers, are taking care of that for me. Polly's obviously doing the flowers and Betty from the tea rooms has already made the cake, a three tiered fruit cake, so I think we're pretty set. I just need to get our dresses sorted and for Max to turn up on the right day and we'll be fine.'

Josie laughed.

'Don't worry, the whole village will make sure Max gets to the church on time.'

Sometimes, after everything that has happened this year, I have to pinch myself to believe that we will finally be married by the end of it. There was a small part of me, a part that I was desperately trying to ignore, that still believed something else was bound to go wrong.

Banishing those thoughts I delved into my bag and brought out the fabric samples I'd picked up from town earlier in the week.

'I've got something to show you actually. I wanted to see what you think of these. With it being a winter wedding, I was thinking of a velvet dress for you girls in one of these three colours. Emerald green, midnight blue or a deep burgundy.'

Josie took the samples from me, her fingers instinctively stroking the rich brushed fabric.

'These are gorgeous, really thick and luxurious.'

I breathed a sigh of relief. So far, so good. I'd deliberately wanted to speak to Josie first because she was the one most likely to have some reservations over what I chose for them to wear. Sasha had model girl looks and would look great in anything, Polly was very girly and shared the same taste as me so I was pretty confident she would love anything I suggested but Josie was more of a jeans and sweatshirt girl who you rarely saw in a dress. I wanted her to feel comfortable and relaxed in what she wore and I knew she would hate anything too fussy or too floaty or that showed off too much skin.

'This is a picture of a dress I found online that I thought would look really lovely on you all.'

Josie took the picture from me and studied it for a few moments, falling silent as she turned the photo round in her hands. It showed a knee length, three quarter sleeve loosely tailored dress that had a sweetheart neckline. It was a classic and simple design, but touched the body in all the right places offering a flattering fit.

'Yep, I like that,' she said in her understated way.

'And do you have a preference for colour?'

I held my breath as she turned her attention back to the fabric samples.

'I like them all but I think my favourite is this one.'

She handed me the lush emerald green sample.

'Ooh, I'm so pleased you picked this one.' I could breathe again. 'It's my favourite too.'

A little frisson of excitement ran through my body.

'Well, that's it settled, then. We have our bridesmaid dresses! Polly is going to prepare the bouquets with cream roses and red berries with some silvery grey foliage, so they'll look beautiful against the green of the dresses. I'll let Caroline know. She'll want to see you, of course. To take your measurements, so maybe if you can pop in to see her in the next day or two, and then she can get started on them.'

'It'll be lovely to have a winter wedding to look forward to, something a bit different.'

Our gazes were distracted for a moment by Stella, who was handing her rag dolls to Noel and beginning to get frustrated when he wasn't changing their clothes as she instructed. She shook her head and frowned, her antics making us smile.

'I think you might have to do it for him, Stella,' I told her.

'He's only little,' reminded her mum.

'You know, I've just had an idea. I don't know why I didn't think of it sooner but it's only just occurred to me. Thinking about the wedding, I've got four lovely bridesmaids but I will definitely need some flower girls as well to hold the baskets of rose petals. Don't you think?'

Josie's eyes widened.

'And Stella and Ruby will have exactly the right cute factor for the job. Plus you and Sasha will be on hand if the little ones become overwhelmed by the occasion.'

'Well, that would be amazing for us, if that's what you really want. You know what Stella's like, she's such a girly little girl and she would absolutely love being like Mummy and wearing a special dress on your big day. Can you imagine the photos?'

'Well, that's settled, then. Come here, Stella.'

I held out my arms to her and she came running over and climbed up onto my lap. I stroked my hand over her gorgeous silky hair. Well, I couldn't get married without my god-daughter taking a leading role, could I? I kissed her on the head, and made a mental note to add another job to my to-do list: finding flower girl dresses.

\* \* \*

After spending a couple of hours chatting with Josie, drinking more tea, including several cups given to me by Stella in her dainty tea set, Noel and I made our way home again. Walking along the high street, my mind was buzzing with everything I still needed to do; I was trying to ignore the sense of panic fluttering in my chest. I would need to organise gifts for the bridesmaids and flower girls, source table linen for the long trestle tables and now source the actual tables too, as ours had gone up in smoke in the fire! We'd need chairs as well, in fact everything that had been inside the barn. I was preparing a mental inventory of its contents when I spotted a familiar figure coming towards me. My heart lurched a little because from a distance I recognised a change in him that I hadn't seen before. He looked different somehow, older and with an aura of sadness wrapped around him. Why hadn't I noticed before?

'Eric!' I tried to hide my surprise. 'Hello again. So, tell me, what's the progress report on the pub? I think sometimes Max gets fed up with all my endless questions, mainly, "*Is it finished yet?*"'

'Well, there's a lot of activity going on down there. There's a way to go yet but Max certainly seems to have it all under control.'

'I do hope so! I don't see much of him these days, he's out early in the mornings, back late at night. All the conversations we do have are about worktops and cupboard sizes.' I laughed. 'I don't mind but I shall be glad when all the work's done and it will be business again as usual.'

'I know. It's only when something like this happens that it makes you take stock and realise what's important to you.'

'You're sounding very philosophical today, Eric. Is everything all right?'

He shrugged.

'Yeah,' he said, not very convincingly. 'I suppose...' His words trailed away and I sensed there was more he wanted to say but was unable to.

'Look, have you got time for a cuppa at Betty's? We can have a proper catch-up if you like.'

Betty's Tea Rooms on the high street was experiencing a boom in business in the wake of the fire at The Dog and Duck. It had become the social hub of the village where people came together for a natter over a cuppa, instead of a pint, to catch up on the latest gossip. In fairness, I'd always made a point of visiting the cafe at least once a week for a chat with Betty and to try out one of her delicious creations, my favourite being the Bakewell tarts, but I was always more than willing to try anything else that might have come out of the oven that day. Betty was a regular visitor to The Dog and Duck and she couldn't come along without bringing one of her scrumptious cakes with her.

Today, Eric ordered our teas and some cheese scones while I got Noel out of his buggy and winter wear. We sat at the round table at the front of the shop overlooking the high street, soaking in the busy atmosphere of the cafe. I popped Noel into the baby rocker that Betty kept for visiting children in the shop.

'Oh, I must tell you. I was chatting to Josie about the plans for the wedding and we're going to have Stella and Ruby as flower girls. Can you imagine how adorable they're going to look?'

Eric chuckled. 'Now, that will be a sight to behold. She loves her pretty dresses and handbags. She'll be so excited.'

'It must be lovely for you seeing her on a daily basis now?'

'There's nothing better but I do feel in the way at times. Josie and Ethan lead such busy lives that when they do have a bit of time to themselves they don't want her old dad getting in the way.'

'I'm sure they don't think like that. Josie was saying how much she loves having you around.'

'That's because she's my daughter and she's a great girl but they've got their own lives to lead.'

'So what you're telling me is that you can't wait to get back to the pub?'

I reached across the table for his hand. When I'd lost my job in London I'd returned to the village for some thinking time to decide what I should do next. Mum and Dad had left to take up a contract in Dubai so it had meant I had their lovely cottage to myself. I'd set up my own little business, dog walking and dog sitting, which had been supplemented by my shifts at The Dog and Duck, courtesy of Eric. It was at that time that I'd learned everything I knew now about running a pub. How to keep a good cellar, how to put orders on at the brewery, how to manage the staff and shift rotas and how to arrange special events nights that would keep the villagers talking for weeks. Eric had taken me under his wing and imparted all his knowledge to me. When he'd announced he would be retiring, and there was the possibility the pub might be sold to an uncertain future, it had seemed like the most natural thing for me to take over the reins.

I had so many happy memories of nights spent working with Eric; he was the most accommodating boss, not like a boss at all, more like a friend, or my second dad as I came to think of him. After a busy night shift we would often share a coffee and a nightcap and talk about the events of the evening, what we'd heard from our customers, often ending up laughing and chatting until the early hours of the morning.

'I'm wondering if I should. It's Dan and Silke's time now. They're youngsters and have their own ideas about running the pub. I'm sure they must get fed up with me, putting my tuppence worth in when it's probably not needed. Perhaps it's time for me to move on, find my own place.'

'Eric, no! To most of our customers, you are The Dog and Duck and, if you haven't forgotten, it is still my pub. I decide what goes on there. Besides, I thought you loved being back there.'

'I do. Or rather, I did, but I'm wondering if I ought to step aside and let them have a free rein at it. I've had my time there, over twenty years.'

'Yes, and that's why we still need you. You have that wealth of experience that no one else does. Dan relies on you for advice and support. He's got the brawn, admittedly, for changing the barrels in the cellar and lugging crates up and down, but you've done your fair share of that. You wouldn't want to be doing that now anyway, especially after that accident you had.'

Eric had slipped down the stairs of the cellar while carrying a crate of Belgian beers and had ended up breaking his ankle. The ambulance people had had one devil of a job trying to get him out again on a stretcher.

'No, of course not. My place is behind the bar, serving customers, but anyone can do that.'

'Pah! You know that's not true. No one can work that bar like you. You're one of the reasons the customers keep on coming in, and all the time Max and I own and run the pub, then you have a home and a job there. Honestly, Eric. I mean it.'

I hated seeing him so out of sorts. It wasn't like him.

'Take no notice of me and don't you go mentioning anything to Josie about me having a grumble. It's good to talk about it though. This fire has thrown me off balance. Made me feel as though I don't really belong anywhere. Miriam's been gone for over ten years now so why suddenly I should be feeling this way, missing her so much, I don't know. I suppose this break from work has made me look at my life and what's missing, maybe.'

'Perhaps you need a dog?' I suggested.

Eric laughed.

'No, love. That wasn't quite what I was thinking of. I can get my dog fix from your motley crew. Nah, once I get back behind that bar, I'm sure I'll be feeling much more like my old self.'

'Right, well, I shall tell Max he needs to get a move on so that we can all get back to normal.'

'Are you two off now?' Betty arrived at our table just as we were pulling on our coats. 'In case you were wondering, Ellie, your cake is maturing nicely in my larder. I'm feeding it every day with a nip of brandy so come December it should be just perfect. I can't wait to start icing it in a couple of weeks' time.'

I couldn't wait to see it. The decorations were going to be in winter berry colours to match the flowers and talking about it with Betty made everything seem so much more real.

'Hang on a minute.' Betty rushed off before returning a couple of minutes later carrying a large wicker tray and handing Eric and me a large paper bag each full of goodies. 'There's some of your favourite Bakewell tarts in there, Ellie, and I've put together a selection of cakes for you, Eric. I hope Josie and the gang will enjoy them.'

His face lit up as he peered into the bag and the wonderful aroma of pastry and almonds and cinnamon and jam wafted beneath our nostrils.

'See, you wouldn't get this treatment anywhere else, Eric!' I gave him a crafty wink and wrapped my arm around his waist for a hug. I hoped Eric had just been having a bad day, one of those where a cake, a cuppa and a good old chinwag with your friends were all that was needed to make you feel so much better about your life.

## 19

As much as I loved living in a busy household like the manor, I still relished those rare moments when I could find a quiet spot for myself or, even more rarely, for Max as well. This evening Arthur had retired to bed early as there was a programme on WWII Spitfire pilots he wanted to watch. Against all the odds Rose and Katy had enjoyed an early supper together before watching *Bridget Jones's Baby* for the umpteenth time in the living room. Hearing them giggle together gave me hope that they might be finding a way to work through their differences, especially as they'd gone to bed now without it being preceded by any door slamming or shouting. The dogs, exhausted from their earlier run across the fields, were curled up in their beds and Noel had gone down happily at his usual bedtime and we hadn't heard a peep from him since.

The conservatory adjoining the kitchen and overlooking the gardens was my favourite place in the entire house. Of an evening, with the low lighting and fairy lights twinkling around the windows, it had a cosy and magical feel. Looking outside, you could see more glistening lights running alongside the footpaths and over the ornamental dwarf trees on the lawns sweeping away into the distance. At any time of day, I liked to sit in the window and gaze outside, picking out new sights that I hadn't noticed before: flowers coming into bud, the trees losing their leaves, the colours changing from season to season. There was also a host of wildlife visitors to the manor, especially when the dogs were safely locked up indoors: squirrels, muntjac deer, the occasional heron and, of a night, hedgehogs, owls and foxes.

Max had come in after nine o'clock so I'd made us an impromptu supper of linguine with king prawns, chilli, wine and rocket, something that I could throw together in a matter of minutes, the scent of garlic and all those other delicious flavours mingling together making us hungry. Max pulled out two glasses from the cupboard and poured the cool, crisp Chablis. Our gazes met as he handed over my wine and I noticed how tired he looked, and grubby too, the result of his hard day's physical labour evident on his dust covered clothes, his face marked with black streaks. I ran my hand over his hair, wiping away some of the debris.

'Should I go and shower?' he asked, clocking my expression.

'No. You're fine as you are.' More than fine, in fact. Downright ruddy gorgeous even if he looked as scruffy as hell and had the subtle aroma of burnt wood about him.

We sat at the small wrought iron circular table and tucked into our bowl of pasta with the green salad I'd prepared and some crunchy white bread. Why was it that a meal thrown together in a matter of minutes could somehow taste better than something you'd spent the whole day slaving over? One of life's mysteries.

'So, how's it going?' I asked.

'Yep, good. Well, in truth it's a bit of a bomb site at the moment but it needs to get worse before we can make it better. We're on schedule though,' he added quickly, seeing my expression drop.

'I saw Eric today. He said he popped by to see you.'

'Yeah, I didn't really have a chance to chat actually. We were just taking delivery of some bricks and materials and then when I turned round to speak to him he'd gone. Is he all right?'

Ah, that made sense, then. Eric had probably thought he'd been in the way again and done his disappearing act.

'Yeah, although I think it's hit him hard having to move out of the pub. He doesn't know anything other than running that place so he's at a bit of a loose end. We went for a coffee at Betty's and I gave him a good talking-to.

Told him everything would be back to normal before we know it. It will be, won't it?'

Max nodded. 'Like you, I want to get this work done as quickly as possible, not only to get the pub open again, but because I've got a whole stack of other work lining up and I really need to get a particularly demanding customer off my back.'

'Really? Who's that, then?'

'You!' he said, laughing, as I suddenly cottoned on.

'Sorry, Max. I know you're doing everything you can. I suppose I'm just impatient, not just for me, but for everyone who's waiting for The Dog and Duck to reopen. I'm sorry, I promise not to ask again.'

'Huh, don't make promises you can't keep.'

'You know, I can always help out if you want me to.' I flexed my muscles. 'I could do some barrowing, mix up the mortar, anything you wanted me to do really.'

Cue more eye-rolling from Max.

'And how exactly are you going to manage that with a baby to look after, a pack of dogs to keep under control and generally managing this house, making sure there are no major fall-outs in my absence?'

'Hmm, well, you know, the two of them were getting along fabulously tonight, so I'm keeping my fingers crossed that we've turned a corner there. Really though, your mum would be more than willing to look after Noel for a few hours if you needed me down at the pub.'

Max shook his head, a smile spreading across his lips.

'I think we'll get by without you, but thanks anyway.' It was probably his idea of hell, me being on site, asking endless questions, querying every decision that was made. No, best leave Max to what he did best, building and refurbishing buildings. My skills were best saved for actually running the pub, when it was eventually open for business again...

'Besides,' Max went on, 'you've got enough to do with organising our wedding. How's it going? Anything I need to worry about?'

'No, it's all under control. Josie and I decided on the dresses for the bridesmaids today and I thought it would be a sweet idea to have Ruby and Stella as flower girls too so I'll need to find some dresses for them. Betty's made the cake already, she just needs to ice it. The menu is agreed so I'll just need to give final numbers to Yardleys a bit closer to the time. Caroline is working on my dress as we speak, although of course that's all top secret for the moment and...'

Max took a sip of his wine, leaned back in his chair, his head tipping backwards, his eyes fluttering closed.

'Hey, are you actually listening to me?' I said, nudging him in the side with my elbow.

'Yep, just resting my eyes, but taking in every single word,' he said, chuckling, although I wasn't entirely convinced about that.

I knew Max wasn't really bothered about the finer details of the day and was happy to leave the arrangements to me, although it would have been nice if he occasionally showed a bit more enthusiasm for our wedding day.

'All you'll need to do,' I told him, 'apart from getting the barn done, of course...'

He flashed me a reprimand in his glare, and I mentally chastised myself for mentioning it yet again, when I'd only just promised I wouldn't.

'...is turn up on the day in a new suit.'

'What? I've got a wardrobe full of perfectly good suits up there. What about the suit I wore to Polly's wedding? That'll do, won't it?'

Admittedly he had looked darned sexy in the soft grey Italian tailoring and when I'd first caught sight of him that day, standing at the front of the church with Noel in his arms, my heart had skipped a beat. It was at that moment when all my doubts had flitted away like a summer butterfly and I'd realised with a burning certainty that I wanted to marry Max more than anything else in the world.

'You know damn well it won't. You only get married once. It warrants a new suit.'

He wiggled an eyebrow at me.

'Always good to keep your options open though.'

'Oi!' I picked up the nearest cushion and whacked it around his head.

He was winding me up, his voice playful and mellow. He pulled me closer to his side, his breathing relaxed and steady. He was exhausted from the physically punishing long days he was putting in at the moment, which was hardly surprising considering everything he had on. Roll on Christmas, when we could all just relax and spend some quality time together chilling out. I closed my eyes briefly too.

'Guess who I heard from today?'

Max grunted.

'Fliss. She texted me to say her aunt and uncle are back so she's staying up there for another week before heading back to Birmingham for a while. Not sure she's looking forward to it, though. Must be hard for her.'

'Yep.'

'Anyway, back to the wedding. I've hand delivered all the invitations locally but I've still got to send off the ones that need to go in the post. I'll do that this week. What else is there...?'

'Max?' I nudged him out of his half-slumber again. 'Am I boring you, by any chance?'

'No.' He stretched out his body and pulled me back into his embrace. 'I still think we should have just gone off and done the deed in secret though.' He yawned lazily. 'We could have been Mr and Mrs Golding by now. Saved all this hassle.'

'It's not hassle,' I said grumpily, pulling away from him. 'We talked about this, Max. I thought it was what you wanted, too.' In my excitement to finally tie the knot had I got carried away with all the arrangements? Had I turned into Bridezilla, thinking only of myself and ignoring Max's desires and wishes? He was clearly stressed at the moment but I'd hate to think he wasn't really looking forward to our wedding day.

'Hey, of course it's what I want. I'm only teasing you. I just want to marry you, Ellie, that's all. I'm a simple guy.' His lips found the fold of my neck and he deposited a kiss there, making me squirm, distracting me from what I was about to say, but maybe now wasn't the time for this conversation.

'Why don't you get to bed?' I suggested, realising Max was in no mood for talking weddings or much else come to that.

'Is that an offer?' he said, his voice low and rumbling against my ear.

'Huh? I don't think you're in any fit state for anything other than your bed. Sleeping in it, that is! Go on up,' I said, disentangling myself from his embrace and taking a surreptitious sniff of his hair. 'I'll tidy up here, then I'll be up in a while.'

'Leave it,' he said, grabbing hold of my wrist as I attempted to stand up.

He pulled me onto his lap, his hands clasping my face, that smoky oaky aroma of his playing with my senses. 'I'll do all this in the morning.' He kissed me gently on the lips, teasing me with his mouth now and I buried my head in his shoulder, relishing the familiar warmth there. Funny how you could miss the closeness of someone even when you were living with them. We'd been so busy, the pair of us, preoccupied with our own hectic schedules, with Noel, Max's mum and the escaping Flora, that recently all we'd managed was a quick kiss on the cheek as our paths crossed briefly in the morning or late at night. Snatching some together time alone this evening had been wonderful even if Max had almost nodded off in the middle of our conversation. Now though, he seemed to have found a second lease of life and was tracing a finger along my collarbone, his eyes devouring me greedily, a look I knew only too well, a look that elicited a response deep down inside me.

'Come on,' I said, chivvying him along. 'Get to bed. You're exhausted, I can tell. And you've got another early start in the morning.'

'Ellie!' The sound of my name from his lips was delightfully seductive. 'Is this how it's going to be when we're married? You being all sensible and straight-laced and more interested in clearing the dishes than spending quality time with your husband?'

'Ahem. We were having some quality time earlier but it seemed only to send you to sleep.'

'A power nap, that's what that was,' he said with that sexy half-smile of his. 'And now I'm feeling, you know, all powerful and raring to go.'

'Just go to bed,' I said, laughing and attempting to get out of the chair again, but Max's touch on my arm was filled with intent. I looked down at it. 'Really, I promise you I won't be long.'

'I think it's important that we make the effort to keep our relationship fresh and alive and spontaneous.' Max was hard to resist when he was in one of these mischievous moods. 'You know, with all the trappings of babies, marriage and domesticity it's easy to take each other for granted, to lose sight of one another's needs and desires.'

'Are you saying I've been neglecting your needs?'

'Well, I don't like to cast aspersions, but we should...' He traced a finger along my arm, making my skin tingle. 'Well, we just need to remember to make time for each other and keep it fun.'

'Fun?' I grinned, and slipped out of his embrace and started collecting the dirty dishes. 'I certainly get my fair share of that living here at the manor.'

'Yeah, but you wouldn't have it any other way, would you?'

'No, of course I wouldn't. As long as it doesn't involve chasing missing dogs across the county, then I don't mind in the slightest.'

'Good. Well, stop doing that right this minute,' he said, whisking away the tea towel from my hand and flinging it across the kitchen in gay abandon.

'Max, I need—'

'You need to do nothing. It will still be here for us in the morning and I'll make sure I clear it up before you're even awake. How does that sound?' I was in no mood to argue with him, not when he was being so persuasive. 'Come here,' he said, slipping an arm around my waist. 'Do you remember that first time you came to the manor and I showed you around upstairs?'

'I do! I was totally in awe. I can remember thinking who is this strange man who lives alone in this mansion in the middle of the countryside? You were so intriguing to me and unlike anyone I'd ever met before. I could never have imagined then that we'd actually end up together and I would one day live at the manor. Back then it was this huge and stunning imposing show house and now, well, it's just my home. It's crazy!'

'Well, that's all down to you. You've made Braithwaite Manor the family home it is today.'

He took me by the hand and led me out into the hallway, switching off the lights in the kitchen as we left. I gazed up the sweeping staircase, marvelling at the huge chandelier above, the sight of it taking me back to that first night here with Max. Then my mouth had literally dropped open at the huge glass construction and the bold abstract paintings on the walls. Half of me had wanted to flee, realising that Max and I lived totally different lives. *What was I even doing here?* had been my overriding feeling. Now, my nostalgic reminiscing was interrupted by Max.

'Do you remember going up these stairs for the first time?' Max looked at me, a devilish glint in his eye, and I knew exactly what he was thinking.

'Don't you dare!'

But it was too late. Before I had a chance to protest further, Max had lifted me clean off my feet, holding me in his arms, my legs flapping futilely, my head thrown back laughing.

'Put me down!' I protested, half-heartedly. Just as I'd done on that first occasion. Then, I'd made some glib comment about Max's sweeping staircase being like something from *Gone with the Wind* and he'd thrown himself into the role of Rhett Butler with masterly assurance. It had been totally surprising, hilarious and maybe a little romantic too, when he'd literally swept me off my feet. I hadn't been able to stop laughing then, but now, well, I only felt self-conscious. I must have put on at least half a stone since those days and I hadn't been feather light then.

'For goodness' sake, Max, you'll put your back out.'

'Nonsense. Where's your sense of adventure, Ellie?' He climbed the steps relatively easily but with a look of grim determination set across his features. Even so I was worried that he would do himself an injury or, worse still, both of us an injury, especially if he dropped me on the steps. The last thing I needed was any broken bones.

At the top of the stairs, Max paused, grabbing hold of the polished oak newel post, breathing heavily for comic effect, I presumed.

'Shhh!' I said, giggling. 'You'll wake the others.'

He staggered along the galleried landing still carrying me, veering one way and then the other, every now and then pretending to lose his grip on me, letting me slip in his arms. I was convinced it was going to end in an unsightly heap and messy tears when the guest room door opened and Rose appeared in front of us.

'Oh-h-h...' she said, unable to stop the smile from spreading across her face. 'It's you. I wondered what the noise was. I thought Flora might have got up here.'

'No, Mother,' said Max, catching his breath. 'Everything's fine. I'm just making sure my wife-to-be gets to bed on time, that's all.'

'Right. Well, um, do be careful. You don't want to do yourself an injury.' She grimaced, clearly imagining that scenario. 'Or else it might spoil your wedding night.'

'Oh, right, thanks for that, Rose.' I giggled.

'I wasn't suggesting you were...' Rose gave a dismissive wave, opting not to say anything further.

'No, don't worry, it's fine. I can manage,' said Max, pretending his legs were buckling beneath him. 'Goodnight, Mother!'

Rose shook her head, laughing, and returned to her bedroom while Max made a mad dash along the rest of the corridor and through our bedroom door. His pretence at struggling to carry me wasn't, I suspected now, so much of a pretence. He careened towards the bed and literally threw me down on the covers before collapsing in a heap beside me.

'Oh, gawd, Ells. I think I might need resuscitating now.'

He flung his arms out wide and closed his eyes, his lips just gently puckering in the air.

'You're mad, do you know that?'

I leant across to give him a reviving kiss and he pulled me on top of him so that my body straddled his. His arms reached up to grab my face and his lips found mine, kissing me gently, all too temptingly, and then more fiercely, rolling me over onto my back so that he was now on top of me.

'You need to get those filthy, dirty clothes off my lovely clean bed linen,' I told him, beginning to undo the buttons on his shirt.

'There you go being sensible again.' This was said in a throaty whisper that sent shivers along my body. 'There's nothing wrong with a bit of filth and dirt between a husband and wife.'

I giggled as he helped me out by undoing the rest of the buttons on his shirt while I concentrated on the fly of his jeans and attempted to wriggle them down over his hips and thighs until he became impatient with my progress and instead did the job himself, depositing his dirty work clothes in a heap by the side of the bed. His body was hard and firm and my hands instinctively reached out for his torso. I climbed out of my clothes too, leaving just my knickers on, the cool air bringing goosebumps to my body. I slipped beneath the covers, relishing the sensation of the clean crisp sheets upon my skin. Max wriggled in beside me, his hands immediately finding the dip of my waist, his thumb sweeping over my hip bone, causing a ripple of anticipation to travel along my body. My legs wrapped around his, my hands feeling the definition of his biceps, the heat inside my body rising rapidly. My eyes closed, my entire being revelling in the sensation of being wrapped in Max's embrace.

He paused to sweep the hair away from my face, looking into my eyes intently.

'Hey, you know I love you so much, Ellie. I'm sorry if I can't show the same level of enthusiasm for the details of the wedding day as you. It's not that I don't care. I do. But what I'm truly passionate about is making you my wife. That's all that matters to me. All that other stuff goes right over my head. But I do want you to be happy and have the wedding day you want and deserve. If you want twenty prancing ponies, a highland band and diamond encrusted glasses, then go for it, Ellie. Honestly, I mean it.'

My mind drifted towards our plans, wondering where the prancing ponies might fit in, although it was hard to focus on anything when Max's fingers were working their magic along the outline of my body.

'Let me get back to you on that,' I said, giggling. 'No, Max, it's fine. I'm happy to concentrate on the detail while you take care of the bigger picture. All that's important is that we're finally getting married and I simply cannot wait.'

'Me neither,' said Max, his voice distant now as he grew distracted by the job in hand.

One hand swept over my breasts, his fingers teasing my nipples, squeezing them gently until I could bear the exquisite sensations no longer. My hand reached out for him, the hardness of his desire clearly evident; I pulled him towards me, wanting more of him. Max left a trail of kisses along my collarbone, each super-sweet kiss making me want more, my mouth growing hungry for his taste. Inevitably, our bodies joined together, moving and swaying in time, forward and backwards, our desire inflaming each other's, working together in harmony. Our bodies were the perfect fit, melding together as one, seeking out the rhythm of the dance, until its inherent passion took over, transporting us both to ever soaring heights, so excruciatingly and tantalisingly out of reach, before finally we reached the summit, coming together in an overwhelming finale.

Smiling, content and emotional, I snuggled up to Max, bathing in the glow of his love and attention.

'Mmm, that was really rather lovely.' I sighed aloud to myself, to Max, to the four walls of my most amazing bedroom, to anyone in the universe who might be listening. All the stresses and pressures of our busy lives had flittered away in those brief intense moments. I turned to gaze up at my handsome husband-to-be, who'd been annoyingly right as ever, and was predictably asleep within a matter of moments. No doubt dreaming about the bigger picture. I lay there in the darkness thinking I should really go to sleep but instead pondered over the entertainment for our wedding reception. Maybe a highland band might do after all.

## 20

My hope and optimism that Katy and Rose had overcome their issues and would be able to live harmoniously together at the manor was short lived. Within a matter of days they were sniping at each other again, over, well, I wasn't sure what exactly. Apparently, Rose had deigned to look at Katy in a certain way over the breakfast table and that was it! It was enough to put Katy back in a full strop and questioning again how much longer her mum intended on staying. As far as possible, I kept out of their disagreements over the next couple of weeks and when the atmosphere inside the house grew too tetchy, then I had the perfect excuse to head outside with the buggy and the dogs.

Today, I was determined to post the last of the invitations, I'd already rung around to those people and asked them to save the date. I wrapped Noel up in his snowsuit, as there was definitely a sharp winter's chill in the air these days, and we headed out, down the lanes and towards the village with the cards held tight in my hand, relieved that I could finally scrub 'send invitations' off my to-do list. Now, with most of the arrangements in place for the wedding, I could start thinking about those other cards I would need to write. The Christmas ones. Thankfully I'd already done a lot of my shopping online and the library was groaning with parcels and packages so when we got home later, I might make a start on wrapping some presents and writing some cards.

It was best not to panic. To-do lists were the way to go. I had one for the wedding. One for Christmas. One for the pub. And one creatively titled, 'general stuff'. If I actually stopped to think about the things I had to do then I might have a major meltdown but putting everything down on my ever growing collection of lists made everything seem that much more manageable. In truth, this was my favourite time of the year even if it was a manic, stress inducing and calorie loading crazy time, and that was without a wedding and warring in-laws thrown into the mix.

At the bottom of the high street I deposited the cards in the post box and walked towards the pub. It had been a fair few days since I'd asked Max directly about the progress on the barn. It had taken a huge amount of willpower and control not to, but I reasoned it was better to leave him to what he was good at, without me badgering him constantly, and for me to get on with everything I had to do. I wasn't sure if he would even be at the pub today or if he was off working on another project. Sometimes he was difficult to keep track of. I pushed the buggy up the cobbled side entrance to The Dog and Duck, reassured to hear what sounded like men at work coming from inside the pub. My gaze travelled up to the window above, which had been my bedroom when I'd been living here, and was where Silke would have first spotted the fire. Every morning when I used to draw my curtains, I would take a moment to look out over the beer garden, seeing the hanging baskets and the climbing roses and the clematis against the old brick walls. I'd always considered it a little oasis of calm and would often take my morning cuppa out there on warmer days, a moment of peace and tranquillity before the customers rolled in and the daily madness began.

Then my gaze travelled across to where the barn had once stood and I felt that familiar twinge of sadness in my chest. The site had been cleared of debris now and a whole stack of building materials stood in its place ready for construction. I'd hoped that they would have started on it by now but I had to trust that Max knew what he was doing. If he wasn't worrying about getting the work completed in time for Christmas, then why should I?

'Hello! It's only me!' I called out to anyone who might hear.

As if he'd been waiting for my arrival, Max immediately popped his head out from the back door of the pub.

'Ah, hello!' He raked his hand through his hair, looking surprised to see me, before composing himself, that familiar lopsided grin lighting up his face. 'My two favourite people in the entire world. Fancy that. I was just coming to see you.'

'You were?'

'Yes. Wait there a minute. I'll be right back.'

He dived back into the pub and I could hear the sounds of a hurried clean-up operation going on with the clanging of tools being thrown into metal boxes. I imagined him mouthing instructions to his team of guys, gesturing to me standing outside, and them all running round like headless chickens. I heard muffled voices too but I couldn't quite work out what they were saying. And there was definitely a female voice in the mix. Had Polly popped in from next door to see what was going on?

'Right.' Max was back, brushing himself down, red dust falling to the floor around him. 'Come on in.' He bowed with a flourish and invited me to step across the threshold. 'I was going to put a ribbon across and get some flowers in but you've beaten me to it. Not that it matters. The kitchen of The Dog and Duck is now complete, ma'am.'

'Really!' I squealed, a real girly squeal from deep down inside, as I clapped my hands together. Although I'd been impossibly impatient for the work to be complete, it hadn't even occurred to me that it might be this soon. I'd expected Max to be tiling or putting the electrics in or installing the new double oven, but no, it was all done, apparently. He took Noel from me and led me inside the pub, instructing me to keep my eyes closed until he told me I could open them. I climbed up the step, the smell of fresh paint greeting me, aware that there were a couple of other people in the room, some of Max's team, I suspected. It was hard to contain the excitement bubbling inside me and I kept my eyes closed even when Max told me I could open them.

'Come on, Ellie!'

My eyes peeled open slowly and that was when there came another squeal, when I saw for the first time the results of Max and his team's hard labour over the last few weeks.

'Oh, my goodness, it's stunning.' My hand flew to my mouth in disbelief. It was a painted oak kitchen in a soft mint colour, not that that bit was surprising in the least as I'd picked out the units and colours myself, but what really took my breath away was the overall effect, which was so perfect it looked like something out of a lifestyle magazine. 'It looks so much bigger now with so much extra storage space.' I opened up cupboards one after the other, peering inside, marvelling at their newness. The old gas cooker had been replaced by a swanky double electric oven and a gleaming new hob. There was much more worktop space too, with Max utilising every spare corner of the room.

'Max, you've done such an amazing job,' I said, throwing my arms around his neck and kissing him on the lips. 'I could kiss you all,' I said, remembering the other guys who were standing there, looking at their feet, shuffling awkwardly. 'But I won't, you'll be pleased to hear. You've all done a great job though.'

I'd made a decision a long time ago, following on from Eric's lead, that we wouldn't become a food establishment because that would have meant changing the whole essence of the pub. But there were occasions on our special events evenings when we liked to serve up food, like our occasional curry nights, or hotdogs on bonfire night, or a soup and pudding supper bash. It had always been a logistical nightmare with just a single cooker but we'd managed somehow. Now with the double oven, it would make life so much easier.

'Ooh, does this mean that Eric, and Dan and Silke, can move back in? When can we open up again?'

'Well, that's entirely up to you. We're moving straight on to working on the barn, so it'll mean a fair bit of noise and disruption, but if you're okay with that, then I can't see why not.'

'Let me have a word with Eric and Dan, see what they say. If they're happy to move back in, then we should be good to go. I don't think the work will affect our customers. It's not as though they'll be wanting to use the beer garden at this time of year. Just think about it, we could be open as soon as Friday night.'

'If that's what you want, Ellie, then that's fine with me.'

'Yes!' Excitement fizzed inside me. With the pub open again, it meant that the rebuilding of the barn couldn't be far behind. I'd cancelled all the bookings for the rest of the year and was only accepting new ones from the New Year onwards. The only event in the diary now was our wedding and Max was confident the new barn would be completed in plenty of time for that.

'Anyway,' said Max, taking hold of my hand, 'are you ready for the big surprise?'

'What? I thought this was the surprise.' My gaze flittered around the newly renovated kitchen as I wondered if I'd missed something but there was nothing jumping out at me. 'What is it, then?'

'There's someone here to see you.' The other guys collected their tool-boxes and wandered outside while Max turned to look into the main pub area. I'd thought I'd heard a woman's voice earlier, but who the hell was it, hiding in the dark shadows? The person wandered out, a big friendly smile on her face, and it took me a moment. That weird sensation when you saw someone outside their normal environment and your poor little brain couldn't make sense of it at all.

'Fliss?'

She threw back her head and laughed. 'Sorry, I hope it's not too much of a shock. I literally just turned up here, moments before you arrived.'

'Oh, my goodness! It's really you! But what are you doing here?' I threw my arms around her for a hug before taking a step backwards to check that my eyes weren't deceiving me.

'Well, you did say I was welcome any time.' She gave a wry smile. 'I really hope you meant it. I went back to Birmingham for a few days to see Mum and Dad but it felt so strange being home again. So claustrophobic, I just had this desire to get away again so I told Mum I was going off to visit a friend. I jumped in the car with no real idea where I was going and somehow I've ended up here. I really hope you don't mind?'

'No, not at all. You are very welcome.'

'I had it in mind I might be able to stay at the pub but I didn't realise it would still be closed.'

'Don't worry about that. You must come and stay with us at the manor. We have so much catching up to do. How long are you intending to stay? Although you know you can stay as long as you like.'

'Just a night or two. I'm only here on a whim and I really need to get back again for the weekend as I've some things I need to sort out.'

'Perfect. I'm going to try and get the pub open for Friday night so you'll be able to see this place when it's open. We can have a bit of a party.'

I grabbed hold of her hand and squeezed it tight. I could just imagine how Fliss felt, going home after everything that had happened and having to face everyone. I understood completely why she'd felt compelled to get away again and felt pleased that she'd turned up on our doorstep. Sometimes you just clicked with people as soon as you met them and that was how it had been for me, Fliss and Max.

In a way, I'd experienced something similar to Fliss when I'd lost my job in London and given up my flat, and had to return to the village. At the time I was pretty down about my situation and had wondered what on earth I was going to do. It had seemed like a failure to come home with my tail between my legs but in hindsight it was the best thing that could have ever happened to me. Hopefully it might turn out the same for Fliss.

Now, my mind was whirring with everything that had happened this afternoon. If we could get the pub open for the end of the week, then we could have a bit of a celebration in the evening, which Fliss would be able to come along to as well. I'd love to be able to show her the pub when it was full to the rafters with satisfied customers. I exhaled contentedly. Finally, it seemed as though things might be looking up.

## 21

The following morning we all gathered around the kitchen table for breakfast and Fliss was able to see the manor for the first time in daylight. She walked around with her neck craned, looking up at the high ceilings and then running across to the floor to ceiling windows to look out over the extensive grounds.

'Oh, my goodness,' she squealed. 'Why didn't you tell me you lived in a stately home?'

I laughed.

'It's funny, I thought exactly the same thing when I saw this place for the first time, but I don't think of it like that any more. Now, it's just my home. But I remember being overawed by the sheer scale of it.'

'It's beautiful,' said Fliss, 'and not at all like a stately home actually. It's warm and welcoming. Just like you and Max. I should have known.'

The good thing about having an unexpected guest was that it brought a ceasefire between the warring factions in the house. Rose and Katy were on their best behaviour this morning and the addition of a new face made for a much more relaxed atmosphere around the table. Arthur always enjoyed having company and would chat away happily to anyone who would listen. Fliss was currently jiggling Noel up and down on her knee, seemingly besotted by our little boy, who was revelling in all the attention.

'As you're all here, I've got some good news for you. Max and his brilliant team have finished the work on the kitchen at the pub, which means we're fit to open again. I spoke to Eric and Dan last night and they're both keen to move back in, which they're doing today, so I'm thinking we'll go for reopening tomorrow night. You'll be able to see The Dog and Duck in action, Fliss.'

'I can't wait,' she said, grinning.

'Brilliant,' said Katy. 'I'll let Ryan and his mates know and get them to spread the word. It hasn't been the same around here with the pub out of action.'

'Too true,' said Arthur, who'd been a regular at the pub for years, visiting at least three or four times a week in his younger days when he would meet up with his best pal, the late Noel Golding Snr, Max's granddad.

With The Dog and Duck being closed these last few weeks it had given us all a taster of what life would be like without a pub in the village and it was every bit as miserable as I'd imagined. So much more than a drinking establishment, The Dog and Duck provided a meeting place for all the villagers, even those who would pop in just for an orange juice or a cappuccino. Although I hadn't done a shift behind the bar for a while now, I still loved my almost daily visits to the pub where I could have a natter with the staff and whichever customers were in that day. It had made me realise just what an important part of my routine it was.

'I'll put on some food as it's a special occasion, nothing too elaborate, just a buffet. And we'll have some music as well in the snug bar. It'll be fun. I really can't wait.'

'Well, I can help out with the food, or anything else you want me to do,' offered Fliss.

'Who's going to look after Noel, then?' asked Katy. 'You could do that, couldn't you, Mum?'

'If you'd like me to,' said Rose, looking at me, but sounding a touch half-hearted.

'No way, you deserve a fun night out as much as anyone.' She'd done more than her fair share of babysitting over the last couple of weeks and I suspected she was getting cabin fever being stuck in the house all the time. Mum and Dad would want to come to the pub too, and so would their neighbours, Caroline and Paul. 'Don't worry, we'll take Noel along with us. We've done it before. There's a travel cot in the third bedroom so hopefully he'll settle down in there. Touch wood, he's sleeping pretty well at the moment and there'll be enough of us around to check on him regularly.'

'You know, you could always invite your dad along,' Rose said to Katy.

'What?' she snapped, her hackles immediately rising.

'It's only a suggestion.' Rose dropped her gaze and reached for a slice of toast. I suspected this was to avoid the scrutiny of Katy's questioning stare.

'He lives miles away.'

'Yes, I know but I thought it would be nice to... for you to see him again, I meant.'

'That's a good idea. Invite him. He's been along to a couple of our dos before,' I said. 'And he's not that far away. I think it takes him about half an hour in the car. He knows lots of the locals now. He always seems to enjoy himself at the pub when he comes over.'

'Okay,' said Katy nonchalantly. 'I'll invite him. I'll get him to bring Jill too. That's his partner,' she said for Fliss's benefit. 'She's really lovely. I haven't known her long but we get on really well together.'

Fliss nodded and smiled, and gave a nervous glance across at me, no doubt picking up on the frisson of tension radiating between Katy and her mum. Rose managed not to rise to Katy's bait most of the time, but I'd come to notice that if she found herself getting riled by Katy's comments then she would normally remove herself from the situation, which was what she did now.

'Right, well, I shall certainly look forward to tomorrow night. In fact, I think I'll go into town and see if I can find myself something new to wear. I think that this special occasion warrants it, don't you? Not that I really need an excuse to buy new clothes.'

Just as Rose got up to leave the kitchen, the telephone rang and I dashed over to answer it. When I realised who it was, I beckoned to Rose to stay in the room.

'Oh, hello, Alan,' I said pointedly so that Rose would hear.

'Hello, Ellie. Could I speak to Rose, please? I've tried phoning her on her mobile and I've left several text messages and emails but she's not answering my calls. I'd really like to speak to her if at all possible.'

There was a plaintive note to his voice that made me feel sorry for him and I hesitated just long enough to give the game away.

I glanced across at Rose, who was shaking her head fiercely, making slicing motions against her neck and mouthing, 'Tell him I'm not here,' but it was too late.

'She's there, isn't she?' said Alan. 'Just a very quick word, if you don't mind.'

'Hang on,' I said lightly. 'I'll just put you on to her.'

If looks could kill. Rose glared at me, snatching the phone from my hand and marching off, closing the door behind her on the way out of the kitchen.

Katy crossed her fingers and held them up in the air.

'Hopefully they'll make it up and Mum will be on the first plane back to Spain. I can live in hope.'

'Somehow, from what your mum's told me, I can't see that happening, but you never know. Stranger things have happened.'

Katy rolled her eyes.

'I just hope Mum won't make things awkward between me and Dad – that's if he's able to come tomorrow.'

'Why would she?' I said as I cleared the dirty crockery from the table and began to load the dishwasher. Fliss took the opportunity to help Arthur out of his chair and accompanied him, with the aid of his walker, into the living room, leaving me alone with Katy.

'I don't know. I would just rather she wasn't there.'

'We can't not invite her, Katy. Besides, I think you're worrying unnecessarily. It's been a long time since the two of them were involved and, honestly, if you'd seen them chatting away together the other day, you'd realise that any ill-feeling between them is now very much in the past. Which is the way it should be. I know how hurt you've been over all of this, but it would be so much better for you and everyone else concerned, if you could find a way to move on and leave all that hurt in the past.'

'That's easy for you to say! You're not the one who was lied to for years.'

'I know that, Katy, and I'm not trying to make light of what happened.

Really, I'm not. But I hate to see you so unhappy and letting all this affect your life still. You're eighteen and you have everything going for you. You're lucky. You have your mum and your dad in your life now and you should be making the most of that while you can.'

'Don't guilt trip me.' She sighed exaggeratedly. 'It's just the constant reminders with her living under the same roof as me now. Every time she says something I'm reminded of what happened and it makes me really angry.'

'Come here.' I pulled her into my body and wrapped my arms around her. 'For your own peace of mind and happiness, you need to let it go. She's your mum and, believe me, she's not going anywhere so you're going to have to learn how to deal with the whole situation in a better way, so that you're not constantly getting yourself into such a state.'

'Oh, God! Do you have any more depressing news?' She gave me a wry smile. 'Look, I'll try harder, but I can't make any promises.' She glanced at her watch. 'I have to go now or else I'll miss the bus.' She picked up her rucksack from the floor and was just packing her keys and phone away when Rose came downstairs and back into the kitchen.

'Well, hopefully now he'll have got the message,' she said, matter of factly. 'I've told him there's no going back for us. I couldn't have made it any clearer and I've told him my solicitors will be in touch.' She pulled on her jacket and slung her handbag over her shoulder.

'Really, Rose, are you absolutely sure? You don't think you're being a bit rash? It hasn't been that long since you separated. Who knows, you might have second thoughts given some time. There's no need to rush into any decisions.'

'It's been long enough for me to realise that my marriage is over. It's sad but it's the right thing for me. I appreciate your concern, Ellie, but really my mind's made up.' She turned to Katy. 'Ah, that's good timing. I'm going into town myself. We can go for the bus together, if you like? How about that?'

Katy opened her mouth as if to protest but then thought twice about it on seeing my expression. Well, it was a truce, but I suspected it might be a short lived one!

Hearing the back door close, Fliss came wandering back into the kitchen.

'Arthur's settled with his newspaper and has the dogs to keep him company, so I think he's happy enough.'

'Good, come and sit down. I'll make us a coffee and you can tell me what's been happening.'

We'd not really had a chance to talk in depth last night. By the time we'd got home and had a cup of tea, I'd had to make a couple of phone calls in preparation for Friday's grand reopening, then bathe and put Noel down to sleep, before preparing supper. Fliss had been exhausted from her long drive and had retired to bed soon after our meal, so this was our first real opportunity for a proper catch-up.

'When did you leave the cafe?'

'Last weekend. My aunt and uncle got home from Australia and so I spent a week with them hearing all the news about Clover and Rob and their little girl, Tilly. They showed me so many photos, it's safe to say they're totally smitten with their new grandchild. Anyway, they've closed the cafe down now for the winter months. They do it every year because trade drops right off, so they take this time to do any repairs that need doing and give the place a general spruce up.'

'Oh, could you not have stayed?'

'Yes, they wanted me to, and I probably will go back soon to help them out, but I just thought for them, and for me too, it was probably best to put a bit of distance between us. They've got a lot of stuff to sort out and I wanted to go home to see Mum and Dad.'

'How was that?'

'Strange! Well, no, it was lovely to see them, obviously, but being back in Birmingham felt odd somehow. I'd only been gone a couple of months but it was as if I didn't have a place there any more. I didn't run into Brad, thankfully, but he was there everywhere around me. In the pubs and restaurants we used to visit, in Cannon Hill Park where we'd spent many long summer days just sunbathing on the grass and eating ice creams. Everywhere I went was a reminder of our relationship. I'm not sure I belong there any more. I don't have a job or a place of my own there so I'm not sure what I would do if I went back home permanently.'

Fliss grimaced and ran a hand through her messy blonde hair.

'The thought of having to find another grotty office job and a little flat somewhere in my home town fills me with dread. Those weeks at The Driftwood Cafe have spoilt me. As soon as I left, I had this really strong yearning to return.'

'I can understand that.'

'The thing is, I don't know if that's just a reaction to what happened with Brad, an escape if you like, and I'm running away from everything I know because it's easier than facing all the reminders of my previous life with Brad. That was another reason why I wanted to get away from both places, my hometown and The Driftwood Cafe. To give myself some distance and some perspective.'

'Sometimes fate has a way of pushing you in a completely new direction when you most need it,' I told her.

Fliss grew thoughtful for a moment.

'Yeah. It's funny, but I felt really at home there. The wild and rugged landscape was just so inspiring. I loved my daily walks along the beach – it gave me a chance to think and get my head straight. I miss that now. The cafe was my bolthole when I really needed it. Mind you, it helped that it was low season so I wasn't completely rushed off my feet.'

'Yes, but you were absolutely in your element. You soon picked it up and were running the place as though you'd been there for years. You were always so welcoming to your customers, especially us. I guess with your aunt and uncle back now and it being the winter season there wouldn't be any work for you?'

'Not at the moment, no, but they did make me a proposition.'

'Really? What sort of proposition exactly?'

'Well, they've come home from Australia and decided they don't want to take on another full season at the cafe next year. I think they've got different priorities now. They've been running the place for over twenty years and they want to slow down a little, get out and enjoy themselves a bit more. Especially now they've got a new little granddaughter to dote on. They're planning more trips out to Oz and there are other countries they want to visit too, while they're still fit and healthy and able to do so. For years they never had a proper holiday. It was impossible for them to get away in the height of the season. When Clover was small that didn't matter as they had that beautiful wide beach on their doorstep. But now, well, I think they have other things they want to do. Can't say I blame them.'

'Right. So where does that leave you?'

'Well, they suggested that if I wanted to I could run the cafe next year. They own the freehold of the property so I could move in and basically take over from them. We could do it on a trial basis just for that season to see how it goes.'

'Really? Well, isn't that the most brilliant opportunity?'

'Do you think so?' Fliss's expression was serious as she fiddled with a silver Celtic ring on her right hand.

'I do. I thought you would jump at the chance.'

'Hmm, well, I said I'd think about it. I must admit it sounds tempting but it's one thing running the place for a couple of weeks in the quiet season and quite another to manage the cafe in the busy summer season. I'd have to employ staff and take care of all the ordering and stock control. I've not done anything like it before.'

'Yes, but you won't know if you can do it until you try. And there's nothing like being thrown in at the deep end for picking something up and running with it. Presumably wherever your aunt and uncle will be, they'll still be available by phone or email if you need any advice.'

'That's true, I suppose.'

'Honestly, Fliss, I felt exactly the same when I was offered the opportunity to take over The Dog and Duck. I'd worked there on and off for years, but I'd always had Eric, the previous landlord, to defer to. I was worried when I took over that the regular customers wouldn't accept me and there were a few, admittedly, who weren't overjoyed at the prospect of having a young female manager in charge, but I soon settled into the role. Hopefully I've proved to those people now that the pub is in safe hands. I've made plenty of changes and we run lots more events than in Eric's day but it's still the same welcoming pub as it's always been.'

'Yes, well, you certainly seem to have made a success of it.'

'If someone had told me a couple of years ago that I would have all this then I would never have believed them. It just goes to show that dreams can come true. And sometimes you have to take a chance. Why don't you give it a go and see if it works out? You've got nothing to lose.'

Fliss shuddered, running her hands up and down over her arms.

'I've got goosebumps,' she said by way of explanation as a smile spread over her face, one of hope and expectation.

I suddenly realised that there'd been nothing spontaneous about Fliss's impromptu visit to Little Leyton. She'd come because she'd wanted some advice about taking over The Driftwood Cafe, knowing the advice she would receive from us would be exactly what she wanted to hear.

## 22

The next afternoon at the manor was manic, to say the least. Fliss and I had been down at the pub for most of the day preparing sandwiches and wooden boards of antipasti for later. It was a totally different experience working in the renovated kitchen as there was so much more space and the old wobbly fridge had been replaced with a spanking new full height one, which made storing food that much easier. We polished glasses, double checked our stock of mixers, although I knew Dan would already have done that job, and put up some balloons and a banner in the snug bar in celebration of tonight's big event. Although it had only been a matter of weeks that the pub had been closed, it seemed much, much longer, and I was just full of relief and gratitude that we could finally reopen.

Now, back at home, after I'd fed Noel and struggled to get him out of his high chair, Max came in from his office just at the right time.

'I'm running late,' I told him. 'I need to bathe Noel and then get changed myself. The dogs need to go out and be fed too.' I could hear the slightly hysterical note to my voice, although I wasn't sure why I was in such a panic. Eric and Dan would be there already so it really didn't matter if I was a little late. I was just keen for everything to run as smoothly as possible tonight.

'Here, let me take Noel. I'll sort out everything here. We'll take the dogs out in the garden together – won't we, Noel? – and then I'll get him ready for bed. You go and get ready.'

'Ooh, Max, you see, this is why I love you so much.' He kissed me lightly on the forehead and I reached up my hands to rest them on his broad shoulders. His eyes, dark in colour and intense, were always mesmerising and I couldn't look into them without feeling the effects of his gaze deep down in my insides. 'Really, thank you for everything. For sorting the pub, the new kitchen makes all the difference and... well, just thank you for everything you do for me. I honestly don't know what I'd do without you.'

He pulled me towards him so that his lips met mine tentatively, teasingly, irresistibly and his tongue swept over my mouth, parting my lips, the taste of him full of promise.

'No, no, no,' I said, pulling back and laughing. 'What are you doing to me?'

Max raised his eyebrows, his mouth twisting in amusement.

'Go on, then. Go and make yourself beautiful. Even more beautiful, if that's possible.'

'Ha, I could be some time, then!'

I ran up the stairs, excitement and anticipation fizzing around my veins, relieved to be free of seeing to the dogs and getting Noel ready for bed. Ordinarily, it was one of my favourite parts of the day, the bed and bath routine. Noel was always at his most scrumptious straight out of the bath, smelling sweet and delicious, dressed in a pair of clean pyjamas. I'd put him down in his cot and sit beside him in the floral backed low chair and read a story in the soft light of his bedroom, while he hung on tight to his muslin, and sucked on his thumb. It wouldn't be long before his eyes, with their impossibly long lashes, would flutter closed.

Tonight, though, was a rare opportunity for me to put my glad rags on and go out to celebrate with all my friends and family at The Dog and Duck. As I walked along the galleried landing to our bedroom the doors to Rose and Katy's bedrooms were flung open at the same time, as they both appeared from their respective bedrooms.

'Ooh, hello. I'm just going to have a quick shower and get ready but don't feel you need to wait for me. You can go ahead if you want to.' I looked from Katy to Rose, and then back again at Katy, whose critical gaze was assessing her mum, sweeping up and down her body, her lips curling in disdain.

'You're not really going out in that, are you?'

'Katy!' I admonished her. 'You look lovely, Rose.'

'Thank you.' Although I could tell by the flush of colour to Rose's cheeks that Katy's nasty comment had stung.

What was Katy even going on about? Rose looked effortlessly glamorous. She was wearing black leather trousers with a silky peach ruffled blouse, which had a plunging neckline. The colour accentuated her golden tan, a legacy from the many years she'd lived in Spain. Her ash blonde hair, normally worn straight, had been curled so that it fell in soft waves onto her shoulders.

'Why are you so glammed up? It's only the pub. And don't you think you're a bit old to wear leather trousers?'

'Oh, for goodness' sake, Katy. Who says I should stop wearing certain things just because of my age? Besides, I'm hardly decrepit yet.' She stuck her chin in the air and wriggled her shoulders. 'I like them. And I think I look good in them so that's all that matters.'

'I think you look great in them too,' I agreed, furious with Katy for being so disrespectful to her mum.

'Well, if you don't mind going out looking like that, then that's absolutely fine.'

Talk about role reversal. I really didn't need this. Not tonight.

'Look, Katy, there's no need for you to be continually snarky towards your mum. It's horrible. And totally unnecessary.' Rose held up her hand and shook her head, as though my protestations were pointless but I couldn't stop myself. 'This is a big night for me and the pub. I've been looking forward to it for weeks and if you spoil it for me or your mum or Max, then so help me, Katy, I don't know what I'll do. Do you understand me?'

Katy shifted backwards and looked at me askance. Rose raised her eyebrows, a smile twitching at her lips.

'Right!' Katy huffed. 'It's probably best if I go, then. I'm meeting Ryan so we'll see you at the pub later. I suppose!'

'Okay, love,' said Rose, looking at her daughter forlornly. My heart ached for Rose. I wished I could wave a magic wand and make everything right between them but it sometimes seemed as though nothing would help.

'It's all right,' said Rose, once Katy had left, obviously seeing my stricken expression. 'I've grown used to it now. I'm not sure coming to live here was such a good idea, after all. I mean, I enjoy being with you, Max and Noel, of course, but if it's making Katy so unhappy then it's not worth it. Something has to change. On Monday, I'll go into town and see the letting agencies, see what's available.'

'I hate to think Katy is forcing you out. You don't have to leave, you know that. It makes me really cross that she's making life so difficult for you. I've tried talking to her but it doesn't seem to make any difference. I'll get Max to have another word, see if he can make her see sense.'

'Don't worry too much. This was never meant as a permanent arrangement, so perhaps it's time I found my own place. Might be for the best. You go and get ready, Ellie. I'll wait for you downstairs.'

Despite Rose telling me not to worry I couldn't help thinking about the situation as I dashed into the shower. Darn Katy for putting a dampener on the evening, and before it had even started too. Initially the tension between her and her mum had been a mild irritation, even sometimes amusing, but it had gone far beyond that now. Something would have to be done because it wasn't fair on anyone, and I certainly didn't want to spend my whole time walking on eggshells and trying to sort out their differences. I scrubbed my arms and legs fiercely with a body puff soaked in orange and bergamot lotion and scrubbed away all those thoughts too. Just for tonight. It would need dealing with, but now wasn't the time.

Thankfully, when I got back downstairs, Fliss, Arthur and Rose were waiting for me and Fliss handed me a most welcome glass of Prosecco. That first sip was delicious and revitalising, the bubbles teasing me on my lips and providing that delicious sense of anticipation for the night ahead. Rose didn't seem to be unduly fazed by her earlier run-in with Katy and was chatting away with Fliss and Arthur happily, so perhaps I was making too much out of what were standard parent-teenager tensions. *Who knew?* I would have all these delights to look forward to one day.

'Are we ready, then?' Ten minutes later, just as we were finishing our drinks, Max appeared from upstairs with a pyjama clad Noel in his arms, causing my heart to swell. My two handsome boys. Max in dark navy chinos, brogues and a white shirt looking too gorgeous for his own good and Noel in his dinosaur print two piece. He was laughing, his little legs kicking against his daddy, eliciting a collective sigh from us all in the kitchen. I took Noel from Max, hugging him tight to my body and inhaling his delicious scent, the sweet smell of all things baby boy hitting my nostrils.

'Here, let me take him,' said Rose. 'I'll put him in his buggy and walk up to the pub and with any luck he'll be fast asleep by the time we get there.'

'Thanks, Rose, we'll see you up there, then. The cot is all ready for him up in the bedroom.'

The good thing about having grandparents and aunties living in your house was that there was always an extra pair of hands to help out when you needed them. Even Arthur took his turn at bouncing Noel up and down on his knee or pulling funny faces at him while he sat in his rocker. If Noel did decide he wasn't going to sleep tonight and wanted to join in the celebrations, at least there would be plenty of people around to look after him.

Down at the pub we parked the Jeep and helped Arthur out. The place was already heaving with so many familiar faces and we got a noisy and good hearted welcome as soon as we stepped through the door and an impromptu cheer. Clearly everyone had come along tonight with one thing in mind. To have a good time. However much I'd missed the pub when it was closed these last few weeks, it seemed our customers had missed it just as much too.

'Ellie!'

It was Polly who came up beside me, slipped an arm around my waist and planted a kiss on my cheek. My hand went instinctively to the now defined bump of her tummy, still small enough not to notice, but definitely nicely rounded beneath my hand. Polly laughed, not minding in the least, just holding my hand to her tummy even tighter. It sent a frisson along my body, a flood of thoughts and emotions filling my mind. Happiness and excitement for Polly, tempered with a little sadness and regret for myself. I couldn't help thinking how my pregnancy would be developing now, imagining the size of my tummy, but it was no good dwelling on what might have been. Tonight was all about new beginnings.

I introduced Fliss to all my friends, Polly and George, Sasha and Johnny, and Josie and Ethan and she smiled and waved, looking bemused as she tried to remember everyone's names. 'This is amazing, Ellie,' she whispered in my ear, a little later. 'Such a great atmosphere. Makes me think I could do something similar with the cafe. I really wasn't sure about the whole idea before coming here but now I'm really excited at the prospect. Honestly, Ellie, you're an inspiration!'

I grinned. Fancy that. Me an inspiration! I didn't see myself that way, but if that was the way Fliss saw me, then why not? And if I could turn my life around, then she could too. Looking around at all my friends and customers revelling in the atmosphere of the pub, I felt a sense of pride for everything we'd achieved here. It wasn't down only to me, of course. Eric had laid down the foundations for making The Dog and Duck the place it was today. I'd simply picked up the baton and run with it. Max had been the pub's financial saviour, we had a fabulous team of staff working for us and our customers were the most loyal and supportive we could wish for. I glided around the pub on a wave of goodwill and several glasses of Prosecco.

'I've just checked on Noel,' Rose told me. 'He's absolutely fine and out like a light. Eric set up the baby monitor in the kitchen so we're keeping an eye on that too.'

'Ooh, you're a star, Rose.'

'Well, I'm glad someone thinks so.' She laughed. 'Do you mind if I go and put some music on in the other bar?'

'You go right ahead, Rose.'

'Hello, sweetheart, how are you doing?'

'Dad! Mum!' It was a big group hug all round. 'Are you all right, Dad?' I asked, peering into his eyes for any evidence to the contrary. Ever since his cancer diagnosis earlier this year I'd been in a constant state of anxiety that his condition might worsen. Despite Dad's assurances that the hospital were satisfied with his progress, it didn't stop me from occasionally waking up in the middle of the night and wondering if those doctors could be wrong. Of course, I couldn't voice any of my concerns to Dad, or Mum. I just had to put a brave face on and pretend to be as positive as them, which wasn't always easy, although I suspected they had their wobbly moments too, Mum especially. It had certainly been a deciding factor in me wanting to marry Max. I was my dad's only daughter, his only child, and I knew it would be a big moment for him to walk me down the aisle and see me married to the man I loved. For me the focus had changed and now it was all about making memories.

'I am perfectly fine, sweetheart,' he said to me, a big smile on his face. 'Very pleased that the pub is now back open. I've been spending an unhealthy amount of time in the shed just to get out of your mother's way, so I'm pleased I've got a valid excuse to get out of the house again.'

Mum shook her head indulgently.

'What is he like? After all these years he's still making out that I'm some kind of ogre that he needs to get away from. I know he doesn't mean it.'

Dad raised his eyebrows playfully.

'Well, I hope he doesn't mean it. Not now we've almost reached the thirty year mark. It's hardly as if he can get rid of me now even if he wanted to.'

'I wouldn't want to, sweetheart,' Dad said, gallantly lifting up Mum's hand and depositing a kiss there. The pair of them had always been very close, but in recent months they'd been much more publicly affectionate, and it was sweet to witness. Dad's illness had been a bit of a wake up call for them both and they were now making the most of every minute, revelling in the time that they were able to spend in each other's company now that Dad had retired. 'And coming here tonight for the reopening of the pub is the perfect way to kick off the celebrations for our thirtieth wedding anniversary, don't you think?'

'I do! It couldn't be more perfect. And on that note, do you think we should have our first toast of the weekend?' I raised my glass of Prosecco to them. 'To my wonderful mum and dad on their pearl wedding anniversary.'

The big day was on Sunday and, after a lot of discussion, Mum had decided she wanted to go to The Four Seasons restaurant in the Manor House Hotel for lunch so a table for twelve had been booked. We'd organised a cake and flowers too, and Dad had shown me the pearl necklace and earrings he had specially commissioned for the occasion, so she really was in for a treat. Then on Monday Dad was whisking her away on a surprise trip to Paris for a few days, travelling in style on the Orient Express. Well, why not?

I tried to imagine where Max and I would be in thirty years' time, the family we might have, a family grown-up and departed, no doubt, but I just couldn't. So much had happened in the space of the last couple of years it was impossible to think much beyond the next twelve months. And perhaps that was for the best. Who knew what fate had in store for us? If there was anything that the last few years had taught me it was that it was best not to spend too much time worrying about the future but to make the most of the here and now.

Just at that moment Max came over and slipped an arm around my waist and I looked up at his handsome face, catching a trace of his woody aftershave. As long as I had this man at my side, then I felt strong enough to face whatever lay in store for us.

Even Katy.

She came bustling through from the back bar with Ryan in tow, her cheeks flushed pink. 'Oh, God, that woman! She is so embarrassing. I don't think I can bear it. Perhaps this has all been some ghastly mistake and I'm actually adopted. Please tell me it's true, Max.'

'What on earth's the matter?'

'It's Mum. I don't know what's wrong with that woman. She's actually dancing now. Doesn't she know it's not that sort of place?'

I laughed and looked at Max, who shook his head, as puzzled as I was.

'Dancing is definitely allowed and it's definitely that kind of place. For tonight at least! There is no dancing ban, if that's what you're worried about,' I teased her. 'And I'm pleased your mum is having a good time. That's what we're here for.'

Katy rolled her eyes and shook her head.

'I was trying to have a conversation with my friends and she's there wafting about like some ageing hippy. You have no idea how excruciating it was. What must they think of me? And what must Andy... I mean Dad... what must he think too? I'm sure all this is for his benefit. You should have seen her. She was all over him. I reckon she's trying to seduce him again.

Come on, Ryan, I can't stay around to watch that. We'll just have to find somewhere else to sit.'

'Lord help us!' said Max, after Katy had gone on her way, dragging a hapless Ryan with her. 'I don't know what's wrong with that girl. She's been impossible to live with recently.'

'Ever since your mum moved in, you mean?'

'Yep, you're right. Those two need their heads banging together.'

I decided it was best not to mention Rose's plans to start looking for another place to stay, not tonight when we were supposed to be enjoying ourselves. That could wait until the weekend. Besides, I had something else to worry about now. From the corner of my eye I'd spotted the front door open and noticed someone slip in quietly who reminded me, for the briefest moment, of Alan, Rose's ex, until I realised why he looked quite so familiar. It wasn't Alan's doppelgänger after all, but Alan himself. In the flesh. What on earth was he doing here? I slipped out of Max's hold, intent on getting to him first, but I was too late.

'Alan? What are you doing here?' said Katy, in a voice so loud I could have sworn the whole of the village heard.

'Hello, Katy. I don't want any trouble. I just want to speak to your mother, that's all.' He was an unremarkable looking man of medium build and medium height with receding hair and glasses.

'Well, I don't think she'll want to talk to you, somehow.'

'Katy!' I frowned at her. 'Alan's come all this way from Spain. Can I get you a drink or something?'

'No, Ellie, thank you. All I want to do is speak to Rose.'

Katy had scooted off, no doubt delighting in telling her mum the good news about Alan's arrival. Sure enough, within moments Rose came marching out from the back bar, a look of serious determination set upon her face. She grabbed him by the arm and led him to one side of the room. Somehow I seemed to have got caught up between the pair of them.

'Alan, what are you doing here?'

We all wanted to know the answer to that question.

'I told you not to come. You've made an unnecessary trip, I'm afraid. We're over, Alan, why can't you see that?'

Alan's face crumpled, but he managed to keep a hold on his emotions and I was in serious danger of feeling sorry for him.

'I wanted to see you face to face, Rose. I wanted to look you in the eye and for you to tell me it was over. I still can't believe it. Why don't you come back to Spain with me, love, and we can forget about all of this?' His face roamed hers beseechingly before his gaze travelled the length of her body, a look of puzzlement on his face. 'Are they leather trousers that you're wearing, Rose?'

'Yes, they are, Alan. Do you like them?'

Distaste spread across his features.

'No, Rose. I'm not sure that I do. They're a bit...' he craned his head, examining them more closely this time, as he searched for the right word '...common, I suppose.'

'Ha! Exactly that! Well, you see, I don't have to worry about what you think any more. I can wear whatever I like, do whatever I want, see whoever I want, when I want, including my own daughter. You were always trying to drive a wedge between us and I was a fool to let it go on for so long.'

'Aw, Mum!' sighed Katy, who had made sure she was in prime position to see and hear exactly what was going on.

'I'm a free spirit now, Alan.'

'Is there someone else, Rose? Is that what all of this is about?'

'Don't be ridiculous. I...'

Just at that moment Eric wandered past and placed a hand on Rose's arm.

'There's a free room upstairs if you two want to talk in private?'

'I don't need to talk,' said Rose, her face flushed now. 'I've said everything I need to say.'

'Just give me five minutes, Rose,' begged Alan. 'Please, that's all I'm asking of you.'

Eric led them through the bar and out of the way of the buzzing melee, the noise levels in the bar rising with people chattering and laughing. I exchanged a look with Katy and shrugged. There was nothing we could do to help Rose. This was something the pair of them needed to sort out for themselves. I was just turning to go into the back bar when someone caught my arm.

'Ellie, hi!' It was Darcy, looking effortlessly glamorous in black skinny jeans, a velvet ruched top, and thigh high boots. My heart sank for the briefest moment, my usual reaction when coming face to face with Darcy, before remembering my manners and plastering a big smile on my face. 'Isn't it great that The Dog and Duck is back open again?' she enthused. 'Did you get the flowers, by the way?'

'Of course, thank you.' I laid a hand on her arm, feeling a pang of embarrassment. I'd been so preoccupied these last few weeks that I'd forgotten to thank Darcy for the kind gesture. She might not be my favourite person in the world, but at least she'd made the effort.

'You didn't have to do that but it was a lovely thought. They were absolutely beautiful. And I should have been in touch to say thank you by now. Sorry about that, it was very rude of me.'

'No problem,' she said with a smile. 'My way of apologising for what I said on the night of the fire. You must have been worried sick and there was me wittering on about all those fit firemen. It was only the next morning that I realised how insensitive I'd been. Sorry!' She shrugged. 'I can only blame it on the booze. I'm meant to be cutting down,' she said, eyeing the flute of sparkling wine in her hand, 'but maybe that will have to wait until Monday now.'

I laughed.

'Honestly, it's all forgotten now.'

'Familiar story, eh? I seem to make a habit of apologising to you the morning after the night before.'

She was referring to the night of Polly's hen party when I'd first met Darcy and she'd flirted outrageously with Max and drunk far too many 'Sex on the beach' cocktails before shifting her attentions to one of the young waiters who I'd hired specially for the occasion. She was in a sorry state by the end of the evening, although I suspected the young waiter had had a wow of a time. We'd made sure Darcy stayed over with us that night so she couldn't get into any further trouble and she'd been very shame-faced the next morning.

'Anyway, where's that sexy man of yours? I really must go and say hello.'

I rolled my eyes, smiling. Honestly, the woman was incorrigible. She really couldn't help herself.

I glanced at my watch and wandered out to the back bar to see to the food.

'Is it always like this?' said Fliss as she came across to help me peel off the cling film from the platters we'd prepared earlier. She'd been an absolute star tonight, helping out with the food, clearing away the dirty glasses and wiping down the tables, not that I'd asked her to, she'd just rolled up her sleeves and got stuck in.

'Not always. We do have some chilled and relaxed evenings too!'

Fliss was seeing the pub at its best. The place was heaving with happy customers, the booze was flowing freely and the fires were crackling noisily. From now on it would be business as usual at The Dog and Duck. Soon the Christmas decorations would go up, which could mean only one thing: Christmas was just around the corner, and, with it, our wedding day too. The celebrations had well and truly begun.

'I can see how much you love running this place,' Fliss said, once the rush had passed and it was our turn to help ourselves to some food.

'Yes, I do. It can be hard work at times and there are always problems that you have to deal with, like the beer being off, missed deliveries, staff being off sick, but I love the challenge of keeping the place running as it always has done. And do you know, none of it actually feels like proper work? It's more like being in charge of a completely dysfunctional family who drive you mad but you love all the same. Embrace the madness, that's what I say!'

Fliss threw back her head and laughed.

'That's good life advice, Ellie. I really must follow that!'

## 23

Over breakfast the following morning, in our weary, sleep deprived and alcohol induced fuzzy state, we lingered over our mugs of tea and bacon sandwiches. Noel was in his high chair babbling away happily. The rest of us, me, Max, Fliss, Katy and Arthur, chatted about the success of the previous night, the turn in the weather – it was bitterly cold outside now – and the startling realisation that Christmas was only a matter of weeks away, for which none of us were really prepared.

'What will you do for Christmas?' I asked Fliss.

'I shall have to go home. Mum and Dad will never forgive me otherwise. It will certainly be different, not sharing it with Brad this year, but I should know by then what my plans are for the new year so it will give me some time to prepare and sort things out.'

'Well, you do know you're always welcome here,' said Max. 'Don't wait for an invitation. If you fancy coming down, then just come. Our door is always open here.'

'Aw, thank you, Max.' Fliss looked genuinely touched by Max's words.

Her visit had passed all too quickly. Her overnight bag was packed and ready to go, waiting for her by the back door.

'What about you two? What are your plans for after the wedding? Will you be going on honeymoon?'

Max and I looked at each other and our mouths contorted to the side, almost in unison.

'I knew we'd forgotten something,' joked Max.

'No, not this year, at least. Christmas is our busiest time at the pub and after the year we've had it will be nice to have a quiet Christmas at home. It's Noel's first birthday too, so we want to be home to celebrate that.'

'Well, hardly quiet with us lot, but that's just how I like it,' said Katy. 'I can't wait. Can Ryan come too?' she asked eagerly, looking from me to Max.

'Yep, sure, the more the merrier,' agreed Max.

Although we'd have a full house for Christmas with Mum and Dad, Eric, Polly and George, Rose, Arthur, Katy and Ryan too, along with any other lost souls who turned up in the meantime, it would still be a relaxed affair as everyone would be expected to do their bit. Of course, there would be a visit to The Dog and Duck for pre-lunch drinks, which meant anything might happen, but we would all rally round to get the Christmas dinner on the table at some point during the day. Mind you, after last year, when Noel decided he couldn't wait and was determined to arrive at the last minute for the celebrations, anything we were faced with this year would be a doddle in comparison.

'Thanks, Max, you're the best. Actually...' Katy looked round the table as though she might have missed something or someone. 'Where's Mum?'

I shrugged. 'I haven't seen her today. She's obviously having a lie-in after all the excitement of last night.'

'Blimey, it's not like her to sleep in so late. Mind you, I think she was well merry last night. What happened with Alan? Does anyone know?'

'I think he went off in a taxi, but I can't be sure.' Some of the events from last night were still hazy in my mind.

'She came home with you though, didn't she?' asked Katy, a touch of concern in her voice.

'No, she must have left before us. I assumed she'd gone back with you.'

Katy shook her head and I saw the panic flitter across her features. 'Let me just go and check she's okay. She's probably feeling rough. Honestly, I don't know why she had to drink so much.'

Katy went off chuntering to herself and Fliss took advantage of the lull in the conversation. 'I could sit here all day, but I must really make a move or else I won't ever feel like going home. Thanks for everything, you two. You've really helped me to get a few things straight in my own head. Best of luck with the wedding. I'll be thinking of you on your big day.'

People kept reminding me that the big day was only a few weeks away but there was part of me that was in denial about that fact. We'd prevaricated for so long about whether it was actually the right thing for us to do, that now the date was almost upon us, I still couldn't quite believe that it would actually be happening. Pretty much everything was in place. This coming week I'd have the final dress fitting with Caroline and I was filled with excitement as to how my outfit would look with all the carefully chosen accessories. There was still the matter of the barn being complete, but Max hadn't said anything to suggest it wouldn't be, and there was always the marquee to fall back on if we needed to.

I couldn't panic about things outside my control, not when there were plenty of other things to panic about, like Christmas itself and Noel's birthday. Who ever thought a Christmas wedding would be a good idea?

'Drive carefully. And let us know that you get back safely,' Max said.

We were seeing Fliss into her car when Katy reappeared just in time for them to have a hug. We waved Fliss off, watching as her little blue car tootled down the long driveway of Braithwaite Manor until it disappeared out of sight, a sense of sadness washing over me. Not that I had any time to dwell on it because as soon as we turned to walk back indoors Katy grabbed my arm.

'Ellie, Max! Mum didn't come home last night. I've checked her bedroom and her bed wasn't slept in. I've tried ringing her but she's not picking up. Have you heard from her at all?'

'No.' Max pulled out his phone to make doubly sure and shook his head.

'Perhaps her phone ran out of battery or something,' I suggested.

'Yes, but where would she be? It's not like her to stay out overnight and surely she would have got a message to one of us if that's what she'd planned.'

'Oh, well,' I said, deciding perhaps I needed another cup of coffee and a cuddle with Noel before I attempted clearing the table and made a start on my list of jobs. I'd got as far as getting the Christmas cards out and finding my address list, now I just needed to sit down and write the blooming things. I loved receiving them, but writing them was a chore. 'There'll be a perfectly logical explanation, no doubt.'

'Ellie! How can you say that? This is our mother we're talking about here.' Katy wiggled her finger to include Max in her comment. 'Anything could have happened to her. Why didn't you take her home with you?' she demanded, as though we were personally responsible for Rose going missing.

'Maybe she and Alan continued their conversation long into the night?' Although even as I said the words it seemed unlikely as the last time I'd seen Rose she'd seemed desperate to get rid of Alan as quickly as possible. 'I just assumed she'd gone home early and gone straight to bed but there won't be anything to worry about, Katy. She'll turn up soon enough, you'll see.'

'Yeah, she'll be fine,' agreed Max, picking up the newspaper and thumbing through its pages.

'This is like Flora all over again.' Arthur's comment didn't do anything to make anyone feel better, so he added with a forced chuckle, 'Maybe she's already found her new place. She was talking yesterday about moving out.'

'Was she?' Katy spun round to glare at Arthur, her question short and terse. She was biting on her lip with her brow furrowed, a telltale sign that her anxiety levels were simmering on explosive level.

'Yes, but then you know she's been talking about that for a while now,' I quickly reassured her, and Max.

'Right. Oh, God! She wouldn't just go without saying anything though. What if she's had an accident or what if...?' Katy's face darkened and she hesitated as though she could barely dare to say the words aloud. Her voice lowered. 'What if something happened to her on the way home?'

'Like what?' said Max, exasperated. 'This is Little Leyton we're talking about here, not downtown Puerto Rico!'

Katy looked at her brother accusingly.

'Terrible things happen everywhere these days. Even in the country. She could have been murdered, or fallen down a ditch and left lying in the cold all night, or been trampled by cows on her way home.'

'I can tell you're not a country girl at heart,' quipped Max.

'What Max means, Katy, is that there wouldn't be any cows around at the moment because they would have gone indoors for the winter. You see cows normally—'

'Grrrr...' Katy stamped her foot on the floor, interrupting Arthur's musings. 'I don't care about the stupid cows. I just want to know where Mum is. And I can't believe you lot don't seem to give a toss about what's happened to her.'

'That's because nothing will have happened to her, Katy. She'll be back before you know it,' said Max. 'Stop getting yourself in such a state.'

The trouble was, when we'd all fallen quiet and were lost to our own thoughts, I couldn't help my mind from wandering. I was making us another coffee and Max was loading the dishwasher, Arthur was playing a game with Flora, throwing a rolled up newspaper for her to fetch, and Katy was crouched obsessively over her phone. It occurred to me that perhaps it was a little odd that Rose hadn't come home. Especially without telling any of us. Where on earth could she be?

'Hang on a minute,' I said, having a moment's inspiration. 'Let me check my phone.'

I'd chucked it in my handbag last night and hadn't looked at it since. A flicker of unease ran down my spine. What if Rose had been trying to contact me?

With a sense of urgency, I scrabbled around in the depths of my handbag and finally unearthed the phone amidst a pile of tissues and old receipts.

'Right, here we go,' I said, relieved to have found it and stabbing at the buttons, quickly realising that the phone was completely dead. 'Damn, I'm going to need to charge it.'

Katy's fevered emotions were definitely rubbing off on me now. She was right: if Rose had made other plans, then why wouldn't she have told us?

I plugged the phone into the charger on the nearest worktop, hovering over it impatiently. It seemed to whir and ping for ages before finally springing into life. My relief at finding my messages was huge.

'Ah, you see. No need to panic at all,' I reassured everyone, but mainly myself. Max cast a glance at me, raising an eyebrow. He knew me all too well. 'There's a message here from your mum. Let me read it.

"Hi Ellie, just to let you know I won't be home tonight. Probably for the best after today's run-in with Katy. Don't worry, I'll be fine. Bye xx'"

'What?' Katy's face was thunderous. 'What the hell does that mean? And why did she send the text to you and not to me or Max?'

'Well, in fairness, you two haven't been getting along that well recently. She probably thought you wouldn't be interested.'

'What? She's my mother. Of course I'm interested.' Katy's face was always so expressive, every one of her emotions clearly etched upon her features so that you had a moment by moment account of exactly how she was feeling. Now, her confusion, hurt and anger were clear to see. 'She's blaming me for everything – that's why she stayed away last night, because of me. And it still doesn't explain where she stayed.' She sighed heavily. You could see the cogs churning, her mind working overtime. 'She was playing up to Dad earlier in the evening. You don't think she went off with him after her run-in with Alan? Maybe she went home with him?'

'Don't be ridiculous!' Max said drily.

'Honestly, if Mum has been trying to get back with him, I don't know what I'll do. She can't just go around picking up people and then dropping them when she feels like it. Just when I get to know my dad and start building a relationship with him after eighteen years of not knowing that he even existed and she wants to get back in there too.'

'Katy, stop it! You're getting into the realms of fantasy now. From what I know of Andy he's totally devoted to Jill. He wouldn't do something like that and neither would your mum. I think you're just making up stories in your head.'

Just then we all stopped and looked at each other when we heard the distinctive laughter of someone coming from outside. It took a moment before I realised why the sound was so familiar. It was Rose and it wasn't laughter either, more like giggling. When she walked through the kitchen door, dressed incongruously in her leather trousers from yesterday and an oversized shirt I didn't recognise as hers, it quickly became apparent that she wasn't alone, but it wasn't Andy accompanying her. It was Eric who was standing behind her, a big smile on his face.

'Just thought I'd make sure your mum got home okay,' he said, tapping his hand on the side of his thigh, as though he might not know what else to do with it.

'What?' said Katy, incredulous. 'After last night? It took an awful long time for you to get home.'

That elicited a snort from Arthur.

'I did tell you I wouldn't be coming home,' Rose said to me.

'Yes, it's fine,' I said, ushering them both in. 'There's some coffee on the go if you'd like some.' Eric nodded and came over to give me a kiss on the cheek. 'It was just Katy was worried about you. I didn't pick up your message until just now so we were a bit concerned when we realised you weren't here this morning. That's all.'

'Ah, you were worried about me. That's lovely. What were you worried about, exactly?'

'Oh, you would not believe the terrible fate that could have befallen you on the walk home from the pub,' Max said drily. He'd gone over to the cupboard to pull out two mugs for Rose and Eric. 'Hypothermia, marauding cows, serial killers. Apparently you take your life in your hands doing that trip.'

Max was trying to raise a smile from Katy but she was still brooding.

'You could have let me know, Mum. Where did you stay, then?'

'At the pub. Eric was very kind to me. I was a bit upset after coming face to face with Alan again. After a while I managed to get rid of him. We put him in a taxi back to the airport. Eric and I got chatting and before we knew it, it was the early hours of the morning. Eric suggested I stay over in the spare room.'

'Oh, is that right?' Katy said the words slowly and accusingly. 'Do you really think I'm that stupid? Can you imagine your reaction if I'd done something similar? Went out for the night and didn't come back and then you find out I've spent the night with some strange man!'

Eric winced at the slight. 'Well, I know I've got some funny habits, love, but I'm not that strange.'

Eric's reaction and Katy's obvious annoyance only made the whole situation that much funnier and I had to look away to stop myself from laughing. Arthur was chuckling, nodding away as though he might be all too familiar with Eric's strange ways.

'Don't be so rude, Katy,' said Rose, who wasn't finding it remotely funny. 'Quite honestly, I didn't think you cared what I got up to. And anyway, I don't need to explain myself to you or anyone else, come to that. I had enough of that with Alan. I'm your mother and a fifty-eight year old woman. If I want to go out with a different man every night of the week, then I can. If I want to wear leather trousers, then I will! It's not up to you or anyone else what I do. I'm a free agent at the moment and that's how I like it.' This last part was delivered with a smile towards Eric. 'When I've found my own place, then you won't need to trouble yourself with what I'm doing.'

'Mum!' Katy's eyes widened and her mouth dropped open. 'What's got into you?' It was a question I'd been wondering too. 'I was only asking. Am I not even allowed to do that now?'

'No, Katy, it isn't just you asking after my welfare. I wish it was! I know you've been unhappy ever since I moved in here and I'm sorry about that. It saddens me that I can't seem to do anything to please you but I can't spend my whole life apologising to you and tiptoeing around trying not to upset you. Despite what you might think, I deserve some happiness too.'

Katy's face reflected her shock at her mum's heartfelt words.

'I was worried about you, Mum,' she said sheepishly. 'Really worried.'

'Right, well, there was no need.' Rose gave a little shimmy of her shoulders and straightened her spine, standing tall. 'Anyway, let's forget about all of that now.' She managed a tight smile at Katy. 'So, what did we all think about the reopening of the pub last night?' she asked, addressing the rest of us. 'Apart from that small matter of Alan turning up, I thought it was probably one of the best nights I've had in a long time.'

And with her eyes shining brightly and a glow in her cheeks, I wondered if there could be another reason, or rather another person, that might have had a part to play in making it such a special night for Rose.

## 24

It was only Monday morning and I was already exhausted, but then again it had been the most hectic weekend. After the excitement of Friday night and seeing Fliss off on Saturday, I'd had to do some last minute shopping for Mum and Dad's anniversary party on the Sunday. What a wonderful day that had turned out to be! We'd been greeted at the restaurant with flutes of champagne and canapés and the fizz hadn't stopped flowing for the entire time we were there. Our table in the orangery overlooking the grounds of the hotel had been laid with white starched linen, fresh flowers and confetti, and when Mum had seen it for the first time she'd gasped in delight. Each of the golden chairs around the table had had a white and pink foil helium balloon tied to the back, bobbing in a celebratory fashion.

In the centre of the orangery had been a magnificent Christmas tree decorated with gingham bows, pine cones sprayed silver and gold, orange slices and candy canes. As I'd walked past, gazing up at the towering Norwegian Spruce, I'd caught a heady whiff of festive scents, including cinnamon, pine and oranges, that had made my nose twitch and brought memories flooding back of Christmases past. And a reminder that I needed to get a move on and put up our Christmas trees at home and at the pub.

The food had been every bit as exquisite as you would expect from a

Michelin starred restaurant, the meals presented on the plates looking like works of art and tasting sublime, the subtle flavours mingling to create a taste explosion in our mouths. There had been a great deal of oohing and ahhing over lunch and Mum had been in her element being the centre of attention among friends and family. Dad had looked on proudly, the love and affection for his wife clear to see in his fond expression. Thirty years of marriage were a wonderful milestone and definitely worth celebrating but for Mum and Dad it was all the more special because there'd been a moment earlier this year when they'd had to consider if Dad would even still be around for their anniversary. That whole episode had taught us how easy it was to take all the good things in your life for granted. To believe that there would be another day, another month or another year to do all those things you wanted to do when none of us really knew what was around the corner.

We'd taken coffees and after dinner drinks with home made petit-fours in the lounge, lingering for as long as Noel would allow. When he'd become fractious someone had suggested a walk around the formal gardens, which, with us all feeling totally sated, would have been a good idea had it not been so perishingly cold. So we'd managed a few brave minutes outside before we'd decided it was a much better idea to climb back into the waiting minibus and head for home.

Back at the manor we had been greeted enthusiastically by the dogs, who had then gone scooting out into the gardens. All possible escape routes for adventure seeking dogs had now been closed off, so I'd been confident to let them roam happily for as long as they'd liked without fear that we would need to send out the search parties again.

We'd all collapsed into the squashy sofas and chairs in the drawing room while Max had made coffee and poured drinks for those that had wanted them. Eric and Rose, after sitting at opposite ends of the table in the restaurant, had been next to one another on the two seated sofa having an animated conversation.

'You know, you should open your cards and presents, Mum and Dad.'

The table had been covered with gift bags, presents, flowers and cards.

'Oh, I feel like the luckiest woman alive today,' Mum had said, intertwining her hand with Dad's. 'Not only did I make the best and most clever decision thirty years ago by choosing to marry this special man here but I'm also very fortunate to be surrounded by my lovely family and friends.'

'Shall we make a start?' she'd said, her eyes alight at the array of goodies in front of her.

Mum and Dad had proceeded to open their cards, delighting in the personal messages written inside. There had been gifts of flowers, chocolates, an engraved crystal vase and theatre tickets, which had all gone down particularly well. They had both been thrilled with the collage of photos I'd put together and framed, charting their marriage over the decades. A photo at St Cuthbert's on their wedding day, the pair of them looking impossibly young and glamorous. One of Dad holding me as a newborn in his arms. Photos from various family holidays over the years, one of us soaked through on a camping trip to Wales when it had rained for the entire week and, in contrast, one of us sipping cocktails on a roof bar in New York City. Happy times and a gorgeous reminder of everything they had crammed in over the years. The last photo had been a recent one of the pair of them taken outside No. 2 Ivy Lane Cottages, the scene of so many happy memories.

'We'll treasure this, won't we, Malc? It will go up on the wall in the living room and whenever I look at it I shall be reminded of today and every one of you here.'

'There's another card for you to open.' Dad had retrieved an envelope from his jacket and handed it over to Mum.

'From you? But you gave me your card and present this morning.' Her hand had instinctively gone to the pearls around her neck, their natural beauty and lustre bringing a light and freshness to her features.

Dad had nodded, not giving anything away. Mum, looking confused, had carefully opened the envelope and pulled out its contents, looking at them and then back again at Dad, as though not completely understanding.

'The Orient Express? To Paris? You didn't? You know how much I've always wanted to do that trip. I can't believe it.'

'Well, you'd better believe it because we're leaving early tomorrow morning,' Dad had said, chuckling.

It had all been too much for Mum. She'd broken down in tears, waving her tickets in front of her face. Everyone, Rose, Eric, Katy, Paul, Caroline, Arthur, Josie and Ethan, had looked genuinely touched by Mum's reaction and I was sure I wasn't the only one who'd shed a tear at the display of her happiness. Noel and little Stella, who had been remarkably well behaved the whole day long, must have picked up on the atmosphere as they'd both started to grizzle too. Any tears had soon turned to laughter though when the dogs had come bounding in unexpectedly, sending all the cards flying and depositing muddy footprints over the carpet too.

Now, sitting in my lovely conservatory, nursing that 'morning after the weekend before' vibe, I glanced at my watch and wondered where Mum and Dad might be right now. Sitting in the lap of luxury on the Venice Simplon-Orient-Express no doubt, sipping champagne and soaking up the wonderful views outside. I felt so delighted for them, and just a tad jealous too, hoping Max and I would have the same opportunity one day.

For now I was more than content to enjoy the peace and solitude of the manor. Having the house to myself this morning was a rare luxury. Max was working down at the pub, Arthur had been taken to a routine medical appointment by Betty Masters, with a promise of a bun and a cappuccino in the tea rooms afterwards, Katy was at college and Rose had taken the bus into town, I suspected in search of places to rent. Whether or not it was because they'd both been on their best behaviour yesterday or if Rose speaking out against Katy the other day had had some effect, but there'd been a quiet calm over the manor this morning. Long may it continue was all I could say.

'Right, Noel, I'm not getting up again until I've finished these Christmas cards. Although maybe I'll have a coffee first, and you some juice. How about that?'

Finally, after much procrastination I opened up my address book, placed Noel on his play mat beside me and started on the job I'd been putting off for far too long. Already today, the first day of December, Andrea our post lady had delivered two Christmas cards, which I'd opened excitedly and placed on the window sill. Admittedly one was from a charity, but the other was the genuine article, a card from a friend I'd made at university. Once we'd had a few more in, I would arrange them over the wooden surround of the fireplace. Mum had brought me a huge blowsy poinsettia, which was on the kitchen table, and I had some lovely mini cyclamens in pinks and whites dotted around the surfaces in little gold pots. It was beginning to look a lot like Christmas and was still relatively low key and tasteful. A few more days and my kitsch side, my 'more-is-so-much-more' design style would kick into place and the sophisticated and classy surroundings of Braithwaite Manor would be transformed into a winter wonderland with tinsel and decorations covering every available surface.

I pulled another card out of the packet and was just writing a message when the back door opened and Max wandered in. When I saw him in the doorway, in jeans, his customary checked shirt and a shadow of stubble across his jawline, my heart jolted and a smile involuntarily spread across my face. Would there ever come a time when Max would no longer have that effect on me? I really hoped not.

'Hello, I wasn't expecting to see you until much later. Look, Daddy's here, Noel!'

His little face lit up to see Max and he reached his arms up, demanding a carry. Max came over and swept him up in his arms before coming across to kiss me on the cheek.

'How's it going?' he asked, looking at the growing pile of cards I'd written.

'Slowly. I seem to have been doing these all morning and I've still got loads to do. Anyway, what are you doing back here?'

'Well, I've been to the pub to make sure they have everything they need and everything's progressing as it should. I've been round to check out the couple of cottages standing vacant in the village. One of them will need a complete refurb but there's another that is in generally good condition. It had a new bathroom and kitchen fitted last year and is pretty clean inside. It will need a lick of paint and the carpets replacing but that's something we can get done fairly quickly. It's worth doing if it means sorting out the problems between Mum and Katy.'

I stood up and wrapped my arms around Max's neck, standing on tiptoe to kiss him on his lips.

'You know, you're such a good son and big brother. I hope those two appreciate everything you do for them.'

'It's what you have to do when it's family, don't you?' he said with a resigned sigh. 'But mainly I'm doing it for you. You don't need the stress of having to sort out all their battles. You have enough on your plate without worrying about them as well.'

'Ah, I love them both, and one on one they're really easy to get along with. It's just when they're together that things can sometimes get a little tricky.'

'Anyway, I thought perhaps we could go down and have a look at the cottage, see what you reckon, if you think it might be okay for Mum. And then go along to Beck's Farm Shop to see if Ryan can sort us out a couple of trees.'

'Really, you've got the rest of the day off? What an unexpected bonus. Spending the day with my husband-to-be! I could drop off some of these cards in the village at the same time.'

After a light lunch of some sweet potato and butternut squash soup that I'd had bubbling on the stove, we wrapped up warm with hats and gloves and our big winter jackets and ventured outside. Max steered the buggy while I held onto Flora's lead and Digby, always totally reliable off lead, mooched around at my side. The cold was biting but invigorating. We walked along the back lanes, the branches of the trees and shrubs stark now, but covered in a sparkling white coating. Scenes so beautiful that they wouldn't have looked amiss on some of those Christmas cards I had in my bag. At St Cuthbert's we lingered by the lychgate and shared a kiss.

'Only a few weeks to go now, Max, and we'll be here for our wedding.'

'I know and it can't come a day too soon. I can't imagine a more beautiful place to get married, can you?'

'No.' I sighed, happily. I'd often dreamt about my own wedding day, of walking through the lychgate on my dad's arm, of my husband-to-be waiting for me at the aisle. Of course, I'd had no idea then who that man might be, but if I'd come up with an identikit of my ideal life partner, then Max would have fitted that profile exactly. I must have been wearing my lucky charm the day he'd wandered into my life. The cold infiltrated my bones as we stood there. 'If the weather stays like this I think we'll all freeze to death.'

'Ah, but it won't be for long. A quick dash from the car into the church for the ceremony and then we'll be back to the pub for the reception. If you're cold, I promise I'll warm you up,' he said with a distinctly lascivious tone.

I laughed and chastised him with an elbow in the side.

'You know, I don't think I'd mind even if it was freezing. Nothing could spoil the enjoyment of our special day now.'

We walked on towards the high street and I was relieved to get rid of some of my cards in the post box, while others I put through the letterboxes of the cottages and shops as we walked past.

'Do you want to go in?' Max asked when we reached The Dog and Duck, and I faltered for a moment. It was a habit of old.

'No, let's leave them to it. Dan and Eric can run the pub perfectly well without me butting in. Oh, look, the wreath looks lovely,' I said, spotting it on the old oak door and going up for a closer look. One of Polly's specialities – she'd supplied us with a couple for the pub and one for home. This one was abundant with fresh holly, red berries, spruce, mistletoe and red and gold ribbons. 'Silke told me she was putting up the decorations around the bar today, so it'll be good to get the Christmas tree in and decorated too. Then it really will feel like Christmas.' I let slip a regretful sigh.

'What's the matter?'

'Nothing. I was just reminiscing, thinking back to how it was when I first took over The Dog and Duck. I did everything then. Living over the shop, so to speak, meant that I was involved in every aspect of running the pub. It was my whole life. I can remember that first Christmas, putting up the tree and all the decorations, organising all the events and working every shift going.'

'You sound nostalgic. As though you miss those times.'

'I do in a way. I loved that sense of accomplishment that came when things went well and people congratulated you on a job well done. Don't get me wrong, I wouldn't want to turn back time because I'm so happy and grateful for everything that I have now.' I grabbed hold of his hand and squeezed it. 'So much has happened since then and I have different priorities, but I'll always be proud of what I achieved at the pub, just for the fact of keeping it standing.'

'You don't have to talk about it as though it's in the past tense. If you wanted to have a more hands on role, then you could do. Noel is that much older now.'

'No, I didn't mean it like that.' We'd talked about this before and we'd agreed that I would take more of a back seat role, leaving Dan and Silke to look after the day-to-day running of the pub. They had the bonus of having Eric living back at The Dog and Duck, so the place was in very safe hands. I basically oversaw what was going on, discussed the orders with Dan, helped organise the special events and tried not to overstep the mark by interfering in matters that Dan and Silke were more than capable of sorting out. To be honest I was probably surplus to requirements now and that feeling was never more prevalent than today, standing outside, observing all the activity going on inside.

'Come on,' I said, not wanting to acknowledge the truth of that fact right now. Instead we wandered along the high street which, with the addition of white fairy lights along all the buildings, had a very festive feel about it. From across the road Betty Masters spotted us from the tea rooms and she came outside to beckon us over.

'Hello! We must have just missed you. I've just dropped off Arthur at the manor. He's had his blood test and a rejuvenating cup of tea and a cinnamon whirl. I think it quite wore him out. He said he was going to have his afternoon nap.'

'Thanks, Betty, for doing that. I know how much he appreciates getting out and seeing different faces when he can.'

'Well, are you two going to come in for a cuppa? I've got some freshly made mince pies with an iced topping, if I can tempt you.'

'They sound delicious but we're on a mission – to choose our Christmas trees, actually. We might take you up on the offer on the way back though.'

'Make sure you do. Even if it's just to collect some pies. I'll put some to one side for you.'

We went on our way and at the other end of the high street we turned off into Friday Street, where there was a row of terraced cottages, two of which belonged to Max and which he let out for rental income.

'This is the cottage I had in mind for Mum,' he said, pointing to the house at the end of the row. 'That's if she's interested, of course. She might have other plans in mind.'

He pulled out some keys from his jacket pocket and I followed him into the little cottage. Despite the whiff of mustiness and a general air of neglect, I was immediately taken with the evocatively named Lilac Cottage, it had a cosy and reassuring feeling about it. It was a small house with a living room that came off the main front door, and a kitchen that looked out on an overgrown garden, but it was easy to see beyond the areas that needed updating. The kitchen was practically brand new, as was the bathroom upstairs. There were two reasonable sized bedrooms and an outlook over the allotments at the back.

'Well, I think it's lovely. It's right at the heart of the village too, so she has the pub and all the shops on her doorstep and the bus stop into town around the corner as well. I'd say it was ideal.'

'Good. I wanted to see what you thought first before mentioning it to Mum. I don't want her thinking I'm trying to get rid of her by offloading her into any ropey old property but I think this will be great once my guys have worked their magic on it.'

'Oh, me too. It's lovely.'

'She knows she can stay at the manor if she wants to, but I can see why she would want to find her own place and get some of her independence back so she's not living under the critical glare of Katy.'

I laughed, and gave him a wry look.

'Yes, I'm hopeful that when they're not living under the same roof, Katy might come to appreciate her mum a bit more.'

Twenty minutes later we'd reached Beck's Farm Shop, which was busy this afternoon with people who had the same idea in mind as us. All the varieties of Christmas trees were lined up in the yard, sweet little ones and huge towering ones, and we spotted Ryan, Katy's boyfriend, lugging the trees around, putting them through the netting machine and then carrying them over to his customers' cars.

The shop was abuzz with customers browsing the extensive Christmas display. There were fancy garlands hanging across the old wooden beams of the barn, buckets full of mistletoe and pine cones, bowls of brightly coloured baubles and handmade wooden decorations hanging from the Christmas trees. The scent of pine wafted in the air. Everywhere you looked there were shiny, gorgeous Christmassy items. I was absolutely in my element. There was a huge selection of tempting seasonal foods too: chutneys, cheeses and fruit infused alcohol, which would make lovely additional presents. Even though I'd done all my Christmas shopping it wouldn't hurt to pick up a few extra gifts for unexpected visitors. Max must have noticed my face lighting up.

'Do you want to stay here, then, and I'll take Noel and the dogs to see if we can pick out some suitable trees? Come and find us when you're done.'

He knew me only too well and I was grateful for the chance to have a mooch at my leisure without having to worry about Noel. The far corner of the shop had been transformed into Santa's grotto and there was a long queue of excitable and expectant children, on what looked to be a nursery school trip, waiting to go inside. Their enthusiasm was so palpable that it rubbed off on me. I glanced at my watch. Perhaps, on another day, without the dogs, I'd bring Noel along so he could experience the magic of meeting Father Christmas for the first time himself.

Twenty minutes later, I'd picked up some tins of shortbread biscuits, some bottles of cranberry gin, some festively decorated gingerbread men, some scented candles and some lovely sets of stationery. Reluctantly, I left the shop, weighed down with my paper carrier bags, in search of Max. In truth, I could have stayed there all afternoon, buying one of everything, but I knew my gang would be waiting for me and I felt certain my bank balance would thank me for it later.

'There you are!' said Max, his face lighting up. 'I thought I was going to have to send out a search party for you.'

'Just picking up a few goodies.' I laughed, trying and failing to hide the bags behind my legs.

'Look, I've picked out these trees, if you're happy with them.' He led me over to where Ryan was manning the tills. 'The big one for the hall at the manor, then the slighter smaller one for the living room and then this one here for the pub. What do you think?'

'Great! They seem fine to me.' I watched as Ryan netted them up. 'How's it going?' I asked him. 'You look incredibly busy.'

'We are and it's only going to get busier with each passing day. I'll put these on the truck and drop them off at the pub and at the manor later. Okay?'

'You're a star, Ryan.'

He and Katy had been going out for over a year and, although they'd had their ups and downs, they seemed much more solid as a couple now. At first, knowing his bad boy past and the fact that he was several years older than Katy, Max hadn't entirely approved of their relationship and had hoped it would quickly fizzle out. But Ryan had shown himself to be a real support to Katy, particularly when she was going through all the trauma of discovering the truth about her dad. He'd encouraged her in her college studies, often dropping her off and collecting her in his truck and bringing her home. He didn't stand any nonsense though, and if he felt she was acting unreasonably or being out of order, then he would tell her so, which sometimes caused fireworks with Katy vowing that Ryan was an idiot and that she would never speak to him again. It never lasted for long though and soon they would be back together, madly in love again.

'You're coming to us for Christmas?' Max asked.

'If that's okay with you?' he mumbled.

Ryan was still wary of Max. He'd known Katy's brother hadn't been keen on him from the off and had witnessed his stubborn nature and authoritative manner when dealing with Katy at times, but actually Max, having seen what a good influence Ryan was on Katy, had really come to like him. Ryan was a man of few words, but he adored Katy, which counted for a lot in Max's eyes.

'Of course. We'd love you to come. It wouldn't be the same for Katy if you weren't there.'

It was only in the last couple of days, and especially so this afternoon, realising that Christmas was very much upon us, that I had felt that first inkling of excitement for the holiday season. Up until now I'd been so preoccupied with our wedding that I hadn't given the festivities a second thought. It was as though December would start and finish with our wedding, but now I could begin to look beyond that to Noel's first birthday on Christmas Day. A double celebration. Even though he wouldn't fully appreciate the significance of all the traditions, I was so looking forward to hanging up his stocking and leaving out some goodies for Santa Claus and his reindeer.

After the hectic and eventful year we'd had, I was almost pleased that we wouldn't be jetting off on an exotic honeymoon somewhere. Christmas at home with our loved ones sounded just perfect – well, that was if we could avoid any family squabbles, which, knowing our lot, certainly couldn't be guaranteed.

## 25

Later that afternoon, back at the manor, I made a pot of tea and we all settled around the kitchen table tucking into the iced mince pies we'd collected from Betty on our way home. They were delicious, the pastry so short and crumbly that it melted in your mouth. So moreish that it was nigh on impossible to eat just one. Afternoon tea had become a bit of a ritual at the manor, a time when we would all gather to share our news, and it was one of my favourite parts of the day. Arthur would wander in from his bedroom after his customary nap. Katy would normally be coming in from college and Rose always made sure she was around to welcome Katy home. They would take it in turns to have a cuddle and a chat with Noel, who absolutely revelled in all the attention. Max wasn't always around to join us, so it was especially nice to have him at home today.

'Good news,' he said to Rose as we all contemplated a second iced mince pie. 'I don't know what your plans are, but Lilac Cottage in the village will be ready from the middle of next week, and you can have first refusal on it. Ellie and I have been down there today and it's in fairly good nick. I've got my guys going in tomorrow and they'll be ripping the carpets up and giving the whole place a new lick of paint. And sorting out the garden too, which is a bit overgrown. Sounds a lot, but they'll be able to get all that done in a couple of days.'

'It's lovely, really pretty,' I added. 'And after the facelift it will be a blank canvas so you could really make it your own.'

'Really? It sounds ideal. In fact, I called round the main letting agencies in town earlier, but there was nothing that really took my fancy, well, not in my price range and certainly nothing in the village.'

'Well, go and have a look at it and see what you think,' suggested Max.

'Yes, and don't think we're trying to get rid of you. It's only an idea and if you don't like it, there's no pressure. You know you're welcome to stay here as long as you like.'

'Thank you, Ellie.' She took a moment, clearly contemplating what she might say next. 'You've both been so kind and supportive to me while I've been here. It can't have been easy having your mother-in-law turning up on your doorstep with all her worldly goods, but you've never made me feel unwelcome or in the way.'

'What, and you're saying I have?' Katy was quick to jump on her mum's words.

'No, Katy, I didn't even mention you,' said Rose in exasperation.

'No, but it's what you meant, isn't it?' Katy's dark eyes blazed.

'Don't be silly. I don't mean that at all. I was very down and low when I arrived, but being here with you all, and seeing little Noel every day, well, it's really helped me to feel more optimistic about the future. I do think though that it's time for me to move on and find my own place. This was only ever meant as a temporary arrangement.'

'I know exactly what you mean, love,' said Arthur. 'I was proper miserable living on my own and Max and Ellie rescued me really. I don't know what would have happened if they hadn't sorted things out for me. Although...' he paused, pensive for a moment, playing with the handle of his mug '...I do wonder sometimes if you get fed up with me being here all the time.'

'NO!!' Katy, Max and I gave our heartfelt and immediate response to that one.

'Don't be daft, Arthur. We've told you, you're one of the family now. We wouldn't let you leave now even if you wanted to.'

'Phew, well, that's a relief,' said Arthur, his eyes lighting up.

'Right,' said Katy, bristling, and turning to her mum again. 'So, when are you moving out, exactly?'

Rose shrugged her shoulders.

'I know you're desperate to get rid of me, Katy, but I haven't even seen the cottage yet. I'll go and have a look and then I can start to make plans. From what Max is saying, it sounds as though it might be ready for me to move into soon.'

'No, I didn't mean it like that.' Katy back pedalled. 'You wouldn't move out before Christmas, would you?' Now her voice was full of concern.

'I don't know. We'll have to see.'

Now it was Katy's turn to fall quiet and thoughtful. 'Well, I don't think you should. What with the wedding and Christmas it's going to be so busy around here and you'd miss out on all the fun if you weren't here. It's not as if there's any hurry, is there?'

We all looked at Katy, slightly bemused by her apparent change of heart.

'Well, from what Max tells me, Lilac Cottage is in the centre of the village so it's not as though you'll be getting rid of me completely.'

'I suppose,' said Katy, a wistful tone to her voice.

At that moment we were all distracted by the sound of a truck coming to a halt on the gravel outside. Katy leapt up to peer out of the window.

'It's Ryan! He's brought the Christmas trees.'

She went running outside to greet him and threw her arms around his neck as he jumped down from the cab. He lugged the bigger of the two trees off the truck.

'I've just dropped the tree off at the pub. So where would you like this one?'

'We'll have it in the hall, please, Ryan, and the other one can go in the drawing room. Katy, show Ryan where to put them.'

'Can we decorate the trees tonight?' she asked, clapping her hands excitedly, as Ryan and Max staggered under the weight of the bigger of the two trees, leaving a trail of pine needles across the floor. 'We could listen to some carols and have a glass of Buck's Fizz while we're doing it. What do you reckon? It will be so Christmassy!'

'That's a great idea!'

In truth I was glad that Katy was so keen. The trees were huge and would need a lot of decorations and fairy lights, so it would definitely be more than a one man job. It was lucky that I'd had the foresight to pick up a load more baubles, tinsel and lights from the farm shop this afternoon.

'Won't it be fun, Mum?'

'Sounds like it, but I'll have to leave you to it, I'm afraid. I've got other plans for tonight.'

Katy's face crumpled, looking at her mum accusingly.

'You're going out? But where are you going?'

'Erm...' Rose hesitated. 'Just into the village, to the pub.'

'The Dog and Duck? But you can do that any time.'

'Yes, but I've agreed to meet up with Eric. He's not working tonight so we thought we'd have a drink and a chatter.'

'Oh... you're seeing an awful lot of him, aren't you? Are you two an item? Is that what this is all about? Don't worry, you don't need to answer that.' She held up her hand as though she didn't even want to hear her mum's answer. 'I don't suppose you'd tell me even if you were. You don't seem to want to tell me anything these days.'

'Oh, Katy, you're being unfair. And not that it's any of your business but Eric is a friend of mine. I've just separated from my husband, it's hardly as if I'm about to rush into another relationship.'

Ryan was back again with another tree in his possession, hovering awkwardly, suddenly aware that he might have arrived in the middle of yet another argument between Katy and her mum.

'Where's this one going then, Katy?' He asked cheerily.

But she totally ignored him, intent as she was on saying her piece to her mum.

'Just through there,' I said to Ryan, pointing him in the direction of the drawing room, eager to get him out of the firing line of mother and daughter.

'No. You're the one being unfair. I thought dressing the trees would be something we could do together. It might be the only opportunity we have. Who knows where we'll all be next year?'

'Katy, I didn't know that we'd be doing the Christmas decorations tonight. This is the first I've heard of it. But you're right, it would be a lot of fun. Don't worry. I'll call Eric and tell him I can't make it. He won't mind. We can always rearrange it for some other time.'

'Oh...' Katy was clearly wrong footed by Rose's change of heart. She'd been ready to have a further rant at the unfairness of it all but there was no need now. 'Are you sure?' she asked, appeasingly now.

'Yes, Katy, I'd really like to.'

With the trees in the required rooms and peace restored for the time being, I left Katy to find the boxes of decorations from the spare room while I prepared supper for us all. I rustled up a quick pasta bake made with bacon, mushrooms and cheese, along with a green salad and some garlic bread. It was a family favourite and everyone tucked in enthusiastically, including Noel. After supper, I left Rose and Katy to start the mammoth job we had in front of us while I took Noel upstairs to bathe him and put him to bed.

Later, with Noel fast asleep, I came back downstairs to find Rose and Katy had managed to untangle the fairy lights, had deposited the contents of several boxes of decorations onto the coffee table and were sitting amongst the disarray surrounded by mountains of twinkly baubles and lengths of tinsel. The trees remained resolutely bare, but they had managed to pour themselves a glass of Prosecco each, which they were sipping on, no doubt in need of a well earned rest just from the thought of all the hard work they were in for.

'You haven't got very far,' I said casually.

'Oh, we were waiting for you,' said Katy, handing me a flute of fizz, which was very welcome. 'We didn't know whether to go for something sophisticated in a single colour theme, you know, all silver or gold, or a two tone effect, red and gold perhaps, or whether to throw everything on and hope for the best?'

'I think we go for the last option,' I said, giggling. 'I don't like things to look too perfect. And if you can't go over the top at Christmas, then when can you?'

'You know what we need?' said Katy, jumping up from her seat. 'Some Michael Bublé to get us in the mood.'

'Uh-oh,' said Max. 'This might be my cue to leave, unless you particularly wanted me to stay for the tree dressing ceremony? I thought I'd take Arthur down the pub.'

'No, you go. Then when you come back again you'll see all our handi-work in its full glory.'

With Max and Arthur out of the way, and Michael Bublé warbling away in the background, we started on the task in hand. First of all we smoothed and tweaked out the branches so that the tree recovered its original shape, the scent of pine wafting around us as we worked. We draped strings of lights around the tree, three sets in total, enough to cover as much of the greenery as possible. When we turned them on we let out a collective gasp.

'I love it, I love it,' squealed Katy. 'You know, we could just leave it like that and it would be absolutely beautiful. And classy?'

Rose and I both shook our heads at that ridiculous suggestion.

'Okay, I'll go and put the rest of these lights on the other tree. Then it can be a free-for-all with the decorations.'

'Let's have a top-up first,' suggested Rose. 'This tree decoration lark is thirsty work.' She laughed, reaching for the bottle of Prosecco in the ice bucket.

That set the tone for the rest of the evening. We would do a bit, sit back to admire the prettiness, drink more wine, have a sing-song and then start all over again. I loved retrieving each of the decorations and with them the reminder from Christmases past. A lot of them were newish but some had come from my grandmother and others I had collected on my travels abroad. Every time I visited a new country I liked to pick up a Christmas decoration as a souvenir, so I was delighted when I came upon the over-sized hand-cut wooden star that I'd found in Copenhagen and then a jolly Santa Claus riding on his sleigh that I'd found at the Cologne Christmas market a few years ago. Rifling through the red hexagonal box where I kept the special decorations, I came upon the sweetest glass angel covered in silver filigree, which had been a present from Mum when she'd been living in Dubai. She'd given it to me on a visit home when she'd known we wouldn't be spending the holiday together, our first time being apart for Christmas. Back then the sight of that beautiful angel wrapped in tissue had made me emotional and just the memory evoked the same reaction in me now.

'Ooh, I've got something we can put on the tree,' said Rose, going off in search of her handbag. 'I picked it up in town today.'

She handed me a paper bag and I peeked inside, pulling out the red and gold bauble, with gold-scripted engraving on the outside.

'I know, strictly speaking, it isn't his first Christmas, but it's the first one he knows about!'

I read the words aloud, my hands running around the shiny bauble sprinkled in glitter.

'"Noel's first Christmas"! Aw, that's beautiful. Thank you, Rose. Let me find a special spot for it,' I said, placing it towards the top of the tree on one of the spiky branches so that it was clearly visible to everyone.

*Making memories.* Wasn't that what Christmas was all about? Especially now our family had grown. I took a moment, remembering the baby we lost, and how things might have been so different. Even though it wasn't to be, I knew Max and I would never forget and she would remain always in a special place in our hearts.

'What do we think about tinsel?' Katy asked, interrupting my musings. She collapsed into a heap on the sofa, draping some purple tinsel around her neck. 'Nice or naff?'

'Definitely naff, but no tree is complete without it, I think.'

'Yay!' She jumped up again and started twirling the tinsel haphazardly around the tree. Rose and I sat back and watched her at work, smiling.

'Gosh, who knew this would be so exhausting?' said Rose, laughing. 'It's been lovely though. Even if I say so myself, I think we've done an excellent job.'

'Do you think?' I asked, still uncertain. There was nothing understated or sophisticated about our multicoloured, all shining, garish tree.

'Oh yeah,' Katy sighed. 'The best tree I've ever seen.' She paused, thoughtful for a moment, and I was beginning to suspect that was what tree decorating did for you. 'Christmas in Spain wasn't really the same, was it?' She glanced across at her mum. 'We only ever had a small tree, a silver threadbare thing, which always looked a bit sorry for itself. I knew exactly how that poor tree felt. I always longed for a traditional Christmas in the cold with a big family around me. Singing carols, going to the pub and going to church.'

'Well, don't worry, we'll be doing all of those this year,' I said.

'Exactly! With just the three of us it didn't really feel like a proper cele-bration.'

'I'm sorry, Katy,' said Rose, sighing. 'You're right, it was pretty miserable at times.'

'Oh, no, I didn't mean for you to apologise. It wasn't your fault, it was... well, just the way it was.'

'I shouldn't have stayed with Alan for so long. He was a bit of a party pooper at the best of times. I suppose I was frightened to leave, didn't know how I would manage on my own, but after you left and came here I didn't have anything to stay for. I knew there was no way you would ever come back to Spain with me and I realised that everything I held dear was back in the UK.'

'Is that why you left Alan?' Katy looked genuinely shocked. 'Because of me?'

'Well, it wasn't the only reason. I didn't love Alan any more. He didn't make me happy. And I suddenly thought, don't I deserve some happiness? But you were a big factor in that decision too.'

'Oh, Mum!' Katy joined Rose on the sofa, curling up into her side and throwing an arm around her mum's waist. The sight of them together, clearly having forgotten all their disagreements for the moment, warmed my heart. 'Do you know something?' said Katy, looking up at Rose. 'I really think with the wedding and Noel's birthday and everyone being here for Christmas Day, this year really is going to be the best Christmas ever!'

As I wandered out to the kitchen to find a well deserved nightcap for us all – a suitably festive Irish cream on ice in chilled shot glasses – I couldn't help thinking that Katy might be absolutely right in her prediction.

# 26

Over the following days, every time I walked past the trees, I would do a bit of careful rearranging. Taking off a bauble here and putting it back in what I thought was a better spot, only to change it back to its original position later, or simply pinching one of the Swiss chocolate Christmas trees, unfurling the foil wrapper and popping it in my mouth. They were far too tempting to resist and would never last until Christmas!

We were all agreed that they were the most magnificent trees we had ever seen. We turned the lights on first thing in the morning and they stayed on until late at night, twinkling their gorgeous festiveness all day long. When I'd brought Noel down the next morning and showed him the trees his face had lit up in wonder and his arms had reached out, his little fingers grasping to feel their branches and the shiny glistening baubles.

Christmas had definitely arrived at Braithwaite Manor.

'Here, look at this,' I said to Max over breakfast later in the week after the postman had been, handing over a thick wad of cards. 'This one's from Fliss. She's going for it. She's arranged to take over the cafe from her aunt and uncle in the new year. Just for six months, a trial period to see how it works on both sides. Good for her. I'm so pleased she's got something sorted out!'

'Me too. In that case, we'll definitely have to make plans to go back.

Maybe March time when the weather's a little better?'

'Yes, a belated honeymoon. I bet she'll make a huge success of it.'

Max glanced at his watch, came across and kissed me on the back of my neck, before blowing a raspberry on Noel's cheek as he sat in his high chair.

'I need to get going. We've got a full day ahead of us at the pub.'

'How's it going?'

'Oh, you know how it is,' he said vaguely. 'We've had some issues, the normal problems that crop up, but we're getting there.' He softened his words with a smile, but I had no clue really how it was and thought it best not to ask further questions. Max was putting in so many hours to get the barn completed in time for the wedding and I couldn't help feeling guilty about the additional pressure this was putting on him. It wasn't the only job he had on and I knew he was spending his days darting from one site to another, trouble-shooting. He rarely spoke in detail about his work but I could always tell when he was stressed because he became quiet and distracted.

'You'll be glad to see the back of that barn, won't you?'

'Well, I'll be glad when it's done because that'll mean it's almost our wedding day.'

Another couple of weeks' hard graft and it would all be worth it. Then Max would be able to have a proper well earned rest over the Christmas period.

He ruffled my hair and was about to leave when the phone rang. He gestured to me to stay where I was and picked it up.

'Veronica?'

Immediately my heart leapt in my chest. Mum and Dad were due home tonight and I couldn't wait to see them to hear all about their trip. I'd had a succession of texts with photos showing me what a wonderful time they'd been having, so why was she calling now?

'What?' Max said now, his brow furrowed with concern. 'Right. But he's okay? Which hospital? Yep, yep, I'll tell her. A-ha, and let us know when you've got any more news.'

'Oh, my God,' I said when Max put the phone down, jumping up out of my seat. 'The hospital? What's happened?'

Before they'd left, Dad had looked the healthiest and happiest since his diagnosis and he'd just sailed through his latest check-up. I couldn't believe something had gone quite so wrong in the space of a few days.

'He's broken his ankle.'

'What?' I felt almost relieved that it wasn't anything else. 'That's awful. How on earth did he manage that?'

'I don't know, your mum didn't say, but they're at the hospital now. He's got to have an operation. It's not a straightforward break, apparently.'

'Oh, no!' Just when I'd thought everything was going smoothly. I supposed it had to be too good to be true to expect no further hitches in the run-up to the wedding. 'Is he in a lot of pain? Did Mum say? She'll be in a right panic. What should I do? Do you think I need to go over there?'

'No, let's just wait and see. Your mum was in a bit of a hurry because they were just about to get him ready for surgery. I think she just wanted to let us know what had happened. She said she'd phone us just as soon as she knows any more.'

I sank back down in my seat, not really believing this could have happened. Hadn't Dad had more than his fair share of bad luck recently? What was supposed to be the trip of a lifetime had ended with an impromptu stay in a hospital in France and who knew how long they would keep him in for? One thing was for sure, they would never make the train home this evening.

'What's Mum going to do? She'll have to find somewhere to stay and arrange transport back again when Dad's fit enough to travel. Whenever that might be.'

'Don't worry, we can help with that if necessary. But they've got travel insurance and they'll advise your mum on what she needs to do.'

Max put down his keys again and went across to the kettle, flicking it on.

'No, you don't need to do that. You go. You've got enough on your plate without having to worry about me and Mum and Dad. I can look after things at this end.'

'If you're sure. But promise you'll call me if there's a problem. I'll only be down at the pub, so I can be home again in minutes if you need me.'

'I will!'

Honestly, I'd never done so much high intensity cleaning in my life. I grabbed my spray and a cloth and swooshed around everything in sight.

Worktops, the sink, and oven, the insides of cupboards, anything to stop me brooding over what had happened to Dad. How did he do it? I wondered. Such bad luck and on their special anniversary trip too, just when they thought they were getting their lives back on track. Dad couldn't have picked a worse time if he'd tried, what with the wedding and Christmas coming up.

Thankfully, just when I was running out of things to clean and was considering whether or not I ought to bathe the dogs, Mum rang back to give me an update.

'He's just come out of the operating theatre and a nurse has said everything went as it should.'

'Phew, what a relief.'

'We'll have to see how he gets on over the next few hours. I'm hoping we might be able to get home tomorrow or the next day but we'll have to see what the doctors say. I've been in touch with the insurance company and I've got a hotel lined up for tonight so there's nothing for you to worry about there. It's a nuisance, but your dad's okay and that's the main thing.'

It was, but I hated being so far away and not being able to see for myself how Dad was. I wanted to look into both their eyes and give them a big hug. Mum was putting on a brave face but this would have unsettled her terribly. The sooner they got home, the better.

'All right, Mum, but anything at all, then please call us.'

After I'd put the phone down, I flicked on the kettle to make a much needed mug of tea and was just pulling out a mug from the cupboard when Katy came sauntering into the kitchen from upstairs, pulling a hoodie over her shoulders.

'Ellie, are you not ready? You haven't forgotten, have you? We're meant to be there in ten minutes. Oh, what's happened?' she said, seeing my dazed expression. 'There's nothing wrong, is there?'

'Oh, shit!' I said, glancing at my watch.

We were meant to be going to Caroline's for the final fitting of the dresses, but all thought of that had gone straight out of my mind when we'd received the telephone call.

Katy gave me a questioning look.

'Sorry, it's just that we've heard from my mum. Dad's only gone and broken his ankle in France.'

'Oh, no! Is he all right?'

'Fingers crossed. He's had to have an operation. They've said it's gone well but I think they want to keep him in overnight, so we're waiting to hear when he can come out and get home again.'

'Do you want me to phone Caroline and tell her what's happened? See if we can do it another day?'

I wasn't really in the mood now, but, thinking about it, there was nothing I could do here and Mum had my telephone number if she needed to contact me.

'No, there's no need. It's probably best if I get out and do something, take my mind off what's happened.'

'What are you going to do with Noel? Are we taking him with us?'

'No, your mum's offered to have him. I think I can hear her coming down now.'

There was no point in sitting at home brooding. Besides, we were running out of time. Getting all of us there today for the fitting had been difficult enough. Trying to rearrange it would be nigh on impossible.

Caroline, Mum and Dad's next-door neighbour and close friend, could hardly believe the news when I told her.

'Your poor dad. He's not having a lot of luck, is he?'

'No, I think he'll be glad to see the back of this year but at least he's had his op now.' I was trying to appear calm and rational, even if inside I was a wobbly mess. 'It could have been a whole lot worse, I know. I'll just feel happier when I've seen him for myself.'

'You look a bit fraught,' said Caroline, 'and I'm really not surprised after the morning you've had. What you need is a glass of champagne. A bride and her bridesmaids need to be totally relaxed and feeling beautiful before trying on their dresses, otherwise there's no point.'

Caroline could be very persuasive when she wanted to be and, to be honest, I was in need of something to soothe my frazzled nerves, so I gratefully accepted the flute of bubbles. It was so lovely to be amongst my best friends knowing that the next time we were all together in our finery would be the day of the wedding. Polly gave me a hug.

'Here's to your dad,' she said, raising her glass to me. 'Wishing him a speedy recovery.'

'He knows how to pick his moments, doesn't he?' I said, able to laugh about it for the first time. 'I was hoping we wouldn't have any more hiccups in the run-up to the wedding but obviously until I get down that aisle and get that ring on my finger I can't take anything for granted.'

'Have you seen the weather forecast for that weekend?' Sasha asked. 'I had a look online today.'

'No, don't tell me,' I said, groaning. 'Torrential rain and thunderstorms?'

It wouldn't surprise me. An image of me soaked through and perishing cold, shivering in my wedding gown, resembling a drenched scarecrow, sprang into my mind. Not really the look I was going for.

'Heavy snow showers, apparently. We could be in for another white Christmas.'

'Surely not,' said Josie with an exaggerated sigh. 'Nothing could beat last year. Do you remember, Ellie? I'd never seen anything like it. It was so thick and heavy outside that we were all snowed in. The whole village looked like a winter wonderland.'

'How could I forget? I mean, I would never have chosen to give birth in the barn, but I suppose, looking back now, it was rather special. Not everyone can say their baby was born in the middle of a snowstorm on Christmas Day.'

'Well, I really hope it doesn't snow because I'm not sure how we'll manage in our heels,' said Polly.

'Hmm, maybe I need to buy us a pair of wellies each, just in case,' I said, seriously considering it.

'Or get the boys lined up to give us a piggyback through the churchyard,' joked Sasha.

'Why did I ever think it would be a good idea to get married in December?' I asked, with a wry smile.

'You know, it's going to be practically perfect in every way,' said Polly in her best Mary Poppins impression. 'And whatever the weather, we'll make sure you have the best day ever.'

After we'd finished our drinks and cleared them away, Caroline said, 'Right, shall we get these dresses tried on? I'll help you slip into yours, Ellie.'

We went behind the modesty screen where my dress was hanging up on one of the panels and I gasped at the sight of it. I'd already seen the finished article and tried it on so I knew how it looked, and how it felt against my skin, but I was still blown away by the sheer elegance of it. In a fetching ivory colour, the dress swept to the floor. With a high rounded neck and long mesh sleeves, the lace bodice was adorned with sequins, giving a shimmering frosted effect, and I honestly believed it was the most stunning dress I'd ever seen. I quickly wriggled out of my clothes, impatient to try it on again. Caroline held it open and I stepped into the glorious creation carefully. She painstakingly did up the myriad bridal buttons at the back and I turned to face my reflection in the mirror.

'Oh, my goodness!' My hand flew to my mouth. 'I just love it.' I twirled around on the spot, admiring the dress from all angles. 'And you're absolutely right – I feel so beautiful in it. You're so clever, Caroline. I knew what I had in mind for my dress but you've taken that idea and transformed it into something I couldn't even imagine. It's wonderful.'

For a moment I was transported to St Cuthbert's church, imagining Max's reaction when he would first see me on our wedding day at the top of the aisle. A shiver of delicious anticipation ran down my spine.

Caroline was looking into the mirror from behind me, not saying a word, and I wondered for a moment if there was something she wasn't happy with, something she might want to change. 'Caroline?' I turned to look at her and then realised. 'Don't you dare!' I chastised her, recognising the moistness in her eyes. 'You'll set me off.'

She was dabbing at her eyes with a tissue now, her cheeks flushed with emotion.

'I can't help myself,' she said, waving a hand in front of her face. 'I've known you since you were a girl and watched you grow up into the wonderful woman you are today. You know how long I've been waiting to make your wedding dress and although I've joshed you about it over the years I never took it for granted that you would ask me. At one time I thought you might opt for a top London designer and I wouldn't have blamed you.'

'Never! In my mind there was only ever one person for the job.'

'Well, it's been a privilege.'

'Oh, Caroline!' I was filled with gratitude, so happy that the dress had exceeded my expectations. 'I'd hug you but I'm too afraid I might mark this dress.'

'Come on, Ellie,' grumbled Polly from the other side of the screen. 'We want to see!'

I took a tentative step out from behind the screen to be met with four expectant faces looking at me, their expressions lighting up in delight, almost as one.

'That is stunning!' swooned Sasha.

'Wow! I've never seen anything like it. You look gorgeous!' gasped Polly.

'Such a beautiful dress!' sighed Josie.

'Max is going to fall in love with you all over again when he sees you in that dress.'

I bit on my lip, touched by their heartfelt reactions. 'Aw, Katy, that's such a lovely thing to say. I just wish the wedding was tomorrow now, so I could wear this for real.' I twirled around on the spot, feeling so happy and pretty, wishing I could bottle that feeling and hang onto it forever. 'Anyway, it's your turn, girls. I need to see you all in your bridesmaids' dresses.'

Caroline handed me the faux fur stole while the others went to try on their dresses. I threw the stole around my shoulders, snuggling into its cosy warmth, although I knew it would only provide the most minimal protection from the elements, especially if we were in for the heavy snow showers Sasha had mentioned. Still, we wouldn't be outside for long, although I wasn't sure my strappy ivory shoes would last even the shortest distance.

'Da-da! What do you think?'

Polly, Sasha, Josie and Katy paraded in their velvet dresses, striking poses and pulling faces, but even their silly antics couldn't detract from the gorgeousness of their suitably festive, lush, verdant green outfits. The dresses managed to flatter each of them in turn and even Josie was surprised at how good she looked as she assessed her reflection in the mirror.

'Hey, that's not bad considering my legs haven't seen daylight for about three years, but, yes, I love it!' She screwed up her face excitedly in the mirror. 'Ethan won't know what's happened to his wife.'

'You look stunning,' I said, squeezing her hand.

Sasha, who was tall and willowy, carried it off with her usual casual elegance, looking effortlessly stylish. Polly was radiant, the dress caressing her now visible bump, accentuating all her lovely curves and highlighting the bloom of her skin. And Katy? The grungy teenager who spent her entire time in jeans and a sweatshirt? Well, I'd never seen her looking so stunning. It took my breath away to see her looking so grown-up and graceful and anticipating how Rose and Max would react when they saw her. I ran my hands over the velvety fabric of her dress and gave her a little squeeze.

'You all look amazing. I am one lucky bride to have you girls as my bridesmaids and I hope you all know, each one of you individually, how much you really mean to me. My wedding day wouldn't be the same without you all there. And you too, Caroline.' I threaded my hand into hers. 'What you've created here, and in such a short space of time too, is nothing less than incredible. I mean it.'

'It's all my pleasure. Anyway,' she said, taking a big restorative breath and bustling around us like a mother hen, 'let's get you out of these dresses then and get them safely stored away for the big day. We don't want any more accidents at this stage!'

Afterwards, keen not to break up the party atmosphere, someone suggested going to the pub for another bottle of fizzy. I'd intended to pop in anyway because I wanted to see Eric to tell him the news about Dad but now I had the perfect excuse to stay a little while with my friends.

'How on earth did your dad manage that?' Eric asked, genuinely concerned, after he'd sorted us out with our drinks order. 'He's supposed to be out there enjoying himself, not doing himself serious damage. Do you think he's trying to outdo me or something?'

I chuckled at the reminder of Eric's accident when carrying the Belgian beers up from the cellar. It had put him out of action for weeks and meant he couldn't make the charity trip to France that we'd organised. Instead, Max had stepped in to take his place and I'd often wondered since if we would ever have got together if it hadn't been for that trip. Perhaps it was one of those things that was simply meant to be.

'I don't know what he's been up to,' I said, brought back to the moment.

'I couldn't believe it when Mum phoned. It couldn't have come at a worse time.'

'He'll be all right, love. Obviously he's going to have a tricky couple of months ahead of him, but he'll get over it.'

'I suppose so,' I said, feeling compelled to check my phone just in case there was any more news from Mum. No news was good news.

'Well, you do know if your dad's not fit enough to walk you down the aisle, then I'm more than happy to step in to do the honours,' he said with a big grin.

'Oh, Eric! Thank you, but I hadn't even considered that. What an idiot I am! He won't be able to give me away, will he? Not with his leg in plaster.'

'I was only joshing you. He'll manage somehow, you'll see.' Eric was clearly trying to allay my fears but I was concerned how Dad would be able to negotiate the uneven terrain of the churchyard in the good weather, let alone without the possibility of snow.

While I adored Eric and was touched by his offer I couldn't even entertain the idea. After everything he'd been through, it was so important to me to have my dad at my side, and I knew it was equally important to him too. It wasn't every day you got to give your only daughter away.

'Are you all right, Ellie?' The girls had been giggling, making their usual racket, which was inevitable when they all got together and there was drink involved. I'd been lost in my thoughts, wondering what we might be able to do to make things easier for Dad on the day, but I shook the thoughts away, bringing myself back to the moment.

'Are you all ready for Christmas?' Josie asked me, trying to pull me back into the conversation.

'Yes, pretty much.' All the cards had been written and sent. All the presents bought with just a couple left to wrap. The turkey, goose and vegetables had been ordered from Beck's Farm Shop, who would be delivering our provisions on Christmas Eve. The champagne was already on ice and Braithwaite Manor was adorned with garlands, holly and ivy, mistletoe, fairy lights and glitter, waiting in breathless sparkly anticipation for the big day.

Christmas would be absolutely fine. All I had to worry about now was whether or not we'd all be fit and ready for the wedding day.

## 27

It was another four days of anxious waiting and phone calls before we saw Mum and Dad again. Max collected them from the railway station in London late one night and took them, weary and very relieved, back to their cottage. The following day Max was at No. 2 Ivy Lane Cottages, bundled them into the car and brought them along to Braithwaite Manor for a welcome home lunch.

When I saw Dad I hugged him so tight I was worried that he might topple over.

'All this fuss, there's really no need,' he said, laughing as he hobbled through the kitchen on his crutches on his way over to the farmhouse carver chair we'd put out for him. We'd also found a padded blanket box for him to rest his leg on.

'We've been so worried about you,' I told him, placing a mug of coffee within easy reach on the table. Mum nodded.

'I can't tell you how worried I was, Ellie, but the hospital were brilliant and the insurance company helped out with all the practicalities. Good job I could remember a smattering of French from when I used to au-pair there, many moons ago.'

It was so lovely to hear Mum's laugh tinkling around the kitchen again.

'You've been brilliant too, Mum.'

'Oh, she has. I don't know what I would have done without her,' said Dad, affectionately.

I glanced across at Mum, amazed at how well she'd handled the situation. Before Dad had fallen ill with cancer, he had been the driving force in the relationship, taking responsibility for most things around the home and providing a steadying and reassuring presence as head of the family. We'd always thought him invincible but in recent months Mum had needed to step up and be the strong one. Although she would never have wished for any of this to happen, it was inspiring to see how she'd grown as a person and proved to everyone, but mostly herself, just what she was capable of.

'Fancy doing so much damage by just falling off the kerb,' said Arthur.

'I know,' said Rose. 'It doesn't seem possible.'

'Ah, well, what we may not have mentioned was how your father came to fall off the kerb in the first place.'

'Dad?' I asked him, curiously.

'Yes, well, it was just a silly accident. One of those things. Could have happened to anyone.'

'Anyone trying to do an Argentinian tango down a Parisian boulevard, you mean?'

'What?' said Katy, screwing up her face in disbelief, spluttering at the thought.

'I was just trying a few dance moves out on Veronica.' Now we all looked at him disbelievingly. Was this really my dad talking? He carried on, and we were all agog. 'We'd been to a show in one of these revue places and it was jolly good. They had a sultry singer and a bit of burlesque going on and then some tango dancing. Oh, my goodness, it was so very passionate and romantic! I suppose the mood overtook me and when we got outside I wondered how easy it would be to recreate those moves. You know, where they snake their lovely long legs around each other and play footsie.'

'Oh, good grief,' I muttered. I was as big a fan of *Strictly* as anyone, but while I could easily imagine some swarthy latino dancer doing those intimate and passionate moves, it wasn't so easy picturing my dad doing the same thing.

'Ha ha,' spluttered Katy.

'You know what's coming, don't you?' said Mum.

'I'm still not sure how it happened. One minute I was in a romantic clinch with my wife and the next I'd tripped over her feet and landed on my side. I heard the crack in my leg as I hit the deck.'

'Silly sod,' said Mum, shaking her head disparagingly. 'It was a good job he didn't take me over with him or we could both have been out of action.'

'All I was doing was trying to keep the romance alive, sweetheart.'

'That's hilarious,' said Katy. 'God, parents can be so embarrassing, can't they?' This was delivered with a pointed but affectionate look at her mum. 'You think they'll grow out of their embarrassing ways, but if anything they just get worse with age.'

'Er, thank you, young lady, but I've got to an age where I'm not going to be apologetic for who I am. Why should we, eh?'

I noticed the conspiratorial glance between Mum and Rose. Perhaps there was something in the water around here because there'd been a similar change in Rose in recent weeks. She was standing up for herself more and had a new resolve in her eyes.

'Too true,' said Dad, chuckling.

'I'm just glad we got home in time for the wedding and for Christmas,' said Mum. 'That's all that really matters.'

Mum was currently balancing Noel on her knee, who was obviously in complete agreement with her as he jibber-jabbered happily.

'I'm worried about how you'll manage, Dad. Are you in a lot of pain?'

'A bit, but as long as I keep taking the pills I'll be absolutely fine. Don't you worry about me.'

I knew he was making light of the discomfort because every time he moved his features scrunched up in pain. The last thing he would want was anyone's sympathy, but I really wasn't sure how he would get around in the coming weeks. Mum would be waiting on him hand and foot, not that she would mind about that, but I could imagine how frustrated and impatient Dad might become over the speed of his recovery.

'You'll never manage walking me down the aisle. We might have to rethink that.'

'What? You're not being serious? Let me tell you something, Ellie. There's nothing that will stop me escorting you down that aisle. Give me another couple of days and I'll have got the hang of these crutches by then.

You'll see, I'll be whizzing all over the place. I really hope you don't think this puts a dampener on things.' He waggled his toes beneath his plaster cast.

'No, I didn't mean that but I don't want you feeling under any pressure. Honestly, I don't care if you have to travel down the aisle in a supermarket trolley. I just want you there, Dad.'

'Well, in that case we're sorted,' he said, with a sincere smile. 'So, come on, fill us in on all the news. What's been happening in Little Leyton in our absence?'

'Well, Max has been working flat out on the barn and I've been getting everything organised for the wedding and Christmas and Noel's birthday. I think I'm almost there. I really don't want any more last minute panics.'

'Knowing you, you'll have thought of everything, and if you haven't, well, it won't really matter. As long as you two turn up on the day and there's drink and food for the hungry masses, then I don't think you'll have anything to worry about.'

'Thanks, Mum. You're absolutely right. I said from the very beginning that it was going to be a relaxed, laid back affair but it's funny how you can get carried away and start thinking, do I need some gold rimmed plates or fireworks or performing acrobats?'

Everyone laughed.

'I used to be able to do back flips when I was a boy,' said Arthur. 'I could always give it a go if you wanted me to.'

'Don't you dare,' I told him. 'I don't want any more accidents before the big day. Do you think we could manage that between us?'

'Ooh, well, I don't suppose you will have heard my news,' Rose said, addressing Mum and Dad. 'I'll be moving on from the manor soon.'

'Really? Oh, Rose. Just when we've got used to having you around here. I hope you won't be going too far?'

'No, actually, not far at all. I'm moving down to Lilac Cottage in the village. I'm not going until after Christmas but it will be good to make a fresh start in the new year.'

'You'll be around the corner from us, then. You know you're always welcome to pop in to see us.'

'Thanks, Veronica. I will definitely take you up on that.'

'Hmm, we're going to miss having you around here, Rose,' said Arthur. The two of them were confidants, often sharing a coffee and a catch-up. 'Aren't we, Katy?'

Katy nodded, twisting her mouth to hide her emotion.

'Yes, well, I'm not sure why Mum's in such a hurry to move out, it must be me, but if that's what she wants to do...' Katy spoke airily, as if she wasn't bothered one way or the other. For so long she'd been prickly around her mother, forever provoking her, but recently the tensions had dissipated, and the pair of them were often found snuggled up on the sofa together or having a hug.

'It's for the best, Katy, and it's not as though I'm going very far. You'll be able to pop in at any time and there's a spare bedroom at the cottage so if you ever want to stay, then you'll always be very welcome.'

'I suppose so. It's good you're not going far though,' she said, smiling, accepting the hug her mum gave her. 'I've got used to having you around again.'

The season of goodwill was already working its magic. Was it really possible that we would get through the wedding and the holidays without any further mishaps or fallings out?

# 28

'Look, Noel, what do you think?' I carried my boy in my arms out into the garden, the dogs running at our side, their excitement palpable as their noses tracked the ground and their paws jumped through the thick white snow. Sasha had been right in her weather forecast but we still had a few days to go until the wedding. Although it looked picturesque and festive there was a part of me that hoped it would all clear up in time for the weekend. It would be no fun whatsoever to have my beautiful wedding dress trailing through mucky slush.

Noel wriggled in my arms, clearly desperate to get down to investigate the white magical frosting for himself. I placed him firmly on his feet, and he wobbled, steadying himself, his face lighting up with the wonder of it all. His big brown eyes grew large and he chattered away excitedly. He tried to move forward, reaching out for the snow, but his wellies and his snowsuit thwarted his progress and he fell with a thud onto his bottom.

'Ooh dear,' I said, laughing. 'Up you get.' And he took my hand, joining in with the laughter.

He'd been walking for a month or so now and ordinarily could make rapid progress across a room, but now, with all these outdoor obstacles to contend with, it was as though he was having to learn all over again.

I took a moment to look around at the landscape. It was breathtakingly beautiful, the sight making me gasp. The air stung at my cheeks and despite the many layers I was wearing, including double pairs of socks and thick mittens, the ends of my fingers and toes tingled with the cold. I wiggled them in a futile attempt to warm them up but I am a chilly mortal at the best of times. The fields in the distance were swathed in thick blankets of snow and the trees dusted in an icing sugar coating.

Noel chuckled at the dogs' antics as they frolicked around us, rubbing their backs into the snow. Their noses burrowed deep into the ground and when they came up for air their snouts were covered in a white frosting. They were so comical, shaking their heads to try and get rid of the snow, but clearly relishing every moment of being out in the wintry conditions. Noel fell over again, but this time made no attempt to get up. He sat, perfectly content, patting at the snow, banging his feet up and down. I crouched down beside him and gathered the snow around me, letting the soft powder fall through my fingers onto Noel's legs. He watched, transfixed, trying to catch it as it fell. Then we formed snowballs together and I threw them into the distance for the dogs to chase after, making Noel laugh all the more.

Back inside, after we'd got rid of all our wet clothes and I'd handed Noel over to Rose, who'd volunteered to go and change him, I dried the dogs with their towels and they disappeared off to find a warm spot next to the Aga or a radiator where they could curl up for the afternoon after all their frenetic activity outside.

Wandering into the kitchen, I could barely see the kitchen table as it was covered with wrapping paper, gift boxes, bows and ribbons and carrier bags full of presents. Katy had broken up from college now for the Christmas holidays and was in full wrapping mode.

'Sorry about the mess,' she said, laughing. 'Do you want me to move it?'

'No, don't worry, we can eat at the table in the conservatory.'

'We've had a lot of wrapping to do, haven't we, Arthur?' Katy said.

'Oh, yes, and I'm so glad you've been here to help me. My fat thumbs can't get to grips with that sticky tape at all and I've never been very good at wrapping presents. They always look a mess when I do it, but you've got the knack, Katy.'

'Ha ha, I'm very happy to be your little helper, Arthur.'

Not only had she wrapped all of Arthur's presents but she'd been out to buy them for him too. They'd sat down together and come up with a list, and she'd done all his shopping, making him feel part of the whole Christmas experience. Arthur and his late wife, Marge, had always bought me a Christmas annual and a selection box each year when I was little and it was still one of my favourite memories of Christmas as a child. So much so that I had bought Noel an annual and a selection box for his stocking, setting up a tradition that we would follow for years to come.

Rose warmed up the potato and leek soup that I'd made yesterday and there was home made sourdough bread too. We sat around the table in the conservatory, the soup warmly comforting after the bitter cold outside. The views overlooking the garden were lovely. There was a little red robin who perched on the bird table, searching for crumbs, right outside the window, who kept us entertained for ages.

'How's Max getting on down at the pub?' Arthur asked. 'Will there be a wedding after all?'

He was laughing but his comment touched a nerve.

'I do hope so!' I sighed. 'They've been held up because of different problems and now this weather hasn't helped but I'm still hoping the barn will be finished in time for the weekend. If not, well, we'll all have to cram everyone into the pub. I don't think a marquee would be such a good choice in these conditions.'

It had seemed so important to hold the reception in the barn, the home of so many happy occasions over recent years, when it was out of action, but now the wedding was almost upon us it didn't seem nearly as important, although now would not be the right time to mention that to Max. The fire at the pub and the subsequent renovation had involved a lot of time and hard work and I would be relieved when it was finished, yes, to have the barn up and running again, but mainly to have Max back. It had definitely been a pressure he could have done without.

Rose went to fetch the mince pies that had been heating up in the oven and brought them in on a tray along with a jug of custard and one of cream. She handed out bowls and spoons and I thought for the briefest moment of resisting the temptation, thinking of the dress I had to squeeze into on Saturday, but the scent of mixed fruits, spices and brandy was far too alluring. Besides, when I'd tried the dress on there'd been just enough mince pie room. I suspected Caroline had made the dress that way specially. I mean, it was Christmas after all.

'Are you feeling nervous for the big day?' Rose asked.

'Not nervous. Excited, and a little bit apprehensive too, hoping that everything goes off as it should, but I'm sure it will. I still can hardly believe that in a few days' time I really will be Mrs Golding. It has a lovely ring to it, don't you think?'

'You've got a lovely ring already,' joshed Katy, picking up my hand to look again at my engagement ring. 'And, just think, you'll be the official lady of the manor then,' said Katy, teasing me. 'I hope all this doesn't change you and you start bossing us all around.'

'That would never happen. Not with our Ellie. She's far too lovely,' said Arthur, backing my corner in the face of Katy's teasing.

'Something smells good.'

Max wandered into the kitchen right at that moment.

'Hello, love, you're just in time for some lunch,' said Rose. 'Would you like some soup?'

'Please, if there's some going.'

'We were just talking about the reception,' I said, thickly buttering a slice of bread. 'I was just saying how we could always use the pub for the reception if the barn doesn't get finished in time.'

'What? Are you kidding? After me and the guys have busted a gut to get the place done.' Max scolded me with a look. 'No way, Ellie. We're having our reception in that barn if it's the last thing I do!'

Out of Max's sight, I grimaced at Rose and Katy. I really hoped it wouldn't come to that.

'Max?' I hadn't intended to annoy him but it was hardly surprising he was rattled. He was exhausted and stressed, working every hour of the day, not the best preparation for the run-up to your wedding. I'd put too much pressure on him to get the barn completed when it hadn't been necessary. I'd been thinking of myself, what I wanted for my special day, but did it really matter? Not when it was negatively impacting on Max and his well-being. How could I possibly explain that to him now though? It was far too late.

'I don't want you working yourself into the ground, Max. It isn't worth it,' was all I managed to say.

Max didn't respond, he just seemed lost in his own thoughts as he contemplated his soup. I wondered what had gone wrong down at the barn today. A major issue that had put the whole project into jeopardy or a minor one that had simply sent Max over the edge. Would he even tell me if I asked?

'Oh, Ells, of course it's worth it,' he said, after what seemed a lifetime. 'It's what you want, isn't it?'

'Yes, but—'

'No buts,' he said, his face breaking out into a smile. 'It's all done,' he said matter of factly, going back to the more pressing matter of his soup. He pulled off a chunk of bread from the loaf and dunked it in his bowl, his tongue running around the edge of his mouth, cleaning his lips. 'We're all ready for Saturday.' I looked at him, aghast. 'Honestly, Ellie, I don't know why you ever doubted me in the first place.'

'Really? You've finished?'

He nodded.

'Ugh, you... so and so.' I'd thought of something much worse to call him, but didn't think it entirely appropriate, not with his mother and his son being in the same room. 'And you let me witter on like that thinking we'd have to make do in the pub?'

He laughed, but I could hardly be cross with him, not when he'd worked so hard to get the barn completed in time.

'That's brilliant, Max, thank you!' I leapt up to give him a hug.

Later that afternoon we went down to The Dog and Duck so I could see for myself the result of his endeavours. Deliberately, over these last couple of weeks, I'd kept away from the building site at the back of the pub so that I wouldn't be able to fret over the progress, or lack of progress. But really I'd had no need to worry.

'Oh, Max, it's lovely, so perfect.' I couldn't find any more words, overcome as I was that we had our lovely barn back in place.

I took hold of his hand and he chuckled.

'Most women get excited about jewellery or designer shoes or handbags, but not you. It's a barn, exactly like the old one.'

'I know, but that's what I love about it. The old stock bricks make it look as though it's always been here. It's not a bolted on extension, it feels like an integral part of the main building. Just as it was before.'

If I needed any further reason why I loved this man so much, then surely this was it.

We walked through the double oak doors and inside the barn and I twirled around across the wooden floor, imagining myself doing the same thing in my wedding dress in a few days' time. Without any furniture in it looked so much bigger than before, but if I looked up at the oak beams of the ceiling, then I could rustle up the memories of all those special times that had taken place in this space over the years. None more special than the birth of our precious little boy, Noel, almost a year ago. We'd done it. We'd finally got here.

Now I had somewhere to hold our reception, a gorgeous dress, a glamorous stole, some pretty shoes (and a pair of wellies just in case), four bridesmaids, two flower girls, a father to give me away – even if he did have a gammy leg – and the most gorgeous and eligible man in Little Leyton, and probably the whole of the country too. Honestly, I had everything I needed to have the perfect village wedding that I'd always imagined.

## 29

Outside, as I'd feared, the thaw had transformed the winter wonderland landscape of Little Leyton into a grey and dreary scene with an unbecoming brown slush seeping over the pavements and roads. Still nothing, not even the uninspiring weather, could dampen my mood, not with just two days left to go until the wedding.

It was all stations go at The Dog and Duck and Braithwaite Manor. As was usual for this time of year, the pub was especially busy with Christmas revellers and had never looked prettier with the tree twinkling in the bay window, the decorations, some of which dated back to Eric's day, draped across the beams and fires crackling in both bars. On the chalkboards we were promoting our winter and festive ales, a festive fizz and an Irish cream cocktail, and just for the month of December we were also offering special Christmas dinner rolls. A white or brown bap filled with roast turkey and stuffing, sausages wrapped in bacon, and cranberry sauce. They were delicious and had been hugely popular with our customers – I'd already had three this week, all in the name of research for my customers, of course – plus there was an endless supply of Betty's marvellous mince pies on offer too.

Josie, Sasha and Katy helped me out with the preparations to turn the barn into an exquisite wedding venue. All the tableware and linen had been ready and waiting for weeks upstairs in the spare bedroom of the pub. There'd been a time when I'd wondered if we'd ever get to use it in the barn but I'd had no need for those doubts. All our original furniture and fittings had been destroyed in the fire so we'd needed to source everything anew. We'd scoured the local auctions and had found items very similar to what we'd had before. Some trestle tables that formed a horseshoe shape and long benches for which we'd had padded calico cushions made for the comfort of our guests. We polished glasses and plates, folded napkins and put together cutlery sets. Josie, Sasha and Polly had done a run to the party shop in town and had come back with black bags full of gold helium balloons, bunting and drapes, which they were keen to decorate the barn with once I was well out of the way.

'Why don't you go home?' Josie insisted. 'We can finish everything that needs doing here and if there's anything we're not sure about we can always call you. I'm sure you've got loads of other stuff to do?'

I could take a hint. I knew when I wasn't wanted. In truth, I didn't have a great deal to do at home because I'd been ahead of myself on the organisational front, and everything, I hoped, was in place now for the wedding and Christmas. Still, it would give me an opportunity to have a chat with Eric on the way out, pop in to see Mum and Dad at No. 2 Ivy Lane Cottages, before collecting some more mince pies from Betty at the tea rooms on the way home. It seemed that everyone was in a heightened state of excitement and anticipation for my wedding day.

The next day, Jennifer, a friend of Katy's from college, who was about to complete her final exams in beauty therapy, arrived at the manor to give me some beauty treatments, including a facial, a whole body massage, a manicure and a pedicure. Normally I didn't go in for a lot of pampering. Scrub that, I didn't go in for any pampering. In the summer I might make the effort to paint my toenails but that was usually as far as it went but a bride on the eve of her wedding deserved some proper pampering, so Katy told me, and I was determined to make the most of this rare opportunity. Katy and Rose were also having some treatments, as were my other bridesmaids, so it was a lovely and rare occasion to have a proper girly day, which inevitably would involve lots of laughter and Prosecco.

Max wandered in at one point but, faced with a gaggle of gossiping and giggling girls and catching the whiff of acetone in the air, he made his excuses and left.

'Arthur and I have got some last minute shopping to do so we're going to head into town, if there's anything you want?' I shook my head. 'Okay, well, have fun. We'll see you later.'

I suspected shopping meant a quick dash into the supermarket to buy a newspaper, followed by a long leisurely pint or two over a roast turkey bap at The Dog and Duck. Still, some male bonding would do them both the power of good.

Much later, when we were all primped and preened, we hugged each other tight, saying our goodbyes, gabbling excitedly about the big day tomorrow. Josie, Sasha and Polly were pulling on their coats when Sasha took a peek outside through the window.

'Look, Ellie! Can you believe it? It's actually snowing again! What did I tell you?'

I joined Sasha, pressing my forehead against the window pane and expecting to see a light flurry of snow dancing outside, but not a chance. Thick flakes fell from the sky relentlessly, settling on the ground and looking as though they weren't about to stop any time soon.

'You really are going to have a white wedding, in every sense of the word,' said Josie.

'Goodness me, you ought to go, before it gets any worse out there. Go on,' I said, shooing them outside. 'And be careful out there. I want all my bridesmaids in one piece tomorrow.'

I watched them go, hanging onto each other for dear life, giggling as they slipped on the snowy ground, their torchlight paving their way into the distance. I couldn't have arranged this if I'd tried but there was absolutely nothing I could do about the weather so there was no point in fretting about it. Max's Jeep must have passed the girls on their way home because moments later he pulled into the driveway and jumped out.

'It's mad out there already. Good job we don't have far to go tomorrow for the wedding.'

'Oh, crikey. It'll be okay, won't it, Max?' I asked, feeling a momentary sense of panic flutter in my chest.

'Of course it will. All we've got to do is get you and me to the church on time, and Trish Evans, and then we've got a wedding on our hands. Never mind anybody else.'

He chuckled, clearly amused by himself, as he trudged through the snow round to the passenger door to let Arthur out. I ventured outside to take Arthur's other arm, and we trod very carefully back indoors.

For supper I'd prepared a simple meal of baked salmon with sautéed potatoes and green beans, and Max and I, Katy, Rose and Arthur sat at the conservatory table watching the steady onset of the snow. I craned my head to look right up at the night sky, remembering when I'd done the same thing as a child, wondering where Father Christmas might be up amongst the stars, imagining the times over the coming years when we'd be doing the same thing with Noel.

After dinner, Rose and Arthur retired to their bedrooms and Katy went to check on Noel before settling in the drawing room to watch *The Holiday*, for what must have been the umpteenth time this year.

Max and I lingered over our wine and then a mug of coffee, happy to sit and watch the mesmerising effect of the snowflakes. I was just thinking I should really get up and clear the table when the phone rang. I jumped up, thinking it was bound to be someone asking after the arrangements for tomorrow, and was surprised to hear Dan on the end of the line.

'Is Max around? He's not answering his mobile.' There were no niceties, no asking after my well-being and no lightness of tone in Dan's voice, as I might have expected on the eve of my wedding.

'One minute.' I passed the phone over and as soon as I saw Max's stony expression, it confirmed that Dan couldn't be ringing with good news.

'Right. Okay. I'll be straight down.'

'What? What's happened?' I asked, when Max came off the phone, wondering what could be so urgent. 'You're not going out now, surely?'

'I have to, Ellie,' he said, sounding resigned. 'Apparently there's a problem down at the barn.'

'But we're getting married tomorrow.' As if he might have overlooked that small fact. 'What sort of a problem?'

'I'm not sure,' he said, pulling on his jacket and grabbing the Jeep keys from the hook. 'As soon as I know anything, I'll let you know.'

'But, Max...?' It was too late. Max had dashed outside and I heard the

Jeep's throaty rumble as it came to life. Luckily, Max had only had a small glass of wine but I was still worried about him driving in these treacherous conditions. What on earth could have happened that needed dealing with right now?

I peered out into the darkness, not really believing that something else could go wrong and at the eleventh hour before our wedding too. We'd been enjoying a moment of calm and mellow reflection together before all the excitement of tomorrow and now Max had to rush out into the cold dark night. Not wanting to think about it and all the dreadful scenarios my mind wanted to explore, I busied myself clearing the table and filling the dishwasher and wiping the surfaces down. I made myself another coffee and sat down at the kitchen table, staring at my phone, willing it to ring. Flora, who'd been curled up in her basket by the Aga, came over and placed her front paws on my knees, clearly sensing something was wrong.

'Oh, Flora. What do you think's happened?' She thumped her tail at me, her big brown eyes looking up at me beseechingly. She'd grown so much in the time she'd been with us. I thought back to that day when Max had brought her home and she'd run riot in the kitchen, scooting around wildly, chasing the other dogs out of their beds and nibbling on my shoes. She'd been a whirlwind but I'd fallen in love with her even before I'd known about the message Max had engraved on her name tag. It was the most romantic proposal I could ever have imagined. It would be heart-breaking, after everything we'd been through, to think that something could go wrong at the very last moment.

Katy had gone to bed half an hour ago and, with still no news from Max, I couldn't bear it any longer. I picked up the phone and tapped in Silke's number, reckoning she was the most likely one to tell me honestly what was going on. With the last of the customers gone, they should be cashing up now so what could Max possibly have been doing all this time?

'Hi, Ellie. Yes, Max is here, they're outside in the barn. Something to do with a leak in the roof. Where it's been snowing I think it's... Oh, hang on, Max is here now. He's saying you're to stop worrying and get to bed. He'll be back as soon as he can.'

How on earth was I meant to stop worrying? I glanced at my watch. It was now the day of my wedding and we were supposed to have got to bed early for a relaxing night's sleep together and instead here I was waiting for my husband-to-be to come home, not knowing when he would be back again. We'd mooted the idea of spending our last night as singletons apart but we'd both quickly discarded that idea. The plan was for Max to slip away in the morning to get changed at Mum and Dad's so he wouldn't see me in my wedding dress but who knew what would happen now? At this rate, I wouldn't get any sleep and I'd be likely to turn up at the altar completely frazzled and with dark rings around my eyes.

Eventually, after what seemed like forever, I heard the Jeep turn up outside and I almost broke down with relief to have Max home again.

'What's been going on?' I asked, running to the door to greet him. 'I've been worried sick about you!'

He took me in his arms and kissed my head, his embrace making everything seem right again.

'You should be in bed,' he whispered in my ear. 'You've got a busy day ahead.'

'What happened down at the barn? Is everything okay?'

'Yep, it's fine now. We think one of the ridge tiles hadn't been affixed properly and with the weight of the snow on the roof, it had caused a huge leak. If Dan hadn't gone in there to take the red wine through when he did, then we might not have known about it until tomorrow and we could have ended up with a proper disaster on our hands.'

'And now?'

'Well, we'll need to get the roofers back on Monday, but we've done a fix which will see us through tomorrow.'

I looked at him sceptically, looking for further explanation.

'We've put a tarpaulin up and a big bucket in the barn to collect any remaining water.'

'Oh, God! How on earth did you get a tarpaulin up there in these conditions?'

'Don't ask. And don't tell Health and Safety!'

I dreaded to think what Max had done there tonight. It didn't bear thinking about but I felt sure ladders, slippery surfaces and calculated risks were involved. I shuddered. It was probably just as well I hadn't been there to see it or else I would have had a hissy fit.

'Do you know, Max, when I found out there was a problem with the barn, I wondered, after everything we'd been through this year, if someone somewhere was trying to tell us something.'

He looked at me blankly.

'How do you mean?'

'You know, if there was something in the stars suggesting that us getting married was a really bad idea? You have to admit everything that could go wrong has gone wrong.'

'Yes, but these things happen, Ellie. You can't read anything more into it than that. Something like this is only too common where building work is concerned. But these things aren't only confined to work. They happen in relationships and in life too. Problems come along and you just have to deal with them. The best way you can.'

He took my hand and squeezed it tight and I was drawn in by his dark attentive eyes. I was tired and emotional and wasn't sure I'd be able to express myself properly even if I'd wanted to. Just that with Max at my side anything seemed possible. I rested my head on his shoulder, filled with love for this man, who later today would be my husband. Yep, he was definitely a keeper.

## 30

Considering the pair of us only managed about five hours' sleep at the most, we were both remarkably fresh faced and good natured the next morning. It must have been a mix of the adrenaline, excitement, caffeine and alcohol that was pumping around my veins on account of a rather lovely breakfast, prepared by Max, of scrambled eggs and smoked salmon with a glass of Buck's Fizz, followed by a cappuccino. Well, if you couldn't be decadent and indulgent on your wedding day, then when could you be?

Peering into my reflection when I went to get ready, I saw no sign of the dark circles I'd feared. My eyes looked bright and full of hope, and my skin glowed in a way that it hadn't in a long while, no doubt down to that facial yesterday. From our bedroom my ears tuned into the chaotic goings-on downstairs, people coming and going, lots of laughter, the phone ringing. Usually I'd be at the heart of it, sorting everyone out, but today I was more than happy to relinquish the responsibility to others. Rose was looking after Noel and she'd taken him into his bedroom to get ready.

Our bedroom window had a view right across the valley, the snow covered fields stretching as far as the eye could see. It was a beautiful picture postcard scene, not perhaps the ideal weather for getting married in, but the photos would be spectacular, at least. Something to regale my grandchildren with one day. My pretty shoes wouldn't be having an airing, sadly, although I'd make sure to have some photos taken indoors with them on. The wellies – and I'd had the foresight to buy pairs for all the brides-maids – would have to do instead.

Last night, when it had become clear that the wedding would be a total white-out, Max had rung around to all our friends in the village who owned 4x4s asking for their help in arranging lifts for guests who needed them.

'I'm off now, Ells,' said Max, coming up from behind me, smiling at my reflection in the mirror.

'Oh, Max, I won't see you now until we're at the church. Can you believe it? Be warned, I'll probably burst into tears as soon as I clap eyes on you.'

'Don't worry, I'll make sure to put some tissues in my suit pocket.' He kissed the back of my neck and my legs went all wobbly. I turned my face up to his, our lips meeting lightly, an electricity sizzling between us. 'I love you, Ellie.'

'I love you too, Max.'

He was off to Mum and Dad's to get changed, taking Arthur with him, and then they would travel together to the church. Johnny would be ferrying me, Katy, Rose and Noel, while Ethan would drive Polly, Sasha and Josie the short distance to the church. Ruby and Stella would be travelling in the care of Ethan's parents.

Shortly after Max left, my gorgeous bridesmaids and flower girls arrived in a flurry of giggles and excitement, which was cause for a celebratory glass of champagne. Still, I didn't need alcohol today to give me that deli-cious light-headed feeling. I felt giddy enough without it. It had been with me ever since I woke up this morning knowing that today was the day I'd be marrying the love of my life. I couldn't imagine a time when I would ever come down off that cloud.

With our dresses on and make-up and hair complete, we had photos taken in the hall, the sweeping staircase and the crystal chandelier providing a suitably romantic background. When Rose had first seen us in our dresses she'd swooned with delight.

'You look stunning, Ellie.' She came to my side and whispered in my ear. 'You do know my son is the luckiest man in the world to be marrying you. He adores you and you make him so very happy. I think he's found a contentment now that he's been searching for a long time. Bless you, Ellie. I'm so grateful for everything you've done, not only for Max, but for Katy and me too.'

'The pleasure has been entirely mine,' I said, basking in the warm glow of affection wafting around the manor today. 'You know, in Katy, I feel like I've gained the little sister I never had, that annoying pesky one who drives you up the wall but you love dearly all the same?'

Rose chuckled.

'I know exactly what you mean.'

'And, Rose, what about us? I love how we've grown closer these last few months. I'm really pleased you've decided to stay in the village.'

'Yep, you're stuck with me now.'

With the cars waiting for us outside we all made our way to the front door, stopping for more photos, this time taken outside against the splendour of the Georgian facade of Braithwaite Manor, wellies 'n' all. We didn't hover for long as it was bitterly cold and we were glad to jump into the waiting vehicles just as soon as we could. I sat in the back with Rose and Katy either side of me, each holding a hand as I felt inexplicably nervous. Noel, dressed in smart navy trousers, white shirt and with a dove-grey waistcoat matching his daddy's outfit, was strapped into his car seat in the front.

Our progress in the car was slow and steady as the country lanes were still thick with snow and I gave a thought to all our guests, hoping that their journeys had been as trouble free as possible in the circumstances. Thankfully, most of our guests were coming from the village so at least they were within walking distance. When we pulled up by the lychgate, George, Polly's husband, was waiting to open my door, and he helped me out, greeting me with a big smile and a kiss on the cheek. Seeing Dad waiting there too, made my heart soar.

'Ellie! You look beautiful,' he said, kissing me on my cheek. 'Come on, sweetheart, let's go and do this.'

With Katy and my other bridesmaids fussing around me, making sure my dress didn't trail in the snow, we made the, by necessity, slow walk through the churchyard to the entrance of the church, Dad and I clinging onto each other, offering mutual support. In the porch we paused so that

we girls could swap our wellies for our proper shoes and I took a breather
to gather myself, overawed by what was about to come. Rose went ahead
with Noel to find her place towards the front of the church where Mum had
reserved her a seat. As we started our walk towards the aisle, nerves over-
came me and I started to giggle at the sound of Dad's crutch tapping noisily
against the tiled floor, the sound resonating around the eaves. I looked
behind me to check my dress and caught Polly's eye; she started giggling
too. I glared at her, shaking my head, urging her to stop because I knew if
we both started then neither of us would be able to stop. I bit hard on my
lip and my gaze searched out the congregation, a sea of smiling familiar
faces welcoming me, caressing me with their warmth and affectionate
glances. I was amongst friends and family here but they all merged
together as one when Max came into view. My heart jolted as his eyes met
mine and that was when the solemnity of the occasion resonated deep
within me.

To say my vows to the man I loved in front of all my friends and family
was something I'd dreamt of for ages and now it was happening. For those
moments as we gazed intently into each other's eyes, repeating the words
said aloud by Reverend Trish Evans, it was as though we were the only
people in the church, our guests only coming into focus again when
Reverend Evans urged us to kiss and a spontaneous round of applause
swept around the church.

'You are looking more beautiful than ever, Mrs Golding,' Max whispered, his mouth nuzzling into my neck, the words on his lips sounding
heavenly. 'I'm one lucky man to have made you my wife.'

'Why, thank you, Mr Golding.' Somehow I'd acquired a permanent
smile upon my face and was still hardly daring to believe my good fortune.
'The feeling is entirely mutual,' I told him, planting a kiss on his cheek.

We wafted back down the aisle on a tide of goodwill, the sound of Dad's
hobbling making everyone laugh out loud now.

Later, when we'd made the short journey through the village and drew
up outside The Dog and Duck, our friends, family and customers had gathered outside to greet us. I didn't know where to look first. There were Paul
and Caroline looking on proudly, Eric was standing with his arm around
Rose, Johnny and Sasha were holding hands and Betty and Ryan and so

many other friendly faces looked on too. And, oh, was that...? No, it couldn't be. Yes, it was! Fliss was here as well. *How?*

'I invited her along. I knew you'd love to see her. I thought it would make a nice surprise.' Max whispered in my ear by way of explanation. I turned to smile up at him in gratitude.

At the edge of the crowd I spotted Darcy, looking unusually demure in a grey sweater dress. She waved at us with a big smile on her face. She hadn't been on our invitation list as we weren't really close friends, so I was surprised she'd turned out in these bitterly cold conditions to see us.

'Congratulations,' she called. 'I hope you don't mind me turning up. I wanted to catch a glimpse of your dress. You look beautiful, by the way.'

'Oh, Darcy!' My heart warmed to her. Funny to think if she hadn't made her comment on that sunny afternoon back in August then we might not have even been here today. 'Will you come in for the reception?' I called.

'Oh!' She was taken aback by the offer, but her face lit up in delight, and she scrunched up her shoulders excitedly, leaving me in no doubt as to her answer.

I barely recognised Ryan in his three piece navy suit. He looked impossibly handsome. With his dark wayward hair cut neatly and his beard trimmed, he really did scrub up well and the expression on his face told me he was taking his responsibilities for the day very seriously. In one hand, he held Flora on a lead and in the other, he held Digby, the pair of them sporting brand new tartan leather collars especially for the occasion.

'Flora!' I called, and her ears pricked at the sound of my voice, her head turning in each and every direction until she spotted me and made a beeline for us, dragging Ryan behind. I laughed and bent down to greet her, giving her a huge hug. She had both her name tags on today, her usual one, and the one that she'd worn that first day I'd met her, inscribed with Max's romantic proposal. I looked up at Max with a big smile on my face at the realisation and the precious memory. Digby, ever faithful and loyal, who'd been with me from the very beginning, stood obediently at Ryan's side, his big brown eyes observing me soulfully, waiting patiently for my attention. I threw my arms around his neck, and tickled him behind his ear in that special spot, just how he liked it. There'd be a special treat for both the dogs once we got inside the barn for the reception.

Max helped me to my feet and everyone around us cheered and clapped as confetti and snow flakes fluttered down on our heads. Hand in hand we walked the last steps towards the pub, pausing to look up at the distinctive sign of The Dog and Duck hanging overhead, slightly obscured now by the white stuff that had been falling all morning. The mistletoe entwined around the sign was clearly visible though and, at the urging of our guests, Max took my face in his hands and kissed me full on the lips, a long lingering kiss which made my toes curl in delight in the depths of my wellies.

We'd done it. We'd come full circle, home to where this mad and wonderful adventure had begun. With Max at my side, my gorgeous baby boy, my friends and my family around me, I suspected this might only be the beginning of a lifetime of further happy adventures ahead.

# ACKNOWLEDGMENTS

It's been such a joy and pleasure to write The Dog and Duck series of books. I've loved being immersed in the world of Little Leyton and having those lovely characters as part of my life these last couple of years. I will definitely miss them!

Firstly, I must give huge thanks to Sarah Ritherdon and Caroline Ridding who were instrumental in bringing these stories to life. It was their idea to take the first book, Winter at the Dog and Duck, and develop it into a four book series of novels. It's definitely been a team effort!

Thanks to Sarah who has been so very supportive and encouraging along the way, and whose editorial advice is always spot on. Thanks too to the amazing team at Boldwood Books for giving the Dog and Duck series a facelift and the opportunity to share the stories with a whole new audience. Special thanks to Rose Fox for her hard work on the copyedits.

To all the book bloggers and author friends out there who have championed the books and shared and promoted them on social media, thank you so much. There are far too many to mention individually, but that's not to say I don't appreciate every single tweet, message and share. I thank you all for being so enthusiastic about the books and for spreading that love across the internet – you're all stars!

To Nick, Tom and Ellie, thank you for everything. On those difficult days, you make me laugh and keep me sane.

Finally, a very big thank you to all my lovely readers. I've been extremely touched by how so many of you have taken these characters to your hearts and contacted me to say how much you've enjoyed the stories, it's always such a thrill to hear from you and receive your lovely comments.

It's bittersweet knowing that this is the end for the Dog and Duck series, but I hope you'll continue to follow my writing, and what comes next. You can reach me on twitter or through my facebook page.

Love Jill x

# ABOUT THE AUTHOR

**Jill Steeples** is the author of many successful women's fiction titles – most recently the Dog and Duck series - all set in the close communities of picturesque English villages. She lives in Bedfordshire.

Sign up to Jill Steeples' mailing list here for news, competitions and updates on future books.

Visit Jill's website: www.jillsteeples.co.uk

Follow Jill on social media:

📘 facebook.com/jillsteepleswriter

𝕏 x.com/jillesteeples

📷 instagram.com/jill.steeples

# ALSO BY JILL STEEPLES

When We Meet Again

Maybe This Christmas?

**Primrose Woods Series**

Starting Over at Primrose Woods

Snowflakes Over Primrose Woods

Dreams Come True at Primrose Hall

Starry Skies Over Primrose Hall

**Dog & Duck Series**

Winter at the Dog & Duck

Summer at the Dog & Duck

Wedding Bells at the Dog & Duck

Happily-Ever-After at the Dog & Duck

## LOVE NOTES

### LOVE IN EVERY CHAPTER

WHERE ALL YOUR ROMANCE
DREAMS COME TRUE!

THE HOME OF BESTSELLING
ROMANCE AND WOMEN'S
FICTION

WARNING:
MAY CONTAIN SPICE

SIGN UP TO OUR
NEWSLETTER

https://bit.ly/Lovenotesnews

# Boldwood

Boldwood Books is an award-winning fiction publishing company seeking out the best stories from around the world.

**Find out more at www.boldwoodbooks.com**

Join our reader community for brilliant books, competitions and offers!

Follow us
@BoldwoodBooks
@TheBoldBookClub

Sign up to our weekly deals newsletter

https://bit.ly/BoldwoodBNewsletter

9 781785 138485